POOR RICHARD'S GAME

POOR RICHARD'S GAME

G. J. A. O'Toole

DELACORTE PRESS / NEW YORK

Published by
Delacorte Press
1 Dag Hammarskjold Plaza
New York, N.Y. 10017

Manufactured in the United States of America

First printing

Designed by Richard Oriolo

Library of Congress Cataloging in Publication Data

O'Toole, G.J.A.
Poor Richard's game.
1. Franklin, Benjamin, 1706–1790—Fiction.   2. United
States—History—Revolution, 1775–1783—Fiction.
I. Title.
PS3565.T6P6   813'.54   82-1356
ISBN 0-440-07025-2   AACR2

FOR MARY ANN

POOR RICHARD'S GAME

Being an authentic account of several intrigues,
treacheries and secret services of the American War of
Independency; and an examination into the true
allegiance of Dr. Benjamin Franklin

Composed by

Pierre-Augustin de Lawless

Drawn from the recollections of his illustrious father,
Chevalier Desmond Cuchulain de Lawless, and
divers others

Edited and verified by

Michael Croft, Col.,
U.S. Army (Ret.)

An Annotated Novel
Presented by

G.J.A. O'Toole

"For life is a kind of chess, in which we have often points to gain, and competitors and adversaries to contend with, and in which there is a vast variety of good and evil events."

BENJAMIN FRANKLIN, *The Morals of Chess*

Introduction

by
G.J.A. O'Toole

ESPIONAGE is as old as warfare and diplomacy. We think of the American Revolution as a war fought in the forests and pastures of colonial America, not the back alleys of European cities. Nathan Hale and Major André were intelligence agents, of course, and Benedict Arnold was a defector, but they were battlefield spies, and the roles they played were part of the armed conflict in North America. But lesser-known intelligence operations were even more important to the struggle for American independence, operations more in the style of present-day espionage, replete with arms smuggling, secret inks and ciphers, political propaganda, and double agents. At the center of these operations was the American mission in Paris, and America's first ambassador, Benjamin Franklin.

The diplomatic intrigue of the Revolutionary War is a fascinating chapter of American history, but one surprisingly little known. Thus, I was delighted to help when my friend Michael Croft asked my assistance in publishing this work. Readers of *The Cosgrove Report* have already met Colonel Croft, amateur historian, professional detective, and former Army intelligence officer. I was pleased to discover that the colonel has once again unearthed an intriguing historical mystery. Those who enjoyed *Cosgrove* will, I trust, be equally engaged by the following narrative, which I have taken the liberty to rechristen with a shorter title in the modern mode—*Poor Richard's Game.*

Foreword

by
Michael Croft

MUCH of this is true, maybe all of it. If I could chase down all the little loose ends I might be certain, I might know exactly where the line between fact and fiction should be drawn. But that could take years—maybe even a lifetime—and there's no guarantee it would settle the question

The final answer is probably locked up in some dusty but well-guarded room in Whitehall where Her Majesty's government keeps the archives of the British Secret Service —the crumbling parchment, the faded foolscap, and the yellowing typescript that tell the story of the oldest continuously operating intelligence service in the world. There, somewhere between John Dee's reports to Elizabeth I of Spanish plans for an armada, and Greville Wynne's debriefings of Colonel Penkovsky of the Soviet GRU, lie the scribbled accounts of British espionage during the American Revolution. But if it's only there the full truth can be had, we'll have to wait until Judgment Day for a look at it.

Meanwhile, we have only Pierre-Augustin de Lawless's tale of the exploits of his swashbuckling father, the Chevalier Desmond Cuchulain de Lawless, plus the evidence I've managed to dig up to support his story.

At first glance the story looks incredible. Double agents, triple agents, dead-drops, and exotic assassination techniques sound more like the twentieth century than the eighteenth. But the spies on both sides in the American Revolution knew all about that stuff, plus invisible inks and cryptology as well.

What do you think of the claim that some high officials of King George's government dabbled in satanism and belonged to a secret satanic cult that practiced the Black Mass? Fantastic? Maybe, but the facts prove they did.

But more than that, how about the idea that Benjamin Franklin—scientist, inventor, Founding Father and patriot —was really a traitor and a satanist, a turncoat who may have sworn allegiance to God and country, but secretly served England and worshiped Satan? Absurd? Perhaps, but a couple of historians claim he did.

Maybe the most surprising thing about the whole business is that these are not just academic questions, not just learned squabbling about things that happened two hundred years ago, of no practical importance today. As a matter of fact, Lawless's story was the subject of a recent five million dollar lawsuit.

That's where I came in.

Meet James Marsh, Esq., sober, respectable and un-imaginative, a junior partner in the Washington law firm of Lawson, Hurley, Clinger and Osburn. Every now and then he needs a private investigator, and he usually calls me. That's what he did six months ago.

"This one is right up your alley, Croft," he said.

"Which one? I hang out in several of them."

"You're a history buff."

"It passes the time."

The last job I did for him involved the memoirs of a late senior partner of the law firm with a new angle on the Lincoln assassination. He asked me to check it out. I got lucky and turned up a few choice morsels.

4

"You were in counterintelligence when you were in the Army, weren't you?" he asked.

"I forget. It was a long time ago. What have you got?"

"We have a client who intends to sue the cities of Philadelphia and Boston for a large sum. More precisely, our client intends to sue the estate of Benjamin Franklin, of which those cities are, in effect, the trustees."

"*The* Benjamin Franklin?"

"Yes. Franklin died in 1790 leaving a will in which he bequeathed one thousand pounds each to Philadelphia and Boston. The money was to be held in trust and invested. After one hundred years, part of the principal was to be used to benefit the cities, and the balance was to be reinvested. After two hundred years, the total is to go entirely to the cities. You see, Franklin understood compound interest."

He consulted some figures on a yellow legal pad.

"After the first hundred years the Boston fund reached $301,000 and the Philadelphia fund amounted to $172,360. Per Franklin's instructions, most of the monies were used to set up a pair of scientific and educational institutions— the Franklin Institute in Philadelphia, and the Franklin Union in Boston. Also, per his instructions, the balance was reinvested."

"How much will there be in the kitty in 1990?"

"Given the present money market, it's difficult to say. But by conservative estimates, at least five million dollars. Our client intends to claim all of it."

"Has he got a case?"

"*She* may have a case, but that remains to be seen. Our client is Ms. Catherine Applegate of New Orleans, who happens to be an attorney herself, but she practices criminal law and this, of course, is a civil action.

"Ms. Applegate was an adopted child. Several years ago she undertook to locate her natural parents. She learned they were dead and that she has no living relatives. Next, she conducted a genealogical study of her natural father's family, which was named Laules. She traced the line to France and discovered the name was originally Lawless, Laules being a French variation."

"Lawless sounds English."

"Irish, in fact. One of her ancestors was a Desmond de Lawless, who belonged to a group called The Wild Geese. The Wild Geese were Irishmen who left Ireland after the English conquests in the late seventeenth century. They served in most of the armies of Europe, but the majority of them went to France, where they formed *La Brigade Irlandaise,* the Irish Brigade of the French Army.

"Desmond de Lawless was born in Kerry in 1743, but he was taken to France by his parents when he was five. He joined the Irish Brigade when he was seventeen and fought in the Seven Years' War and in the American Revolution. Later, during the French Revolution, he was regarded as an aristocrat, so he was forced to move to Spain. Still later, he emigrated with his family to America—Louisiana—and settled there.

"Desmond de Lawless had a son, Pierre-Augustin, who wrote an account of his father's exploits during the American Revolution, which was published in 1836. Ms. Applegate located a copy of it in the course of researching the family history, and it is the basis for her claim. This is it."

He took out an old book from his desk drawer and handed it to me.

"In this book, Pierre-Augustin states that his father lent Franklin two thousand pounds, exactly the amount Franklin left to Philadelphia and Boston. Now, if Franklin ever repaid this supposed debt to Lawless there is no record or receipt of the payment among the Franklin papers, which have been collected by the Yale University Library. Thus the presumption that the debt was outstanding at the time of Franklin's death, and Ms. Applegate's claim that, as Lawless's only living descendant, she is entitled to the two thousand pounds Franklin left to the cities, plus all accrued interest."

"And you think she can make that stick?"

"Possibly. I don't really know. There is not much precedent for this sort of action, except, of course, in the general sense that the federal courts recently have countenanced much stranger arguments. But this case hinges entirely on the authenticity of Pierre-Augustin de Lawless's story of his father's adventures. I'm afraid it's the only evidence she has to offer that Franklin ever actually incurred the debt."

"And that's where I come in."

"Exactly. We are at a great disadvantage because Pierre-Augustin was not a witness to the events he recounted; he wasn't born until three years later, in 1785. He claims he learned of the matter from his father and other surviving witnesses. I don't have to tell you this presents us with a tremendous burden of proof."

"No, you don't. You think it's a pretty long shot, but with a possible five million dollar payoff, why not play it?"

"I wouldn't use those words, but yes, that is substantially the firm's position in accepting Ms. Applegate's case."

"But why me? Why an amateur? You know this thing is probably going to end up in the Supreme Court. Why not get yourself a professional historian, some college professor who can put his academic seal of approval on your evidence?"

"If and when we take the case to trial, that is what we intend to do. But for the moment we need your own curious blend of expertise. The matter of the loan, you see, is rather incidental to Lawless's story. The principal matter of the account happens to involve counterintelligence. According to Pierre-Augustin, his father was sent to France to investigate suspicions that Benjamin Franklin was in the employ of the British Secret Service. That sort of thing— spy hunting, I mean—involves patterns of thought and action that are unfamiliar to most historians; they might be better understood by someone with your own intelligence background who also has an avocation toward history. After we have your report we will review the case and determine whether or not to advise our client to pursue it."

"All right, I'll see what I can do. Is there anything in particular I ought to be looking for?"

"First of all, we'd like to know if you can prove that Pierre-Augustin de Lawless invented the whole story. Quite obviously we hope it's impossible to prove that, but if it's not, we'll save a great deal of time and trouble if we find out now."

"I see. I'm to play devil's advocate."

Marsh smiled. I'd never seen him do that before.

"A very apt metaphor, as you'll see when you read the story. If you find nothing to prove conclusively the thing is a fraud, we want you to determine whether any part of the story is supported by historical fact. Some elements of the account seem particularly dubious, and I think we'll need some additional corroboration if we hope to win our case."

"Such as?"

"The idea that Benjamin Franklin was in any way involved in espionage, and especially the idea that he was ever suspected of being a traitor."

8

"I can confirm that last one right now," I said. "Franklin was accused of treason on at least two occasions: once during his own lifetime, and once just a few years ago."

"How can you possibly know that?"

I put the book in my briefcase and got up.

"As you say, I'm a history buff. I'll be in touch."

It had been a few years since I came across it, this theory that Benjamin Franklin had been a traitor, so I didn't have the details at my fingertips. They weren't in my office, either, so I locked the door and went home, which is where I keep my collection of historical mysteries. I spent the afternoon rereading several books and articles I hadn't looked at for a while. By dinnertime most of the case had come back to me.

There were so many chapters in the life of Benjamin Franklin we overlook the most important one, which came near the end. He was seventy years old when the man who was a philosopher, a scientist, an inventor, and a statesman became a diplomat. When Franklin sailed for France in December 1776, he undertook the most important diplomatic mission in American history, because the only hope of victory and independence lay in a military alliance with France. In spite of the gallantry of General Washington's army of farmers and tradesmen, it could never have triumphed over the professionally drilled and well-equipped troops of King George without French aid. Bravery can win battles, but it takes logistics to win wars. The American leaders understood this; so did the British Secret Service. Franklin had hardly set foot on French soil when his arrival was noted in Downing Street.

"I look upon him as a dangerous engine," wrote Lord Stormont, the British ambassador in Paris, using the quaint idiom of the eighteenth century, "and am very sorry that some English frigate did not meet him by the way."

Franklin was well known to King George and his prime minister, Lord North, and they did not doubt his ability to bring the French into the war on the American side. The Sage of Philadelphia soon became the prime target of British intelligence. And some historians claim he soon became its most valuable agent.

The case against Benjamin Franklin goes something like this:

1. In France, Franklin was lax to the point of recklessness about security. He left secret diplomatic correspondence and other documents lying around his office where they could be read by any casual visitor, and he always ignored the warnings of friends and associates against the danger of British espionage.

2. Throughout the war, Franklin received frequent clandestine visits from British agents. While some of these contacts were undoubtedly British overtures to negotiate a peace agreement with the rebellious colonies, others were attempts to bribe him. Whether any of the latter succeeded remains an open question.

3. Franklin's bookkeeping on the ministry accounts was less than satisfactory to his associates across the Atlantic. After the war, he was unable or unwilling to account for more than 100,000 pounds of government funds. If it can be inferred that Franklin stole from his country, the theory that he also sold it out becomes more plausible.

4. Franklin's friend and Paris colleague, Silas Deane, switched sides and participated in a propaganda operation run by the British Secret Service. Franklin ignored obvious evidence of Deane's treachery and defended him against his accusers.

5. On Franklin's orders, his protégé, Dr. Edward Ban-

croft, was hired as secretary to the Paris mission, in which position he served throughout the war. Bancroft, too, was shielded by Franklin against accusations of disloyalty, but unlike Silas Deane, Bancroft did not switch sides; he was working for British intelligence from the beginning and throughout the entire period of hostilities and afterward. He was a professional agent of the British Secret Service, and little that transpired in the American embassy was not soon reported by him to London.

6. Secret Service documents released from British archives a century after the Revolution revealed that British intelligence chiefs referred to Franklin by the code number 72 and the code name Moses, disclosures which seem to imply Franklin was indeed a British agent.

7. Franklin is alleged to have belonged to the Hell Fire Club, an English society devoted to sex and satanism, which one historian believes was a cover for the recruitment of spies by British intelligence.

What does it all add up to? Was Franklin really a traitor? After two hundred years, it didn't seem likely the thing would ever be proved either way. The historical debate had been put on the shelf, and it might have remained there indefinitely. But then Marsh's client, in search of her ancestors, stumbled across Lawless's book.

I took it out of my briefcase and looked at it again—new evidence in a very old case. I settled back, opened it, and began to read. It was almost dawn when I turned the last page and put it down.

I could see my job wasn't going to be easy. On the other hand, when you're getting paid to pursue your hobby, you shouldn't complain about hard work.

Desmond de Lawless, an Irishman serving in the French Army, may have fought in the American Revolution, may have been given a spy-catching assignment, and may have lent two thousand pounds to Benjamin Franklin. If I could prove the story true, Ms. Catherine Applegate would collect five million dollars, Marsh's law firm would pocket a big slice of the award, and I would have the answer to a mystery as old as the Republic: Which side was Benjamin Franklin really on?

I caught a few hours sleep, then headed for the Library of Congress. I was back to the library the next day, and the one after that. In fact, I showed up in the Main Reading Room bright and early every day for five months, and I usually didn't leave until I was kicked out at closing time.

As I said, much of the story turned out to be true, but we'll probably never know whether some of it might be false. I wish I'd been able to nail the thing down completely, but it doesn't matter to Marsh and his client; I've settled the question of Franklin's two thousand pound debt to her ancestor. And I think I've also settled the question of whether Benjamin Franklin was a traitor.

I'll tell you what I think, but first I want you to read Lawless's story for yourself.

A True History of the Secret Services Rendered by
The Chevalier de Lawless
During the American War of Independency

Composed by

Pierre-Augustin de Lawless

Drawn from the Recollections of His Illustrious Father,
Desmond Cuchulain de Lawless, and others witting
of these affairs

CAREY & HART
PHILADELPHIA
1836

Preface

by

Pierre-Augustin de Lawless

IT will be neither surprising nor amiss if the ensuing
sheets find favor among those readers who take pleasure
in the romantic novels that have lately become so popular.
Those who revel in the swash and derring-do of Scott may
find here some of that same gallantry. Those whose patriotic
pride is stirred by Cooper's tales of our nation's infancy
(one is especially put in mind of his *Tale of the Neutral
Ground**) may find like inspiration in these pages. Even
those whose delight it is to shudder at Mrs. Shelley's dark
imaginings may find here something to their taste. And
while the author of this history may only emulate, and
never duplicate, that felicity of style commanded by those
to whom the pen is a lifelong calling, he makes so bold as
to claim one supreme advantage over his fellow scribblers,
to wit, every single word of his tale is true.

If it seem audacious for one who was yet unborn at
the time of the events herein recounted to warrant so
positively their truth, let him beg to assure his readers

---

* *The Spy, A Tale of the Neutral Ground,* by James Fenimore
Cooper, 1821. (The full citation is given here because this work
is not cited again. Works I have cited often to explain or support
Lawless's story, or which are especially relevant to its background,
are identified in the notes by author and page number, and fully
identified in a bibliography I have added after my own final com-
ments.)—M.C.

15

that the tale he tells is not the mere recitation of one learned at his father's knee (though the word of the illustrious Chevalier de Lawless is credential enough). Some of what will be recounted here transpired beyond the eyes and ears of the Chevalier, and so, to render a complete and authentic relation of the tale, the author has been at pains to search out other witnesses to these matters and beg their reminiscence.

The compilation of the facts presented in this history has been a life-long preoccupation of the author, and he thanks a kindly providence for the propitious impulse that sent him early to the portals of those principal deponents who have since passed to their reward.

I was scarcely more than a boy when my beloved godfather and namesake, M. Pierre-Augustin Caron de Beaumarchais (who is perhaps better known to the world as the author of those splendid plays, *The Barber of Seville* and *The Marriage of Figaro,* and to horologists as the inventor of the principle employed in all modern timepieces), shared with me his recollections of the Chevalier's secret services.

I was barely a man when the late president Thomas Jefferson welcomed me to the White House and recalled those matters of the secret diplomacy of the War of American Independency of which he was perforce witting by reason of his service in the Committee of Secret Correspondence.

Yet later, Mr. William Temple Franklin, grandson of the celebrated Sage of Philadelphia who plays so great a role in this history, graciously shared with me his remembrances of his days at Passy when, as Dr. Franklin's personal secretary, he witnessed many of the events herein recounted.

The brave Major Benjamin Tallmadge, the noble Count O'Toole, the enigmatic Chevalier d'Éon, and a host of

16

others whose names cannot be familiar to the reader, all furnished this plodding scribe with fragments of the dissected puzzle* which he has been at pains to reconstruct with care and accuracy.

It must be allowed, of course, that only the eye of God sees all, and where, on occasion, a scene is recounted herein of which no living testimony was possible, the author begs the reader to indulge him with that same license granted other literary artists, and he hopes to assure him he has exercised the same rigorous deduction of the true event as that employed by the celebrated Cuvier,† who demonstrated the power of sheer reason to infer the entire form of an ancient animal, given but one of its bones. Dead bones are all that is bequeathed to us by the past, and what is history, but the pathetic strivings of memory to breathe life into them once more?

NEW ORLEANS, 1836

---

* Jigsaw puzzle.—M.C.
† Georges Léopold Chrétien Frédéric Dagobert Cuvier (1769–1832), French anatomist and founder of the sciences of paleontology and comparative anatomy.—M.C.

1

Tyburn Fair

IT was the year of Our Lord 1781, the third week of July, and a bright summer morning. The bells of London rang out across the City, summoning lord and lackey alike. In Berkeley and Grosvenor squares, gentlefolk arose from their breakfast and began to dress. In the coffee houses of Exchange Alley, stock jobbers put aside their jottings and went into the street. From the tailor shops of Spitalfields to the halls of Westminster, from the hovels of Rope-makers' Alley to the tenements of Chick Lane, the bells called out the people of London. Tailors and tanners, brewers and brickmakers, pimps and pickpurses streamed from every court and alley to swell into great human rivers that flowed along Piccadilly, the Strand, and Cheapside. A festive air was abroad, for on this day, as on seven others the year round, there was to be a fair on the Tyburn Road, a festival of human mortality.

Tyburn Fair, a hanging day.

Troops of Life Guards and foot marshaled in St. James's Park and marched to Tower Hill. Then came the sheriffs of London, the undersheriffs, the sergeants-at-mace, the yeomen, and last of all, the executioner. A sheriff struck his staff upon the Outward Gate, and the lieutenant of the Tower appeared.

"We come for the French spy," declared the sheriff.

A brace of Tower warders marched out. Between them

strolled a debonair fellow of middle years, finely dressed in a new suit of clothes, with large, square cuffs and great flaps to the pockets. He walked with a lively step that ill became the occasion, for he walked toward his doom.

As those assembled before the Tower moved off in prescribed formation, the throng of onlookers parted to let the procession pass. The constable of the Tower marched in the van, followed by the knight marshal's men and tipsters. Next came the sheriff's officers, then the sheriffs and the executioner. A team of oxen drew a rude cart, and atop it stood the prisoner, straight and silent. The Tower warders marched behind, followed by columns of Life Guards and foot. A hearse, drawn by a pair of black horses, brought up the rear.

It was a pageant much finer than that commonly seen on a hanging day in London, for this was not the ragtag caravan of thieves, pickpockets, and highwaymen that regularly passed from Newgate Prison to the Tyburn gibbet. The hanging of a prisoner from the Tower was done with splendid ceremony.

The tide of onlookers filled the streets and flowed over the rooftops, and not a window overlooking the procession was empty of curious faces. Some jeered the prisoner, others called out encouragements, and yet others toasted him with beer and gin. To all he replied with a lift of his hat and a sweeping bow. The parade turned into Oxford Street. The Tyburn gibbet stood but half a league beyond.

The scaffold stood near Bryanston Street, where it crosses Edgware Road. A multitude waited there, straining for a glimpse of the approaching parade. Mother Proctor's Pews (as the Tyburn grandstands were called, after their proprietress) were filled with those who would pay for the vantage, while a greater number of their meaner fellows contented themselves with the inferior view. Peddlers

hawked ale to the crowd, and beyond the gibbet a flesh-
monger had set up his stand. The redolence of spirits and
burning pig mingled with the stink of the human stew and
filled the air of Tyburn.

A howling cheer greeted the procession as it approached.
The constable of the Tower called a halt, while a squad of
Life Guards cleared a path through the mob, driving it back
from the foot of the gibbet, which then was encircled by a
troop of horses. The parade resumed, and the prisoner's cart
passed within the circle. A priest of the Roman Church
mounted the cart, and the prisoner knelt to receive his
blessing before stepping down to take his place with the
warders and march the final steps to the gibbet.

The dismal ceremony was halted for a moment, while a
sedan chair borne by four liveried footmen was carried
through the throng to the grandstand. An elderly gentleman
emerged, and was guided to a preferred place that had
been saved for him. A murmur rippled through the crowd,
and here and there a voice was heard to remark, "Selwyn.
It's him."*

At the edge of the mob, two gentlemen regarded these
proceedings from within a fine carriage. One was a portly
fellow of some fifty years, and his companion was a leaner
man of similar age. Few in the throng should have failed
to recognize the first man as Lord North, and some might
have known the second to be Lord Stormont.†

---

* George Augustus Selwyn (1719–1791), noted wit, conversationalist, bon vivant, member of parliament, sadist, and necrophile.
Executions were among Selwyn's favorite amusements, and he
often traveled great distances to witness them. We'll see more of
him later.—M.C.

† Frederick North (1732–1792), Second Earl of Guilford, and
George III's prime minister from 1770 to 1782.

David Murray (1727–1796), Second Earl of Mansfield and

"Indeed, it *is* Selwyn," said Lord Stormont. "I've heard it said of him that he never misses a Tyburn Fair."

"No doubt," said Lord North. "But, Stormont, my good fellow, I'd no notion *you* took such a gust for a hanging. I've not been to Tyburn since Ferrers was hanged, and that must be twenty years past." He drew a perfumed handkerchief from his sleeve and held it to his face. "The air about this place is quite as vile today as then."

" 'Tis to be more than hanging for the Frenchman, my lord," said Stormont. "His crime was treason, and it earns a harsher punishment."

He recited the sentence of the court.

" 'To be hanged by the neck, but not till dead; then to be cut down, and his bowels taken out and burnt before his face, his head to be taken off, his body cut into four quarters, and to be at His Majesty's disposal.' "

"Barbaric!" shuddered North. "No doubt the fellow has earned it, but what virtue can there be in witnessing the spectacle?"

"Shopkeepers come to watch when a filcher climbs the Tyburn tree, and teamsters turn out to see a highwayman hanged. Is it not then mete that we who practice statecraft should witness the punishment of a spy?"

Lord North made no reply, but fixed his gaze upon the scaffold. The executioner made to bind the prisoner's hands, but the Frenchman stopped him and, removing his hat, scaled it out over the heads of the cheering crowd. Then

---

Seventh Viscount Stormont, a scholarly patrician with a distinguished career in government and diplomatic service. He served as ambassador to France from 1772 until the French entered the war in 1778, when he returned to London to serve as North's secretary of state for the Northern Department until 1782. During this period he also quietly served as senior intelligence officer and chief of the British Secret Service.—M.C.

he lifted the periwig from his head and presented it to the hangman, as though to say "Here, take this; it is too fine and costly a thing to sit astride a head so shortly due to roll in the dust." A chorus of huzzas applauded these brave gestures.

"A curious sort of sin is spying," mused Stormont. "In Paris, little more than a hundred leagues distant, this man La Motte should be esteemed hero for the same labor that has earned him a felon's death here in London."*

"We punish felons," said Lord North. "That the French choose to employ them may be singular, but it is also infamous."

" 'Tis not quite singular," said Stormont gently. "There are some in Paris and Versailles who risk this Frenchman's fate for English gold. Were they to lose their heads, I should lose my eyes and ears."

Lord North looked at his companion with displeasure.

"Make a vitrue of necessity if you will, Stormont. Perhaps you must traffic with rogues, but do not boast of it to me."

---

* Henry Francis de La Motte (or La Mothe), aka Baron Deckham, Mr. Soyez, "B," and "D," a colonel in the regiment of Maréchal de Soubise during the Seven Years' War. La Motte went to England during the American Revolution to run a spy ring for French intelligence. La Motte's apparatus included a clerk in the British Admiralty named Ryder, and a couple—Rougier, a Frenchman, and an Englishwoman named Dobrey, who lived together in Greek Street in Soho, serving as couriers and forwarding La Motte's reports to Paris by way of Margate and Ostend. La Motte's downfall came in January 1781, when he was caught after dropping a handful of confidential British Foreign Ministry documents on a staircase while leaving the office of Lord Hillsborough, secretary of state for the American colonies. La Motte's ring was rounded up, and La Motte was tried for treason and convicted. He was hanged, drawn, and quartered in July 1781 (Morris, pp. 132–133).—M.C.

"Oh, some are far from rogues, my lord. One is a gentle-man of even greater degree than this unhappy Frenchman. You have often shared in the intelligence he sends me."

"But I do not wish to share the knowledge of his name!"

"I do not speak it," said Lord Stormont. " 'Tis safer if the names of such men are never spoken, for their necks are ever at risk. The one of whom I speak is called Moses, even in the highest councils and the most secret papers of His Majesty's government. I thank God we troubled with such precaution, for this Frenchman, La Motte, stole some of those very documents before he was found out. Had we entrusted the true name of 'Moses' to paper, it should have been discovered to the French, and even our man's exalted station could not have saved him. Treason earns the same reward in every land, no matter how high the traitor's station."

North made no reply, but gazed through the carriage window. The Tyburn mob had gone suddenly silent. With horror and fascination, the two gentlemen watched the drama played out upon the scaffold. Abruptly North snatched down the curtain, covering the view.

"Are you ill, sir? You've gone so pale!"

" 'Tis nothing," North replied. "Nothing but the stink of this place. The atmosphere fair reeks of roast pig!"

Lord Stormont nodded. "Of course, my lord. It must be the roast pig. I think they roast a fresh one now."

He thrust his head through the window and called to the coachman.

"Drive on, fellow! To Downing Street!"

A black and unctuous cloud rose over Tyburn as the carriage drew away. A long scream of anguish rent the strange silence.

It was as the cry of a damned soul in the deepest pit of hell.

2

Madame Brillon's Bath

FOUR weeks later, in a fine house in a suburb of Paris, a knight advanced and stood before a queen.

"I present you with a gift, my dear," said Benjamin Franklin, who was seated comfortably upon a fauteuil. He removed his spectacles and polished them on his sleeve. The moist air of the chamber had coated the lenses with mist. Mme. Brillon reclined in the warm bathwater and considered the chessboard.

"Ah, *mon cher papa,* do not think to delude me with false generosity," she said. "I have read Vergil, and I fear the Greeks when they bear gifts."

"I, too, have read Vergil, madam," replied Franklin, as he replaced the spectacles upon his nose, "but learned a different lesson: Greeks bearing gifts need not be feared, for it was gifts bearing Greeks that proved Troy's undoing."

Mme. Brillon laughed delightedly.

"Then I must look into the mouth of your gift horse," she said, modestly passing an arm across her breast as she reached for the chessman. "I see no Greeks, but *mon Dieu!* It is a wooden horse! I think you conspire to conquer me, *monsieur!*"

"I besiege the citadel, dear lady. And while I may dream of conquest, I am content merely to prolong the siege, for there is great delight even in contemplating the object of my design from beyond the walls. When you play at chess with me in your bath, my strategy is neither to win nor lose, but to prolong the game."

Mme. Brillon slid down until the bathwater covered all beneath her chin.

"Is this scandalous, then, *papa?*" she asked brightly.

"Scandalous? I cannot say what might be scandalous in Paris, but in Philadelphia 'tis deemed scandalous for a gentleman to call upon a ravishing lady when her husband is away. And in Philadelphia it would be thought scandalous indeed for that lady to receive the gentleman in her bath. But Paris is not Philadelphia. Paris knows a different scale of scandal. When a charming lady grants a gentleman every favor save that one for which he most yearns, that is a Parisian scandal. But forgive me, madam. I fear I've brought you blushes."

"Ah, must I surrender my virtue to preserve the honor of France? I think you misprise the nature of French hospitality, *papa.* But you tease me. You know my love for you is that of a daughter for her father."

"But my feelings for you, dear lady, are far from paternal."

"Then if I cannot be your daughter, I shall be your comrade. Tell me, *papa,* how goes the war?"

Franklin paused and studied the chessboard. He moved a piece and sat back.

"The war? The war goes on. There lately have been battles in the South, in Carolina and Virginia. The story continues to unfold, but I think the denouement is near at hand."

"Ah, a glorious victory!"

Franklin smiled. "Perhaps. Or perhaps an inglorious bankruptcy. Were the English king to see the game is not worth the candle today, I should be better pleased than by the most glorious of victories tomorrow. We wish not conquests, but independency."

"But the peace, it must be an honorable one," insisted Mme. Brillon.

"Madam, there hardly ever existed a bad peace or a good war. At all events, there seems a mood for peace in Philadelphia. The Congress appoint commanders to make peace, even as they commission generals to make war. They have named me as one of those who will bargain with the English for a peace."

"But, *papa,* have you not resigned?"

"The Congress have done me the honor of refusing my resignation."*

Mme. Brillon abruptly rose, toppling the chessboard. A shower of droplets and chessmen fell upon the floor.

"But this is the most wonderful news! You do not joke, *papa?*"

"I do not jest, my dear, but I blush for us both. Have a care you do not take a chill."

Madame folded her arms modestly and submerged once more.

"This victory is quite as glorious as any won upon the field," she said. "You have vanquished your enemies at Philadelphia, and your Congress have proclaimed their

---

* On 2 January 1781, a committee of the Continental Congress, which had reviewed charges made against Franklin by his enemies, called for a congressional session to consider Franklin's recall from France. Perhaps with this in mind, Franklin wrote to Congress on 12 March and offered to resign, citing poor health. By August, Franklin had learned that his resignation had been refused and that he had been appointed one of the five peace commissioners who were to negotiate with the British.—M.C.

love and respect for you by naming you general of peace. We shall have a great banquet to celebrate Dr. Franklin's victory at the battle of Philadelphia."

Franklin smiled and shook his head. "Thank you, my dear, but no. I think it indiscreet to send word abroad that we prepare to make peace before we have been more successful in making war. One solid victory in the field, and we shall bargain in strength. Until then, you must say nothing of this. Great designs should not be made public till they are ripe for execution."

"Ah, you are very wise, *papa*. And you must be cautious, for the English have their spies everywhere."

"Oh, I do not fear the English spies," laughed Franklin.

"But you must! You are such a trusting old *grandpère!*"

Franklin arose and took the lady's hand.

"When I have a good game, madam, I guard against presumption. But tonight I have lost the game, for in a single breath you have advanced me from your father to your grandfather, and so put my ardor in check."

He bowed, turned to leave, then stopped.

"I hope I shall fare better when next we play."*

---

* The flirtation between Franklin and Mme. Brillon, and her penchant for playing chess with him in her bath, are recorded in their correspondence. This and other details of Franklin's Parisian dalliances can be found in *Mon Cher Papa: Franklin and the Ladies of Paris,* by Claude-Anne Lopez (Yale University Press, 1966).—M.C.

3

The Chevalier de
Lawless

THE breath of horse and rider misted the frosty air of
the bright October morn. The Chevalier had been
a-saddle since first light and put behind a dozen leagues of
the rolling Maryland countryside. The hoofs of his mount
beat a smart cadence on the frozen earth as he galloped
eastward, crossing into Pennsylvania on the Old Post Road.
He passed the sleeping hamlets of New Garden and Kennett
Square, and traversed the icy flow of Brandywine Creek at
Chad's Ford. Dawn enlightened his way through frosted
meadows and woods festooned with autumnal ribands of
crimson and ochre. He reined his mount atop a rise.

The Schuylkill River wound through the valley below,
and beyond rose the spires and chimneys of Philadelphia.
Immediately before him the road dropped gently to the
riverbank, where a ferry cable girded a stout tree trunk.
On the farther shore the ferryboat rode tethered against
the current. The rider drew his cloak about himself and
urged his steed forward.

The Chevalier wore the regimentals of the Irish Brigade
—a red coat faced with gold, breeches and waistcoat of
buff, and high-topped boots. A black tricorn rode at a
jaunty angle atop his head, which was adorned with no
periwig, but his natural hair, instead, slightly powdered

and tightly queued. He was a well-made fellow of eight-and-thirty years, with the white trail of a rapier cut from his left temple to the base of a stubborn jaw. He owned the countenance of a seasoned soldier, yet he looked out upon the world through a pair of laughing eyes.

As he neared the riverbank he saw a figure huddled beside a fire. The stranger had the look of a gentleman, though he seemed scarcely more than a lad, and might have been a young schoolmaster or student of divinity. The young man looked up from the fire as the rider approached.

"I present you with the top of the morning, *monsieur*," the Chevalier called, saluting him with a sweep of his tricorn. "May I beg your advice, if you chance to know the designs of the master of yonder vessel?"

"Good morning to you, sir," answered the young gentleman, rising. "I've seen no sign of the ferryman; I'll warrant he's still abed. Come warm yourself by the fire, if you like."

The Chevalier thanked the young man, dismounted, and tethered his horse.

"Have you come far?" asked the youngster.

"Six days in the saddle, from Yorktown," replied the Chevalier. "It is a grand madness, is it not, to tarry three weeks beyond the walls of a town, entreating the Englishmen within with great stores of shot and powder to remember their hospitality, and then, when the gates have at last been opened, to gallop away through the wilderness? Ah, *c'est la guerre*. A soldier must obey. And if I did not see a town, I saw a world turned upon its head, and an English general deliver up his sword."*

---

* The allusion is certainly to the eighteenth-century song, "The World Turned Upside Down," which tradition says was played during the surrender ceremonies at Yorktown.—M.C.

The young man declared his interest in the recent and famous victory at Yorktown and pressed the Chevalier for particulars of the siege and the battle. While the two conversed, a post chaise approached along the same road the Chevalier had recently traversed, and drew to a halt at the ferry landing. The coachman jumped down and held open the door, while two elegant young gentlemen alighted, bedecked in the martial raiments of the Pennsylvania Militia—blue coats with red facings, buff waistcoat and breeches—and wearing badges of the rank of captain. One of the Pennsylvanians was a short, thick fellow, while his companion was nearly as tall as the Chevalier (that is, well above the average height) and long of limb. The bantam looked about and, catching sight of the Chevalier, placed his hands upon his hips, cocked his head to the side, and strutted forward.

" 'Pon my word! A Redcoat!" he exclaimed.

The Chevalier glanced at him, then turned back to the young gentleman.

"Here, fellow!" persisted the bantam. "Are you indeed the king's man?"

The Chevalier turned again.

"*Oui, monsieur,*" he gently replied. "His Most Christian Majesty, Louis, the king of France. I am indeed his man."

"He doesn't *sound* like an Englishman," ventured the taller captain, joining his companion.

"Then why does he dress as one?" demanded the bantam. "Why do you wear the king's colors, fellow?"

"I do not sound like an Englishman because I am not an Englishman," said the Chevalier. "You, *monsieur,* on the other hand, sound like an Englishman, although you wear the dress of General Washington. That seems a greater mystery."

"He studied at Eton and Oxford," ventured the taller militiaman. "We were classmates," he added proudly.

"*Voilà!* Now it is clear! You sound like Englishmen because you lately *were* Englishmen. Myself, I have never been an Englishman, though I wore these same colors when you were but little English mannikins at the English knees of your English mothers. They are, as you say, the colors of an English king, but one of the house of Stuart, a king long dead.* I, *messieurs,* am of The Wild Geese."

The bantam frowned, baffled by the Chevalier's words and affronted by his tone.

"Wild Geese?" he echoed, turning to his companion. "Wild Geese?"

"I think he *is* a Frenchman," ventured his companion.

"*Parbleu!*" exclaimed the Chevalier. "Can it be these rustics are ignorant of *La Brigade Irlandaise?* Ah, I have been deceived, but now I comprehend. They are not soldiers, but children dressed up to play soldier. When you grow to be men, *mes enfants,* should you ever play soldier in earnest, should you ever know war, then you will also know The Wild Geese. And you will know that we all are Irishmen."

While the travelers engaged in this colloquy, the ferry-

---

* King James II, whom The Wild Geese followed into exile. Curiously, these expatriate Irishmen, who fought the English and served in the French Army, never abandoned their original English military regalia. Not only did they wear red coats, their regimental colors were red and white, and included the Red Cross of St. George, along with the Irish Harp. For a detailed description of the colors of the Dillon Regiment (Lawless's unit), see *The Irish Sword* (Dublin, The Irish Military Historical Society), Vol. I, p. 19.—M.C.

man had appeared on the distant bank and brought his barge across the river. The Chevalier, seeing this, got his horse and joined the young gentleman at the landing. But the militiamen were stung by the Chevalier's words, and were loath to eschew a reply in kind.

"What a fable!" exclaimed the tall one. "He dresses as an Englishman, speaks as a Frenchman, and claims to be an Irishman! I think he is a madman or a liar!"

"Tell us, Mr. Goose," cried the bantam, "of your horse. Is it an Irish horse? It has an Irish look to it."

The Chevalier, who was leading his mount aboard the ferry, paused to reply.

"I comprehend your error, *monsieur,*" he said, placing a hand beneath the head of the animal, "for the creature is of a noble countenance, and might well be Irish. But it is, indeed, an American horse, as you can discern if you but view it from the proper aspect."

With this he led the horse about and presented its hind quarters to the militiamen. Lifting the mare's tail, he continued. "Aha! So extraordinary a resemblance to your own lineaments, I think I recognize a kinship!"

The bantam trotted forward, his hand upon the hilt of his smallsword.

"Insolent rogue! Will you apologize?"

The Chevalier shrugged and turned to his horse.

"*Très bien.* I apologize, Mme. Horse."

Both militiamen drew their blades.

"Sir," cried the taller one, "we demand satisfaction!"

"And you fancy it will satisfy you to be run through the body?" the Chevalier inquired.

"It will satisfy me to scatter your giblets upon the ground!" roared the bantam.

The Chevalier nodded. "I see," he said; then he turned to

the tall one. "And you, *monsieur?* You, too, wish to scatter my giblets?"

"I do, indeed!" answered the militiaman earnestly. "And I mean to!"

"Ah, you mean to, as does your comrade. But, *messieurs,* I fear I am equipped with but one suit of giblets, and so can satisfy but one of you. Let the pleasure of scattering my giblets go to the one who is the better swordsman."

"That is I," announced the tall one.

"No, Arthur," declared the bantam, " 'tis I."

"I must differ, Ralph!" protested the tall one.

"You are mistaken, sir!"

"No, you!"

"*Messieurs!*" exclaimed the Chevalier. "Shame upon you! There is but one way for two gentlemen to settle such a controversy, and it is with action, not words. An *assaut d'armes,* and whichever draws first blood, it shall be he who scatters my giblets."

The two militiamen faced each other uncertainly, sword in hand.

"Do you insist, Arthur?"

"I must, Ralph."

"So be it, Arthur. Guard yourself!"

While the Chevalier looked on with folded arms, the pair crossed swords, and the slither and tinkle of steel upon steel filled the icy air. Bantam Ralph advanced with his guard in carte, engaging the blade of tall Arthur, who parried and whirled his blade into tierce. Ralph answered with a parry and riposte, engaging Arthur once again in carte, and attempting a flanconade, but Arthur retired before Ralph could gain his feeble.*

---

* Even a reader schooled in modern fencing must find these terms strange, because eighteenth-century fencing was different in both

In much this manner, the two militiamen engaged and disengaged repeatedly, moving back and forth across the ferry landing while the Chevalier and the others watched. The pair seemed evenly matched, neither a better swordsman than the other, and the bout promised to last until one or both dropped from exhaustion. At last the Chevalier struck up their swords with his own and stepped between them.

"*Assez!* Enough! Are these the lessons taught by Monsieur Angelo?* Then he should call himself *maître de danse,* and pray he never meets a true *maître d'armes.*

"Here, *mon petit Capitaine.* God has made you small of limb, a disadvantage in a swordsman which must be overcome by learning to advance and retire smartly. But you, *monsieur,* burden your left leg with an unequal share of your weight, and so cannot retire beyond the advancing blade of your larger adversary."

"It is the proper guarding stance," Ralph objected. "I retire quite smartly."†

---

terms and technique. Fencers may be interested to know that "carte" is merely a variation in spelling and pronunciation of the familiar *quarte*; "tierce" has about the same meaning as it does in modern saber competition; while "feeble" is the same as *foible,* i.e., the thinner and more flexible part of the blade or foil, near the point. There is no modern equivalent of "flanconade," a maneuver in which one swordsman tries to grab his opponent's blade with his left hand in order to disarm him. A complete exposition of eighteenth-century fencing may be found in *The School of Fencing* by Domenico Angelo (London, 1787).

The reader with no knowledge of the blade, either ancient or modern, is advised to recall to mind the films of Errol Flynn or Douglas Fairbanks, Jr. or Sr.—M.C.

* Domenico Angelo was fencing master at Eton.—M.C.

† In fact, the militiaman was adhering to the precepts of most eighteenth-century fencing masters in resting most of his weight

"*Oui?* Then I invite you to strike," replied the Chevalier, dropping his point and bending both knees equally.

Ralph advanced a step with great quickness and thrust in carte. The Chevalier did not parry but, keeping his point upon the ground, skipped backward. Ralph repeated his advance, and then once again, but to no avail, for the Chevalier retired with great agility, preventing his smaller adversary from coming within distance.

"*Voilà!* That is how one retires when both legs bear equal burdens. Observe, now, the difficulties you make for yourself."

The Chevalier lifted his blade and advanced. Ralph retired, but the Chevalier's blade stayed within distance. A feint in tierce, a thrust low in carte, and the bottommost button of the militiaman's waistcoat flew through the air. Ralph hopped backward, but he could not outdistance the point of the Chevalier's advancing blade. A second button arched through the air, then a third, and a fourth. Ralph made to parry, but could not engage the Chevalier's blade, nor could he evade its tip. A trail of buttons marked Ralph's retreat across the ferry landing, and his waistcoat hung open. The militiaman stumbled and sat down upon the frozen ground, devoid of buttons and dignity. The Chevalier lowered his blade and helped the fellow to his feet.

---

on his left foot and leaning away from his opponent. Only Captain John Godfrey (*Treatise on the Useful Science of Defence,* London, 1747) seemed to appreciate the fact, basic to all modern fencing, that the best stance consists of balancing the body's weight equally between both feet. The Chevalier may have read Godfrey, or else discovered this useful point through hard experience, perhaps in whatever engagement left him with that facial scar described by his son in an early paragraph of this chapter.—M.C.

"There, *monsieur*. You must take my advice to heart and put it into practice."

Then he turned to the other militiaman.

"And you, *mon grand Capitaine*. God has blessed you with a largeness of limb and shoulders, but you turn this to your disadvantage by offering so much of yourself to your adversary's blade. Your left foot, *monsieur*—it should be behind the right one; and your left arm—it should be held back and raised, so. In this way you will make yourself a smaller target. Why do you present yourself this way?"

"Why, the better to disarm an adversary," ventured Arthur uncertainly.

"Ah, *oui*, the flanconade. A demonstration, *s'il vous plaît*."

The Chevalier engaged the tall militiaman in carte, and permitted the fellow to grasp the feeble of his blade. With the blade of his adversary thus held in check, Arthur ventured to plunge his point under the Chevalier's elbow and into his flank (from which the name of this thrust derives). But the Chevalier pulled his sword back smartly, then beat his opponent's blade in tierce, sending it spinning from his hand. Arthur fell back, disarmed, and with the Chevalier's point at his throat.

"Do not look to grasp two blades when you have not learned the proper method of holding one. Keep your left arm behind you. Balance yourself with it, and if it pleases you to disarm an adversary, seek one who holds his sword as you do, as though it were a fragile bird. Then do as I did, and send the bird on the wing.

"Now, then, *messieurs*, resume your combat, and perhaps we shall see if either of you is a swordsman at all."

The bantam, who had regained a measure of his dignity and composure, addressed his comrade.

"The fellow has an unnatural advantage of me, Arthur,

for he holds his sword in the left hand.* You have exercised often with left-handed adversaries, as I have not. I must leave it to you to settle with him."

Before the startled Arthur could find his tongue, the Chevalier spoke.

"Ah, *mon petit Capitaine,* for snatching unnatural advantage I do apologize. It is my habit to hold the sword in the right hand, but an English musket ball causes a temporary inconvenience."

He drew back the right sleeve of his coat to reveal a bandage wrapped about his forearm.

"I make no objection if you, too, grasp your sword in the left hand," he said.

"Well, then!" exclaimed Arthur in evident relief. "That is a different matter. We did not know you were wounded, and we certainly cannot fight a wounded man, for it would be an unequal match."

The Chevalier stepped forward and embraced each of the startled militiamen in turn.

"Such *noblesse!* It brings tears to these eyes. But I will

---

* Fencing is one exercise in which a left handed person has a distinct advantage. In his *School of Fencing,* Angelo put it this way:

It often happens that the right handed fencer is much embarrassed in defending himself against a left handed one, occasioned by the constant habit of fencing always with right handed fencers, which gives the left handed fencer a considerable advantage. You seldom have occasion to fence with a left handed man, because the number of these is but small; and for the same reason, when two left hands meet, they are equally at a loss with one another.

Angelo, along with many other eighteenth- (and twentieth-) century fencing masters, advised his students to practice fencing with the left hand as well as the right, and be ready to switch when confronted by a left-handed opponent.—M.C.

not accept. To deny you your satisfaction, *mes* brave gossoons, should make me dwell in sadness. Now, resume your combat to the first blood. One of you will be wounded, and then we shall have an equal match. I shall meet the loser! *Allez, messieurs!*"

The two turned and faced each other uncertainly. The Chevalier watched with twinkling eyes as the two crossed swords again.

Hesitantly at first, but then with growing vigor, the militiamen fenced. Ralph profited by the Chevalier's words; he bent both knees and moved to and fro with alacrity. Arthur, too, had learned his lesson, and he kept his leftmost parts far from the tip of Ralph's blade, but presently he left an opening in his guard, through which his adversary plunged his point, striking him in the shoulder.

"First blood!" proclaimed Ralph.

Arthur clapped a hand to the wound and bit his lip.

"No," he answered. "You but wounded my coat."

"Then remove it, sir," demanded Ralph, "that I may see for myself."

"What? Call me liar?"

"If I am wrong, sir, remove your coat!"

"Fie upon you, sir! Apologize, or I will shed your blood in earnest!"

"My blade is the only apology I offer!"

"So be it! On guard!"

The two resumed combat with a new grimness and ferocity.

"Have a care for your giblets, *messieurs!*" the Chevalier merrily cried. "I am pledged to meet the loser, but I cannot fence with a corpse. It would be—how did you say it?—an unequal match!"

While the Chevalier watched this entertainment, he failed to observe that the ferryman had cast off his line, and the barge bearing the young gentleman, the militiamen's post chaise, their coachman, and the Chevalier's valiant horse had commenced its voyage across the Schuylkill River. But the beast, seeing her rider left behind, whinnied and drew his notice.

"*Revenir!*" cried the Chevalier, but the ferryboat continued into the stream.

"You kidnap my horse!"

The Chevalier waded into the icy water and quickly overtook the barge before it had passed beyond the shallows near the bank. With the help of the ferryman and the young gentleman, he climbed aboard.

"Take care, Major Lawless," warned the young gentleman. "This ferryboat has already drowned one great soldier of France."*

"You seem to have the advantage of me, *monsieur*. And you have my horse, as well."

"Accept my apologies, Major, and your horse, as well. I but meant to draw you from the landing and so remove all need for those lads to assassinate each other. I am Ben Tallmadge, major of the Second Light Dragoons."†

The Chevalier bowed.

---

* Probably a reference to the Chevalier de Coudray, a French aristocrat who served as general of artillery and ordnance in the Continental Army. If so, it places this scene at Gray's Ferry, below Philadelphia and near the mouth of the Schuylkill, where Coudray's horse jumped from the ferry on 15 September 1777, drowning the general, who had not bothered to dismount for the crossing. —M.C.

† Benjamin Tallmadge (1754–1835), Yale graduate, schoolmaster, and friend of Nathan Hale. Tallmadge was commissioned as major in the Second Light Dragoons on 7 April 1777. However, in October 1781 he was no longer serving as a dragoon, although he may have claimed to be; since 1778 he had been chief of General Washington's intelligence service.—M.C.

"I salute your wisdom, Major, and I envy it. I, as you seem to know, am Desmond Cuchulain de Lawless, major of the Regiment of Dillon."

"Your splendid reputation has preceded you, sir."

"And traveled in the company of a likeness, one might think," replied the Chevalier with some bemusement. "But I do not recall sitting for one."

"I should need no portrait to recognize one whose swordsmanship is his signature," said Tallmadge, smiling. "At all events, your arrival was expected."

"*Oui,* in a certain house in Philadelphia," ventured the Chevalier carefully.

"A house that is our common destination," said Tallmadge.

The ferryboat had gained the eastern bank, and the travelers disembarked.

"A happy conjunction, *monsieur,*" said the Chevalier, "for I am a stranger to this place. Lead on, *s'il vous plaît,* and I shall follow."

4

A Secret Service

THE house of M. de La Luzerne stood upon the north side of Chestnut Street and was of a magnificence befitting His Most Christian Majesty's emissary to the American Republic.* Had we arrived some minutes in advance of the Chevalier and his companion, we should have found the minister taking leave of an early visitor, an earnest gentleman of some forty years, whose manner was marked by great intensity and want of good humor.

"I fail to understand, sir, why this matter cannot be dealt with by your secret police," said Arthur Lee.†

---

* Anne-César de La Luzerne, French minister to the United States from 1779 to 1784, of whom it has been said, he "wielded so much influence that he may almost be considered one of the heads of the American government" (*Reluctant Rebels: The Story of the Continental Congress, 1774–1789,* by Lynn Montross; New York, 1952; pp. 314–315). His house was on the north side of Chestnut between Sixth and Seventh streets (*The Story of Philadelphia,* by Lilian Rhoades; New York, 1900; p. 195).—M.C.

† Arthur Lee (1740–1792), of the aristocratic Lee family of Virginia. In 1776, Lee, together with Benjamin Franklin and Silas Deane of Connecticut, was sent to Paris to procure French aid for the Revolution. An irascible and, perhaps, paranoid personality, Lee quarreled with Franklin and Deane, accusing them of profiteering and treason. He returned to America in 1780, serving in the Virginia House of Delegates and the Continental Congress, where his indictment of Deane and Franklin split the

"*C'est impossible,*" replied M. de La Luzerne. "Recruit to your mind, *monsieur,* the power of this person. Dr. Franklin has many friends in France, as does he here. Consider what might ensue should Monsieur Le Noir* fail to discover the proofs of which you speak, and Dr. Franklin should discover that the police spied upon him. It should be a great embarrassment to His Majesty."

"Then let me send an American on the errand. Major Tallmadge, or one of his men."

"No, Monsieur Lee. That could bring a worse calamity down upon our heads, should it get abroad in Paris and Versailles that the Americans mistrusted their own minister plenipotentiary. If you would permit me to say so, *monsieur,* the alliance between our two countries is often a fragile one, and might not survive the spectacle of the Americans laundering their soiled linen in the hotel at Passy."

"Very well. I see that it cannot be an American. Yet neither may it be a Frenchman. But, damme, sir, is this fellow you propose not one of Rochambeau's men?"

"He is, *monsieur,* but he is not French. He is an Irishman."

"Ah, a mercenary! Can we trust such a man?"

"*Oui,* he is a soldier of fortune, but he is one that takes his pay in English blood. We may trust such men, so long as we keep England as our enemy."

"He has the sound of a rascal."

"We should send a rascal to catch a rascal, *n'est-ce pas?*

---

government into two opposing factions. In January 1781 Lee tried unsuccessfully to have Congress recall Franklin from Paris. —M.C.

* Jean-Charles Le Noir, chief of the Paris police and hence responsible for French internal security.—M.C.

If he fails he is an Irish rascal, not a French rascal or an American rascal. Irish rascality is less an embarrassment to His Majesty or a hazard to the alliance."

A servant entered the chamber and whispered into the minister's ear.

"Ah, the rascal has arrived, together with your Major Tallmadge. Do you wish to meet him?"

"Tallmadge? Here?"

"A courtesy between allies, Monsieur Lee. It would be unseemly for me to examine into the allegiance of the American minister plenipotentiary without consultation with American leaders; and it would be imprudent to share such a secret with as many as sit in Congress. Thus I have assumed the liberty of advising General Washington and Monsieur Jefferson of the affair through Major Tallmadge. They have given their blessing to the undertaking."

"But that is splendid news, sir! If you have awakened such persons to Franklin's treachery, you have already done us a great service."

M. de La Luzerne bowed in reply.

"The matter seems well in hand, then," said Lee. "I shall take my departure by your back door and leave it to you to wish your Major Lawless godspeed."

After the American was gone, Major Tallmadge and the Chevalier were ushered into the chamber. The minister, who knew the Chevalier very well and did not, in truth, regard him as a rascal, greeted his friend with affection.

"It is a delight to glimpse an old, familiar face in this foreign land, *mon ami*! Where did you find him, Major Tallmadge?"

"On the far bank of the Schuylkill. I think he meant to establish an academy of fencing there."

"Indeed?"

"A school of civilities, perhaps," laughed the Chevalier.

"Bad manners and poor swordsmanship make a fatal compound. If those puppies learned nothing of the blade from me, perhaps they learned a lesson in courtesy."

"Shame upon you, Desmond," reproved M. de La Luzerne. "It is not suitable for a soldier of France to go about quarreling with His Majesty's allies."

"But quarreling is a soldier's stock-in-trade, dear friend," replied the Chevalier. "I am content to leave diplomacy to able diplomatists, such as yourself."

"Ah, but I am not content that you should do so. A secret diplomatic service is the very thing I wish of you; it is the reason I asked you here."

The Chevalier glanced at Major Tallmadge. Turning back to M. de La Luzerne he lifted an eyebrow but said nothing.

"Major Tallmadge is in my confidence," said M. de La Luzerne. "He is, in fact, in the secret service of General Washington."

"Since when does a dragoon serve in secret?" inquired the Chevalier.

"When he puts by his regimentals and captivates naught but intelligence," Tallmadge replied.

"Aha!" exclaimed the Chevalier. "A *dragon* in the clothes of a sheep.* But the sheep might call it spying."

"Call it what you will, Major Lawless," said Tallmadge, "but it is a necessary part of warfare and, I think, an honorable one."

"Perhaps," acknowledged the Chevalier, "but it is not a part of the warfare of my acquaintance."

---

* The Chevalier's pun may seem less labored if it is noted that the French *dragon* refers to both the mythical beast and the mounted infantryman. Dragoons originally took their name from that of their principal weapon, a large musket which, like a dragon, belched fire.—M.C.

"Then, Desmond, you must complete your education as a soldier," said M. de La Luzerne. "You are not yet such an old dog you cannot learn new tricks. Major Tallmadge, unfold for my friend a map of this new battlefield he is to fight upon."

"The grounds upon which secret war is made are not to be found on any map," said Tallmadge. "They are grounds for suspicion, belief or disbelief, inference or absolute knowledge. The object of such warfare is not ground, but intelligence of the enemy's strength, his situation, his intentions. Its soldiers are not grenadiers, dragoons, nor infantry, for secret service may be rendered by any man, or even woman, blessed with eyes and ears, and if he is ever to be found in military dress, it will be the enemy's coat he wears."

"*C'est-à-dire,* he is a turncoat, *un traître,*" the Chevalier remarked.

"Or a brave masquerader," M. de La Luzerne observed dryly. "It depends upon one's point of view."

"Whatever your point of view," said Tallmadge, "there is such a one concealed within the American ministry at Paris."

"And it will be your task, Desmond, to discover his name."

"My task? *Morbleu!* Am I to quit the field, then, so I may journey to Paris to count the Americans' silverware and catch some errant *valet de chambre?*"

"The Americans have not been betrayed by their servants," replied M. de La Luzerne. "The traitor that must be unmasked is an august personage, a member of the American delegation whom the English call Moses."

"Moses? *Très joli.* But how is it you know this *petit nom* of the English for their spy?"

"Through a spy of our own—Colonel La Motte, who

purchased the information at the price of his head. He obtained secret papers of the English Foreign Ministry which disclose the existence of this Moses and discover the depths of his treachery. Not a word of any consequence has been uttered at Passy* which was not soon whispered into the ears of the English king and his ministers. And the ink had scarcely dried upon the most secret state papers of the Americans before copies were beheld by English eyes.† No, Desmond, Moses is no *valet de chambre.* I fear his name may be Benjamin Franklin."

"*C'est incroyable!*" exclaimed the Chevalier.

"You are acquainted with Dr. Franklin?" inquired M. de La Luzerne.

"*Mais non,* yet I have seen him many times walking the streets of Paris, with great crowds at his heels straining for a glimpse of the American Voltaire. They say he is a good and wise man, and they call him the Sage of Philadelphia. I cannot believe such a man would betray his country and his allies."

"Yet that is what some believe and have charged. One who knows him very well sat in that same chair not an hour ago and accused Dr. Franklin of treason. I speak of Monsieur Lee of Virginia."

---

* A village one half mile from Paris, where the American ministry was established in a wing of the Hôtel de Valentinois.—M.C.

† Remarkably, this is not an exaggeration. When the Treaty of Alliance between France and the United States was signed in Paris on 6 February 1778, a copy was in the hands of King George and Lord North within forty-two hours, which was an extraordinary feat of communication at a time when the overland trip from Dover to London alone required a full day. The details of this coup were later recorded by the British agent who accomplished it, and a copy of his memorandum appears in full in Currey (*Code Number* 72), pp. 319–322.—M.C.

The Chevalier dismissed this with a gesture of contempt.

"I have heard of Monsieur Lee," he said. "He is a famous accuser, who himself is accused by others of petty jealousy."

"He is a quarrelsome fellow," M. de La Luzerne admitted, "but his accusations have proved true before, as he reminded me this morning. I speak of Monsieur Deane, who, having betrayed his country even as Monsieur Lee claimed, has now betrayed himself. And who defended Monsieur Deane when these charges were first made against him? Who vouched for him? None but his dear friend Dr. Franklin."*

"That may be," said the Chevalier, "but loyalty to a friend is not treason to one's country. If Monsieur Deane would betray his country, would he cavil at betraying the trust of Dr. Franklin? Where is the proof of Dr. Franklin's treachery?"

"In Paris, if it is to be found at all," replied M. de La Luzerne. "That is where you must look for it, Desmond. A French corvette clears port today, bound for Brest. You must be aboard her when she sails. Here is a letter you will deliver to the foreign minister when you reach Ver-

---

* Silas Deane (1737–1789). Deane had been recalled from Paris in 1778 to answer Lee's charges. Two years later he returned to Europe as a private citizen, angry and resentful at his treatment by the Congress; apparently he was recruited by British intelligence at this time, and was paid to write letters to friends in America arguing against the cause of independence. These supposedly private letters were to be "intercepted" by the British and published for their propaganda value. In fact, Deane submitted them directly to Lord North and King George, who reviewed them before they were published in *Rivington's Royal Gazette,* a Tory newspaper printed in New York City, which was still in British hands. The letters were published between 24 October and 12 December 1781, a period which includes the date of this scene.—M.C.

sailles. He will arrange that you be posted *en second* to the American ministry as aide to Dr. Franklin. Then it will be up to your own eyes and ears."

"Listening at doors and peeking through keyholes!" exclaimed the Chevalier. "This is no work for a fighting man of *La Brigade Irlandaise*."

"So it may seem, Major Lawless," ventured Major Tallmadge, "but in fact there is no work more vital to victory over the English."

The Chevalier cast a doubtful glance toward the American.

"Perhaps, *monsieur*," he said, "but I trust you will take no offense if I esteem such a claim to be somewhat extravagant."

"It is perfectly true, Desmond," said M. de La Luzerne. "You should not judge Major Tallmadge's words extravagant if you shared all he knows. Major, I think we must let Desmond into the secret."

"As you wish, sir," said Tallmadge. "Major Lawless, the defeat of Lord Cornwallis at Yorktown has brought this war to a decisive juncture. There shall likely be no more great battles fought."

"What is this you say?" demanded the Chevalier. "Are the English not yet strong at New York and in the South?"

"They are," Tallmadge admitted, "but not so strong they can undo what has been done. Yorktown has broken the back of the British military adventure in America. It remains only for King George to see that."

"Ah, *oui*," laughed the Chevalier. "That, indeed, is what remains. Perhaps you should send a messenger to the English king to explain that his back is broken, before he sends more soldiers to replace those he lost at Yorktown."

"He will send no more soldiers," said Tallmadge. "Nor is there any need for such a messenger, for his Parliament will soon tell him that this war must end. King George may wish more war, but the English people will no longer bear the cost of it. We have our friends at Westminster, you see, and our intelligence on this point is most reliable."

"Très bien," said the Chevalier. "But if this is so, what can it matter if a dozen English spies lurk within the American ministry?"

"It is a matter of the greatest moment, sir," the American replied. "When the English see, as soon they shall, that they cannot prevail by making war, they shall be ready to sue for peace. Then they will strive to secure with bargaining that which they have been unable to hold by force of arms. Foreseeing this, the American Congress have appointed several commissioners to treat with the English and establish satisfactory terms for a treaty of peace. And chief among these peace commissioners is Dr. Franklin."

"Dr. Franklin?" remarked the Chevalier. "But is it wise to send a man you do not trust on such an errand?"

"The Americans could not do otherwise," said M. de La Luzerne. "Dr. Franklin's many friends in the Congress believe him loyal and esteem him most able to treat with the English. If they are not mistaken in the former, they are also right in the latter."

"Yet, if they are wrong, if Dr. Franklin is indeed a traitor," said the Chevalier, "then that which has been won upon the battlefield may be lost at the conference table."

"Just so," said Tallmadge. "You see our dilemma. If Moses and Franklin are one and the same, then we must discover it and denounce him to the Congress. And we must do it before the bargaining begins!"

The Chevalier considered Major Tallmadge's words for some moments before he spoke.

"My apologies, *monsieur,*" he said, "for making little of this matter. Now that you have clarified it, even a simple soldier such as myself can comprehend the magnitude of the difficulties presented by this affair of Moses. A few moments ago I thought this task unworthy of myself; now I fear it is I who am unworthy of the task. It is indeed a vital matter, as you say, Major Tallmadge, and it demands one with greater wit than I command. You must send another to discover this Moses, for the deed wants a cunning head more than a mighty arm. I am not seasoned in this secret war of which you speak, and I fear I know nothing of intrigue."

"Yet Major Tallmadge and I *are* veterans of such clandestine warfare," said M. de La Luzerne, "and we esteem you more suitable than any other for this mission, Desmond. If we know more of such matters than do you, must you not therefore defer to our judgment in this case?"

"I will defer to your wishes in any case, *mon ami,*" the Chevalier replied, "for it is a soldier's duty to obey his orders. General Rochambeau has sent me to you; therefore your wish is my command."

"Well spoken, Desmond," said M. de La Luzerne. He took up a book from his desk and presented it to the Chevalier.

"You say you know nothing of intrigue. *Très bien.* Here is the intrigant's canon, the works of Niccolò Machiavelli. They are the manual of arms of the secret war. You have a long voyage before you; pass the time in study. God go with you, Desmond."

"*Merci, mon ami,*" replied the Chevalier. "I shall pass the time in study, and in prayer, as well. I shall study the ways of the secret war, but I shall also pray you are not greatly mistaken in sending me upon this errand.

"*Au revoir.*"

5

Engagement at Sea

RISING and falling on the long Atlantic swells, the *Aurore* ran before a freshening westerly. She was twenty-six days out of Philadelphia and, by the reckoning of her master, Captain La Rochelle, within a hundred leagues of the French coast. A crimson dawn broke over the waters and discovered to the lookouts a sail on the western horizon. The hue and cry brought the Chevalier to the quarterdeck, where he found La Rochelle observing the stranger through a perspective glass.*

"Friend or Englishman?"

"I cannot say, Major Lawless," the master replied, "and I do not think I shall put about to please my curiosity."

"That is a pity," remarked the Chevalier. "If they are friends they will think us churlish; if they are English they will judge us cowards."

"When, indeed, we are merely prudent, *monsieur,* for we have been too generous with our powder and shot at Philadelphia, and have left ourselves little with which to engage an English warship. My orders were to supply General Washington and avoid the enemy at sea."

"Very well," sighed the Chevalier, "but I mourn a respite from my boredom."

---

* Telescope.—M.C.

"Then restrain your grief, my friend," said the master, folding his glass. "You yet may have your respite, for she has seen us and gives chase."

The three masts standing above the horizon had narrowed to one as the stranger came about. La Rochelle called for more sail, and the watch climbed aloft to shake out top gallants and royals.

"Two points to the windward!" he called. The helmsman spun his wheel, and the *Aurore* yawed to the new heading. Reaching before the wind with canvas stretched taut, the corvette gained two knots. La Rochelle extended his glass.

"She has done the same," he said.

"The same wind fills her sails," said the Chevalier. "We shall see which of us is the swifter."

"I fear the question may be settled," said La Rochelle, handing the glass to the Chevalier. The stranger was a three-decked frigate of some forty guns. Uncommonly swift for a vessel of such burden, she drove before the wind, spray flying from her bow. La Rochelle barked an order to the boatswains, and the watch again went aloft to crowd more canvas onto the groaning yards.

Throughout the long hours of the forenoon watch the Chevalier remained at the rail, looking on as the frigate slowly overhauled the *Aurore*. By noon the stranger had advanced to within five leagues, and at three bells in the afternoon watch she came within long-cannon range. A scud of smoke billowed from her bow and the ball spouted in the *Aurore*'s fleeting wake as the dull thud of the frigate's bow chaser reached her quarry. The English jack now flew at the stranger's topmasthead. La Rochelle called all hands to quarters.

"She insists upon an engagement," remarked the Chevalier.

"Then she shall have one," replied the master. "About ship!" he cried.

The helmsman spun the wheel, and crewmen ran to the mainbraces and swung the yards. With a deep groan the *Aurore* began to lay over and come about.

"Run out the guns on the weather side!" ordered the master.

The trucks roared as tons of iron rolled across planking, countering the warship's heel as she swung around. The Chevalier steadied himself on the tilting deck and watched the English frigate bearing down upon them.

"As close to the wind as she'll lie!" called La Rochelle.

With sail shortened, the *Aurore* hauled into the wind, the Englishman now broad on her port bow. The master's maneuver caught the frigate by surprise, and she fired a ragged broadside as she passed abeam. The English gunners aimed badly, and a cluster of fountains erupted harmlessly amid the spindrift in the sea between the two vessels.

"Once again, and quite smartly!" cried the master. "Hard over! About ship!"

Again the *Aurore* heeled steeply. The Chevalier grasped the rail to keep his footing on the sloping deck.

"Faith and by blue!" he cried. "Do you seek to turn us turtle?"

"No, Major, it is the weather gage* I seek, and with the help of the good God and the dull wits of the English captain, I will have it."

---

* In the days of fighting sail there was a great advantage to being upwind of an enemy ship. This position, called the weather gage, enabled the ship that had it to steer straight for her opponent, who was forced to tack against the wind, often blinded by the smoke from the other's guns. Sea battles were often preceded by lengthy maneuvering for the weather gage.—M.C.

The Englishman began to come about, but too late. She stood fine on the starboard bow of the *Aurore,* broached to, her canvas luffing, and rolling broadly on the quartering seas.

"Run out the starboard guns!" called the master. "Stand by to fire! Steady as she goes!"

Driving before the wind, the *Aurore* bore down upon the frigate. The gunners stood ready, their linstocks smoldering. From his vantage on the quarterdeck the Chevalier could make out figures clambering into the Englishman's rigging as she strived to make headway, beating against the wind.

"A sitting duck!" he exclaimed.

"Yes," replied La Rochelle, "but we have scarcely the wherewithal to bag her. Enough shot and powder to put one broadside into her. Not what is wanted to sink her, but, if it please God, enough to dismast her and leave her behind."

A mass of smoke erupted from the side of the frigate as her guns roared in salvo. The broadside fell short of the charging *Aurore.*

"She wallows too badly for fine aiming," remarked the master. "Hold your fire, my children!" he called to his gunners. "Let us first see the whites of their eyes."

The frigate loomed large above the *Aurore*'s forecastle, and the Chevalier could see the English officers standing on the quarterdeck and crewmen running to the braces.

"Three points to the windward!" called La Rochelle.

The *Aurore* swung to port, putting the frigate upon her starboard beam.

"Prepare to fire on the upward roll!" he called. "Her rigging is your target! Ready! Fire!"

The *Aurore* shuddered as a dozen eighteen-pounders roared in unison. The smoke cleared, revealing the broadside's result. The mainmast of the frigate lay among the braces and shrouds of the mizzen, and the fore and main topsails flew tattered in the wind. The crew of the *Aurore* burst forth in a hearty cheer.

"Good shooting, my children!" cried La Rochelle. "The English will still lick those wounds when we are long safe in port."

The *Aurore* drew away from the frigate and came to starboard, the wind once again filling her sails. She made way to the east and passed before the crippled Englishman, which stood dead in the water.

"The English make to offer us a farewell salute," said the Chevalier. A gun crew had appeared on the frigate's forecastle, tearing the tarpaulin from a cannon and readying it to fire.

"A carronade!"* exclaimed La Rochelle.

The *Aurore* swung two points to port, putting the frigate dead astern, and presenting the smallest target to her gunners. Crewmen ran aloft to shake out more canvas, the sooner to withdraw beyond the reach of the dread carronade. The Englishman's gun thundered, but the pitching, rolling forecastle thwarted the gunners' aim, and the shot fell harmlessly into the sea, short and starboard of the *Aurore*.

"They bid us stay," laughed the Chevalier, "but clumsily."

"Please God, they do not become more adroit," said La Rochelle. But the next shot from the Englishman tore through the *Aurore*'s mizzen topgallant.

"Their luck surpasses their marksmanship," remarked the Chevalier.

---

* A short-barreled cannon introduced by the English in 1779 and named after the Scottish village of Carron, where it was first manufactured. It fired a heavy load over a short range and possessed tremendous smashing power against masts and crew.—M.C.

"They enhance both with chainshot,"* said the master.

The Englishman fired a third round, which whistled over the *Aurore*'s taffrail and smashed the mizzen. The mast toppled, wrenching the mainsails from their braces as it thundered to the deck. Crewmen rushed to pull their injured comrades from the wreckage of canvas, yards, and rigging.

"We are undone!" cried La Rochelle.

"We are yet afloat, *monsieur*," replied the Chevalier. "Let us come about and board the Englishman."

"Are you mad?" demanded the master. "We are fewer than one hundred, while they are likely thrice as strong!"

"A trifle, my captain," proclaimed the Chevalier. "They are, after all, only Englishmen. Moreover, if we have not the canvas to flee, nor the powder to fire, it seems we must either board the Englishman or wait for her to blow us from the water."

La Rochelle recovered his wits and saw the wisdom in the Chevalier's words. While he made to bring the *Aurore* about and close with the frigate, the Chevalier sought out the ship's master-at-arms and saw that the small-arms lockers were opened and that pistols, muskets, and cutlasses were dealt out to the crew.

"Is there a rifleman among you?" the Chevalier cried.

Several crewmen came forward, and the Chevalier spoke to them and, selecting five who were Germans,† allotted the ship's furniture of rifle-muskets to them.

---

* A pair of cannonballs linked by a length of chain to increase their destructive power against masts and rigging.—M.C.

† The rifled gun barrel was developed by the Germans and Swiss during the seventeenth century but had not found wide military use by the end of the eighteenth. Infantry tactics of the day placed little importance on accuracy (since battles were fought at

"Follow me!" he commanded, and led the five ahead to the fore rigging.

"To the foretop with you, my friends, and do not suffer the English gunners to fire their carronades!"

The rifle-muskets slung at their backs, the five marksmen climbed aloft. The crippled *Aurore* had come about and was slowly making way toward the frigate, which now lay dead ahead. The English gunners stood by their carronade on the forecastle, waiting for the *Aurore* to come within reach of the short-ranged gun once again. A sharp crack split the air, and one of the gun crew grabbed his head and fell to the deck. The carronade barked, but the load fell short of the bow of the *Aurore*. A volley from the marksmen in the foretop dropped two more of the gunners and drove their comrades from the forecastle before they could reload.

As the *Aurore* closed upon the crippled frigate, the English captain made to turn and present a broadside to the approaching vessel, but the frigate only wallowed in the seas, the wreckage upon its decks thwarting the maneuver. The rattle and smoke of musketry filled the air as the two ships closed, bow to bow, and came into pistol range.

"Prepare to board!" cried the Chevalier, and the crewmen of the *Aurore,* armed to the teeth, crouched in the shelter of the rail on the main deck. On the frigate, the

---

close range), and stressed the greater firepower of the smooth-bore musket. Many commanders of the American Revolution viewed the rifle as nothing but a hunting piece, although the German troops who fought in the war brought their rifled weapons with them and used them to some advantage. Without the opportunity to use more scientific selection criteria, the Chevalier seems to have chosen the German sailors as more likely to be proficient with the rifle.—M.C.

English crew did the same and made ready to repel the invaders.

As the two warships passed abeam, no more than a yard of ocean between their broadsides, a pair of French sailors, one forward and the other aft, cast grapples onto the Englishman's deck. Timber groaned against timber as the two craft heaved together.

"Boarders away!" cried the Chevalier, as he leaped to the frigate's deck, firing his pistol into the face of an English officer and laying about him with his sword. Cursing, roaring, and cheering, the crew of the *Aurore* swarmed after him.

The crew of the frigate numbered over three hundred, but the warship's main deck, cluttered with wrecked canvas and rigging, offered scant room for the English to profit from their superior strength. Pistols and muskets were fired point blank and then, there being no time to reload, grasped by their still-smoking barrels and made to do duty as cudgels. Steel rang upon steel amidst a din of shouts, screams, and curses. Inspired by the Chevalier's wild fury, the French crewmen fought with abandon and pressed the enemy back. A segment of the main deck, from the port rail to the starboard, soon fell to the boarders, cutting the English company in two. Half of the defending force fell back toward the forecastle under the onslaught of a party led by the master, while the rest of the Frenchmen followed the Chevalier in an assault upon the quarterdeck, where the English officers watched the battle in dismay.

"They are like the very demons of hell!" exclaimed the English captain.

"And led by a madman," rejoined a lieutenant. "That fellow in the lobster coat."

"There seems a method to his madness," observed the captain. "He means to take the quarterdeck, and so capture the ship in one blow! I think he may do it if he isn't stopped! Take a party of marines and rid the deck of that fellow. We shall see how well the Frenchmen fight without their mad leader!"

The lieutenant and ten marines descended to the main deck and joined the fray, pressing toward the place where the Chevalier stood, his sword engaging the cutlasses of five English tars.

"Ha, *messieurs*! You make to hack and cut, but there is not sufficient room to swing the cat! No, gentlemen of the cutlass, the day will go to the point, not the edge!"

And so saying, the Chevalier swiftly skewered two of his adversaries, while the others fell back in terror. As the three tars retreated, the lieutenant and the marines stepped in and pressed the attack upon the Chevalier.

Five royal marines engaged the Chevalier and made to encircle him, but he wounded three, then withdrew smartly to the frigate's foremast, which he made to shield his back. The lieutenant, meanwhile, had ranked the balance of his party and prepared to fire a volley at their formidable opponent. But the marines had scarcely raised their muskets when a salvo from the riflemen in the *Aurore*'s foretop cut them down.

"Thank you, my friends," cried the Chevalier. Then he turned to meet a new tide of English tars that swarmed around his station at the foremast.

The English captain, having witnessed the defeat of his marines, conceived a new design to overpower the Chevalier. Taking a pair of crewmen aside, he instructed them with great precision and sent them aloft to the foreyard, above the head of the unwitting Chevalier. Moving along the yard, the pair worked swiftly.

"Have a care, Major Lawless!" cried La Rochelle, who saw the stealthy move from the vantage of the forecastle.

The Chevalier looked about himself in puzzlement, but could spare little attention from the ring of flashing steel encircling him. A rifle-musket in the *Aurore*'s foretop cracked, and one of the seamen fell from the yard, but his fellow continued his work.

"Beware above you!" cried La Rochelle, but too late. The Chevalier looked up toward the yard and saw the foresail as it fell upon him. The English tars seethed forward as their adversary struggled beneath the canvas snare. The Chevalier made to draw his dagger and cut the hindrance from about him, but the emboldened foe surged over him, crushing him to the deck, and the blow of a belaying pin to his skull drove him into oblivion.

6

Windsor

IN Berkshire, some half-dozen leagues from London, the
Oxford Road passes through a pleasing woodland, a
place of ancient groves and bubbling streams, rich in every
kind of game. There is a place where, for a league or more,
lofty elms stand at regular stations to either side of the
road, so the way seems to run between endless colonnades.
The summer traveler, from his vantage a-saddle or at a
carriage window, may catch fleeting glimpses through the
bosky veil, of walls and towers high upon a hill. But he
who comes this way when the trees stand winter-naked
against the sky may gaze without obstruction upon the
magnificent battlements of Windsor Castle. Yet the lone
passenger in the coach that lurched and joggled over the
frozen ruts on this December morn had no eye for the
castellated ramparts that marked his destination; Lord
Stormont had looked upon them often, and on this day his
attendance was captive to those papers of state he had
spread upon his lap robe.

Let us leave Lord Stormont to his wintry meditations
and fly ahead upon the wings of thought to the summit of
Castle Hill, to seek out among Windsor's sundry chambers
the drawing room of the king, where we find His Majesty,
George III, in conference with his most loyal subject and
prime minister, Lord North.

"Your Majesty is well apprised," said North, "that, in

this country, the prince on the throne cannot, with pru-
dence, oppose the deliberate resolution of the House of
Commons. And Your Majesty well knows that the opposition has long called for a peace with the Americans. Now
the tidings come from Yorktown like a ball in my breast,
and Your Majesty's affairs grow worse by every hour that
my removal is delayed. I must, once more, beg your leave
to step down."

The king gazed long into the fire before making his reply.

"Ah, Freddie," he said, "good and loyal friend. When
success crowns our strivings a thousand men claim paternity, but failure is an orphan, and only my dear friend
would adopt this malformed and embarrassing child as his
own, and remove it from the royal bedchamber. I thank
you, my friend, but there is much more at stake than royal
repute.

"You say you would resign your office, Freddie. I, too,
would resign mine, to abdicate in favor of my eldest son.
Then we both of us should be quit of this wearisome
business. But then, what of England?

"A great state may not subsist as a small one might, by
giving up the game. A great state moldering does not simply submit itself to an inferior situation; it invites its own
annihilation. No, to give up the game in the name of pre-
serving ourselves shall do nothing but destroy England.
It cannot, it must not be."

"I should gladly surrender my life that it should not be,
Your Majesty, but I fear that it already is."

"Come, come, my friend. Of course the loss of my forces
in Virginia has put us all in a very gloomy cast. But if we
despond, ruin shall ensue. And I believe a good end may
yet be made to this war."

A servant entered the room and presented the king with
a paper upon a silver salver.

"Very good. Stormont is here. Show him in. We shall hear his thoughts. Perhaps they are less melancholy than our own."

Lord Stormont entered and began to make his obeisance to his monarch. The king motioned him to come forward and join them by the fire.

"There's no need for ceremony here, Stormont. Sit you down with us. It is your kingdom, not your king, that requires your good offices today."

"I should give the very heart from my breast for them both," declared Stormont, as he took his seat.

"I do not doubt it, dear Stormont," replied the king, "but it is the brain in your head that can avail us best. Better than any other you know the unhappy state of the war. The Americans have given Cornwallis a sound drubbing in Virginia, and Lord North and I are quite at a loss for the means to preserve my American colonies. Have you any thoughts to offer?"

Stormont cleared his throat and considered the question.

"To begin," he said, "I beg to point out to Your Majesty that the victory at Yorktown was not an American victory. It was a French victory."*

---

* Precise estimates vary, but it is generally agreed that Cornwallis's force at Yorktown numbered about 9,750 men, and that he faced a combined force of about 11,000 Americans and 9,000 French (Boatner, p. 1248). Thus, the most ardent American chauvinist cannot deny that the presence of the French caused Cornwallis to be outnumbered two to one. While it is, of course, impossible to prove that the American forces could have taken Yorktown without French aid, it is a matter of record that the French, who arrived first, believed they could do it without the Americans. The Marquis de Lafayette had to persuade the French commander, Admiral de Grasse, to wait for Washington's army, which was still marching south from New York and Philadelphia

"Of course," agreed the king. "Our enemies have seen in our colonial troubles a splendid opportunity for mischief. They have allied themselves with the rebels, so we face not one foe, but four—the French, the Dutch, the Spanish, and the Americans."

"The Spanish and the Dutch are of little account in this war," said Stormont. "Spain has not allied herself with the Americans but with the French, to whom they offer little else than some paltry coin that does not begin to supplant the treasure Louis has already lavished upon his American mischief. And the Dutch! They war with us in the most tepid way, and at our own instance. We were forced to make war upon them only because they could not resist the temptation of commerce with our enemies. But they are a nation of peddlers and of no military consequence. No, Your Majesty, it is France and none other that has swung the balance in the Americans' favor."

"That may be," said Lord North. "But as a practical matter I fail to see what difference it can make at this juncture. Whether Lord Cornwallis was defeated by the Americans or by the French, the melancholy fact remains that he was defeated."

"Quite so, my lord," Stormont agreed, "and that defeat marked the death of our hopes for victory upon the field in America."

"Is it your counsel, then, Stormont, that I must needs surrender my American colonies?" inquired the king.

"It is not, Your Majesty," replied Stormont earnestly. "I counsel only that further military adventures in America

---

when the French were already prepared to strike (Bendiner, pp. 206–207). Viewed from this perspective, Lord Stormont's characterization of Yorktown as a French victory is not completely untenable.—M.C.

can have no result, except to squander more blood and treasure. The war must be pursued elsewhere, and in a different way."

"What?" demanded Lord North. "Would you have us invade France, then?"

"Not at all," replied Stormont. "I propose quite a different design. I say we have been thwarted by an unholy union between a handful of malcontent and traitorous Englishmen and our ancient French enemy. I say that the proper object of our belligerency is not some field or fortress an ocean distant, but that pernicious union, the heart of which may be found but a hundred leagues distant, across the Channel in Versailles."

"Divide and conquer, is that it?" asked the king.

"It is, Your Majesty," Stormont replied. "And it is a happy species of campaign, for in it our foes are our unwitting allies. The Americans have divided themselves, through jealousy and suspicion—a falling-out among thieves. And there are many in Versailles who would put an end to this costly business before the French treasury is emptied by it; Louis receives a nightly lecture on his extravagant war, for his queen is the most outspoken of those who say it costs too much. To Mr. Adams, the French are a nation of libertines, while to Monsieur de Vergennes, his American allies often seem no more than a band of ungrateful mendicants. No, this alliance is infallibly doomed, and all that falls to us is to hasten the day of its demise and ensure that day dawns before the American rebels have wrested their cherished independency."

"Splendid words, dear Stormont," said the king. "What measures have you undertaken to hasten this salutary situation of affairs?"

Lord Stormont glanced about the chamber.

"This is a secret war, fought by secret men. Your

Majesty knows the names of many of his secret servants I have sent to the Continent to sow disunity between the Americans and the French—Wardlaw, Swinton, Forth, Digges; names I scruple to recite even within the precincts of these royal apartments."*

"Quite so," agreed the king. "The names of such men should not be spoken, even within these walls. I trust those you named shall do their utmost to bring about a falling-out between our enemies, but there is one name—a *nom de guerre*—you did not speak, and it is the name of one who above all others is best situated to sunder the alliance between the Americans and the French."

"You speak of the man called Moses, Your Majesty?" asked Stormont.

"I do," said the king. "Those secret men you have named are concealed within the walls of Fortress France, and are well situated to light fires of jealousy, fear, and discontent in her barracks and stables. But Moses dwells within the

---

* William Wardlaw, aka George Smith and Baron d'Issola, a British double agent who neutralized French agents, stole diplomatic correspondence, and worked to destroy the French-American alliance (Morris, pp. 128, 133ff).

Samuel Swinton, black propaganda agent of the British, who published *Courier de l'Europe,* a French-language newspaper aimed at inspiring French discontent with the war (Morris, p. 138).

Nathanial Parker Forth, British agent and courier who carried a British offer to the French of Canada and part of India in return for a separate peace (Bendiner, p. 210; Morris, pp. 254–256).

Thomas Digges, a Maryland native and British agent who tried to befriend John Adams in Amsterdam and so divide the alliance (Bendiner, p. 209; Morris, p. 255ff).

Stormont names only a few of the agents he dispatched to disrupt the French-American alliance.—M.C.

very powder magazine of the enemy. A single spark from his flint could loose so mighty an explosion not a single stone would remain of the bridge that carries French succor to American rebels."

"I fear that Moses himself might not survive such an explosion," remarked Lord North.

"Then he will share the glory of that heroic legion that has sacrificed everything for king and country," replied the king.

"With all respect, Your Majesty, I must counsel against this," said Stormont. "True it is that Moses, at his vantage within the American ministry, might well put a spoke in the wheel and halt the French engine of war. Yet the man is not above suspicion, and some of his countrymen have already said he plays a double game. Were we to use him thus, the shot might backfire, discovering our own design as well as his. Then we should have accomplished nothing but the loss of a supremely valuable spy, and perhaps have helped cement anew the alliance between our enemies."

"I am baffled by your argument, Stormont," said the king. "What does it profit us to have the best intelligence of our enemies' designs if we do nothing to thwart them? You have said it well: Our foe is this alliance between the French and the Americans, and our best hope lies in its destruction. And if sundering that union requires we hazard Moses, why then I put it to you, sir, of what benefit can he be to us if the alliance survive?"

"Should such come to pass, Your Majesty, and I fervently pray it does not, but should the alliance survive our best efforts to put it asunder, why, Moses' value to us shall have appreciated a hundredfold—no, a thousandfold.

"The Americans know they have the better of the game for the moment, and they are in a mood to make peace while they retain their advantage. The American Congress have appointed a commission and authorized it to bargain with us toward that end."

"I have no wish to hear of the Americans' hope to bargain," said the king heatedly. "I do not propose to bargain with traitors and rebels. When the Americans have authorized a commission to surrender, you may inform me of it!"

"Your Majesty," said Lord North, gently, "I do not think we can hope for the Americans to lay down their arms without condition, no matter how well blessed may be our efforts to divide them from the French. This war, like most wars, will be concluded, not upon the battlefield but at the treaty table."

"And the better of any bargain," ventured Stormont, "goes to the one who knows just what the other is prepared to give. That is how Moses can serve us best, for not a word of the Americans' deliberations is unknown to him, and through him we shall learn to the penny the price the Americans are willing to pay for peace."

"It seems imprudent to hazard the man now," agreed Lord North.

"I do not much like this talk of bargaining and conditions, gentlemen," said the king. "A great state does not win victories by preparing for defeat. Lord Stormont, you have my approval of your design to divide the French from the Americans. I leave to you to choose the means of executing it. The question of how Moses may best be employed is one you must decide. Now, have you other business, or may we adjourn?"

"There is another matter, Your Majesty," said Lord Stormont. "We have spoken of the one called Moses. Unhappily, that name is also known to the enemy, for all but the true name of the man was discovered by the French spy La Motte and conveyed to Versailles before he was apprehended. The French and the Americans know they have a traitor in their midst at the American ministry at Passy."

"But they have not discovered his name, you say," said Lord North.

"Not yet. But some three weeks past a British frigate met and captured a French vessel bound for Brest. One of Rochambeau's officers was aboard, and secret letters were found disclosing a plan to second this man to the American ministry with the aim of ferreting out a spy named Moses."

"And pray, what became of this fellow?" inquired the king.

"He is in the Tower. It transpired he was not French, but one of Louis's Irishmen."

"Those rascals!" exclaimed Lord North.

"He has been tried and convicted of treason and piracy, and sentenced to death."*

"Well, then," said the king, "the matter seems to have come to a fortunate conclusion for Moses. Why do you mention it?"

"Because, Your Majesty, I propose that this man— Lawless is his name—be set free so that he may resume his mission. He could be paroled and sent to Ostend as a yuletide gesture."

"My good Stormont," said the king, "I confess you have baffled me utterly. You earnestly argue against risking Moses under any circumstances; next you ask I set free the

---

* In February 1776 the British Parliament passed a law authorizing the king to treat all Americans captured in arms at sea as "traitors, pirates and felons" (Jones, p. 15). Although Lawless served in the French Army, the fact of his Irish birth would cause the English to regard him as a British subject and therefore a captured traitor, rather than a prisoner of war.—M.C.

very man our enemies have sent to catch him. I cannot think what your design might be."

"Your Majesty, I reason thusly: Neither the French nor the Americans know we have discovered the mission of this man Lawless, so if he is again set at large, I make no doubt he shall resume it. But if we hang him, another whose name we do not know will infallibly be sent upon the same errand. Willy-nilly, the enemy will try to catch Moses, but Moses is less likely to be caught if he knows his hunter."

"A devious line of reasoning," said the king, "but I own it seems sound enough. What think you, Freddie?"

"I have heard of this man Lawless," said Lord North. "I do not pretend to know the art of intrigue, but I hope I comprehend simple justice. This scoundrel slaughtered some forty of Your Majesty's officers and men in this sea battle, and maimed a dozen more. I say he has earned his sentence, and it ought to be carried out!"

"Forty English sailors murdered!" exclaimed the king. "No, Stormont, I think this man Lawless must hang."

"And be drawn and quartered?" inquired Stormont. "That was the sentence."

"No, not that!" exclaimed Lord North. "That is barbaric! 'Tis enough he hang, I say."

"So be it," said the king.

7

The Theater of the Dead

THE fog rose from the river and crawled into the city, curling through streets and alleys to conspire with the night. Its dank and fetid embrace smothered into dimness the light of lamp and windowpane, imprisoning all for whom the darkened byways of London held a special dread. Yet there dwelt behind some doors things more frightful than any that might be met abroad in the dismal streets.

Within a great hall in Warwick Lane* there had been constructed a kind of theater. Ascending ranks of rounded galleries encircled a pit, a design affording an unobstructed view to those who watched from above that which was done below. The darkened galleries were empty, but the light of a guttering lamp disclosed three figures down in the pit. Two men stood and gazed upon a third, who lay naked on a stone table.

The man on the table had no eyes. The top of his skull had been cleanly cut away, and his brain laid out above his head. He had been neatly cleaved from breast to groin,

---

* Surgeons' Hall. The Royal College of Surgeons stood on the west side of Warwick Lane, near Newgate Street, around the corner from the Old Bailey. The bodies of felons and paupers were brought there to be "anatomized," i.e., dissected for anatomical study.—M.C.

and much of what God had packed within now reposed in a wooden bucket on the floor of the pit.

"Darkmans,"* whispered Jack Bolt, the new porter. He turned away from the thing on the table and shuddered. "I own I'll fancy this work more when the sun shines," he said.

" 'Tis commonly done by day," said the beadle. "We've no resurrection men here, but for one upstairs, grinning in a glass case.† No, my good Bolt, the carcasses you fetch for me you shall fetch lawfully. Each morning you will take the dungcart and make your rounds, calling in turn upon each of the Saints."

"The Saints?"

"The Saints," repeated the beadle with a crafty smirk. "St. Thomas's, St. Bartholomew's, St. George's, and the other hospitals. But mind you, don't pass up Guy's or London Lock, or any of the other places that ain't been canonized. They're all of a oneness to Old Mr. Grim, and wherever he may stop, there also must you stop. He favors

---

* The night. (For the meanings of eighteenth-century slang, jargon, and cant words, I have resorted to *A Classical Dictionary of the Vulgar Tongue,* by Captain Francis Grose, originally published in 1796, and edited and republished in 1963 by Eric Partridge. Partridge's *A Dictionary of Slang and Unconventional English* [seventh edition, New York, 1970] was also very useful in deciphering some of the language of Lawless's text.)—M.C.

† In the seventeenth and eighteenth centuries, grave robbers, called resurrection men, filled the burgeoning demand of medical schools for cadavers by plundering churchyards by night. Ironically, some of this occupation were caught, hanged, and sent to the dissecting tables themselves. The skeletons of some dissected cadavers were kept on display for anatomical instruction; the eighteenth-century phrase for such a fate was "to grin in a glass case."—M.C.

the little hours of the morning, so you must be up with the sun to gather the night's harvest of soul-cases while they're yet fresh."

"Aye, better they be fresh," said Bolt with distaste. "I shouldn't fancy carting any stale ones. But what answer shall I make to widows and others as been bereaved, should they think a churchyard a more fitting place for the departed than a table in Surgeons' Hall?"

"You'll meet no mourners on your rounds, Bolt," answered the beadle, "for you'll claim only the unclaimed, those that haven't the price in their pockets to pay for a bed to die in, much less the cost of a Christian burial, nor any ready to stand it in their behalf."

Bolt nodded. "I'll be the beggars' coachman," he said.

"Beggars' and felons'," agreed the beadle. Then, striking his knee, he exclaimed, "Damme! I near forgot! There's to be a Tyburn Fair tomorrow, so see you hie yourself early up Holborn Hill and gather the fruit that falls from the Tyburn tree. Then bring 'em here directly."

"There's but one cove being stretched, I hear," ventured Bolt.

"Never mind. The surgeons see a plenitude of them that's been ailing, and they're always keen to stick a knife into one that's hale but for a touch of hempen fever. It's to be a pirate, I think, and an Irishman, at that, so I'll warrant he's a healthful specimen. See that you fetch him, Bolt. One rogue is worth a dozen almsmen."

"Very well," answered Bolt. "And by your leave it's me for home and bed now, the better to make an early day of it tomorrow. Tyburn Road is long for any but them that rides over it standing in a tumbrel."

"Stay awhile," said the beadle, drawing his watch from the pocket of his waistcoat. "I expect a visitor." An uneasy cloud passed over his countenance. Bolt looked on expectantly.

"A visitor that wants something fetched or carried?" the porter asked.

The beadle shook his head. "A visitor with stranger wants than that. Oh, a fine gentleman, mind you. Holds a seat in Commons, in fact. But 'tis a passing queer hobby horse he rides. To put it plainly, he is allured by the dead. Scarce a week goes past that he fails to come here by night to look upon the carcasses."

"Your gentleman must be named Mr. George Selwyn," Bolt remarked.

The beadle started as one stricken. "Hold your tongue, Bolt! His name is secret!"

"A secret shared by half of London, then," answered Bolt. "Mr. Selwyn's horrid fancies are famous, and his face is known to any that's been to a Tyburn Fair."

"That may be," allowed the beadle, "but his name must never be spoken here."

The porter shrugged. "Then I shan't speak it. And I think your nameless gentleman might be better pleased if you greeted him alone."

"He would that," the beadle agreed.

"Yet you bid me tarry?"

"For mine own sake, Bolt. 'Tis your company and not your back that's wanted. Oh, the gentleman is agreeable, and generous as well—ten guineas whenever he visits, and a fine Christmas box each year. And there's many a gentleman that makes private studies of natural philosophy and the like, so why should such a one not pursue anatomy?"

"Why not?" Bolt agreed. "But . . . ?"

"But he quite makes my hair stand up upon my head!" the beadle exclaimed. "Listen!"

A slow, dull tattoo echoed through the hall.

"He's at the door! Show him inside, Bolt!"

The porter left the dissecting room and crossed to the main door. He swung open the massive portal and lifted his lantern. A wizened little man of some threescore years stood framed in the portico, his cloak wrapped round himself. A nimbus of fog twisted about the gaunt figure like a cloud of infernal smoke, and the lantern's light glistened brightly in a pair of darting eyes.

"Who are you?" demanded the apparition in a raspy whisper.

"Bolt, sir. The new porter. Come inside, if you please."

The little man turned and signed to a pair of sturdy chairmen that stood with a sedan in the foggy lane, then stepped through the doorway.

"You'll be wanting the beadle, sir," said Bolt. "He's in the main shambles. Come this way, sir, if you please."

"The main shambles,"* repeated the little man. He cackled hideously and followed the porter.

"Oh, good evening to you, sir," said the beadle, coming forward to greet his visitor. "I've had your note and was expecting you."

"Then why are you not alone?" demanded the caller.

"This is Bolt, sir, the new porter. He's a trusty fellow with a short tongue and a shorter memory."

The beadle's answer did not quite satisfy the little man, but he remarked no further on the matter. "I've come to see the wench you got from Bridewell† today," he said.

---

* In the eighteenth century the word still retained its original meaning of slaughterhouse, or butcher shop.—M.C.

† A prison located on the west side of the present New Bridge Street and just north of Tudor Street. It was originally an exclusively women's prison, but later male prisoners were also incarcerated there.—M.C.

"Fetch her here, Bolt," said the beadle. The porter departed and some minutes later returned with a barrow upon which rested a tiny figure covered by a shroud. The beadle turned back the sheet while his visitor fixed his spectacles upon his nose and stepped closer.

"Ah, what a shame!" the beadle remarked. "Such a pretty little thing, no more than a child."

"Is she poxed?" demanded the little man. The beadle was startled.

"Why, she was no strumpet, but a lady's maid that stole from her mistress. She was flogged today, and 'twas more than her little body could suffer. I think she died of an apoplexy."

"I know she was flogged, you fool!" hissed the little man. "I *saw* her flogged.* I asked you if she was *poxed*!"

"There's not a mark upon her but those left by the cat,"† the beadle replied. "You may see for yourself. Clear the table, Bolt."

The porter removed the dead man and, after swabbing down the table, placed the child's body upon it. The little man poked and prodded the corpse and found, as the beadle had promised, no blemish but for a score of long, dark red welts upon the child's back and shoulders.

"Ah, a fine little tabby kitten with purple stripes," cackled the little man. The beadle made an uneasy smile, but the porter did not disguise his horror.

"Now leave me!" ordered the little man. "Both of you! And do not return until you are summoned."

The two men departed the amphitheater to wait in the hall beyond.

---

* The flogging of women prisoners at Bridewell was a spectacle available to any of the public that cared to watch.—M.C.
† The lash.—M.C.

"What might he be about in there?" demanded Bolt.

The beadle shook his head. "I dare not guess. It may be he prays for her soul."

Jack Bolt made no reply to this.

The beadle added, "When he spoils 'em he pays a premium."

"Spoils 'em?"

"Aye, cuts 'em open and takes away liver and lights, or some other part. They're little use to the surgeons then, so he pays full price for the carcass."

"By God's wounds!" exclaimed Bolt. "What can he want with their parts?"

" 'Tis no business of mine, Bolt, nor yours either. Mayhap he preserves 'em in pickle for later study, as the surgeons do. Or it may be he holds with them country folk as say such things are canker cure."*

" 'Tis ungodly and wicked," muttered Bolt.

"That may be, Bolt, but it ain't our business," reproved the beadle.

"And I praise the saints it ain't," Bolt replied. The two men lapsed into silence, and a quarter hour passed before the door to the amphitheater opened and the little man emerged.

"Ah, there you are," he said, a horrid smirk twisting his mouth. "The good beadle and his trusty porter. Waiting for your pay, no doubt."

---

* Belief that the corpse of a felon, especially one who had been hanged, possessed magical therapeutic powers was widespread in English folklore of the eighteenth century. Skin disorders, withered limbs, goiter, tumors, ulcers, and even sterility were among the ailments thought curable by contact with the body of a hanged person (Hay, pp. 109–110).—M.C.

He drew a purse from the folds of his cloak and threw it at the beadle's feet. The beadle swiftly seized it up, his tongue wetting his lips. The little man threw a golden guinea at the porter.

"There, trusty Bolt. See that your tongue and memory stay short."

He was turning to leave when the beadle found his voice.

"Thank you kindly, sir. Will you be coming on the morrow?"

"Tomorrow? Why should I come tomorrow?"

"A pirate's to be scragged at Tyburn. He'll be brought here directly for the surgeons to ottomize."*

"Pirates are hanged in chains at Wapping," said the little man. "The rascal of whom you speak is a traitor, and so will be half-hanged, drawn, and quartered. His tripes will be torn out for all to see at Tyburn. Do you think to cheat me, man? To make me pay for that which I'll have already seen?"

"Begging your pardon, sir," said the beadle. "Traitor he may be, but by the king's mercy, there's to be no drawing or quartering. His sentence was changed to sus per coll."†

"I see," said the little man. "That is a pity. 'Tis hardly worth a trip to Tyburn to see one rascal hanged without some added diversion. Very well, keep a place for me and send word round to my house of the hour at which the slicing is to be done."

He waited while Bolt drew open the door.

"Five more guineas for you, beadle," he said. "You should be grateful for the king's mercy, but not so greatly obliged as I fancy the rogue must be."

---

* Anatomize, i.e., dissect.—M.C.
† *Suspensus per collum* (hanged by the neck).—M.C.

Cackling at his wit, the little man disappeared into the fog.*

---

* The disgusting little man who visits Surgeons' Hall in this chapter is identified by Jack Bolt as George Selwyn. The reader may recall that Selwyn was seen briefly on the sidelines during the execution of Henri de La Motte in Chapter One, where I noted that he lived from 1719 to 1791. Did the historical Selwyn resemble the monster we met here? The answer seems to be that Lawless's portrait of Selwyn, however lurid, is accurate, or at least consistent with the reputation the man earned during his lifetime.

The staid British *Dictionary of National Biography* notes, "Selwyn's fondness for seeing corpses and criminals and for attending executions was the subject of frequent comment during his lifetime, but it was warmly disputed by intimate friends." Several accounts of Selwyn's life mention a trip he made to Paris to watch the execution by slow torture of Robert François Damiens, a lunatic who stabbed Louis XV in an assassination attempt. Bayne-Powell (p. 222) says Selwyn remarked, after watching the hanging of some fourteen-year-old boys, "I never saw boys cry so much."

The *Dictionary of National Biography* notes that Selwyn was expelled from Oxford University in 1745 and forbidden to come within five miles of the campus "for a reputed insult to the Christian religion; he [Selwyn] contended that the freak (of using a chalice at a wine party) was merely a satire on the doctrines taught by the church of Rome." (It would have been a "satire" on the Church of England, as well, which also employs sacramental wine in its services.)

There may have been a little more to this "freak" that went unrecorded but was sufficient to warrant the obvious horror of the Oxford administration, because it suggests an early experiment with what was later to become another of Selwyn's amusements, i.e., the Black Mass. There is no question that Selwyn was a principal member of Sir Francis Dashwood's satanic order, the Hell Fire Club, a distinction that makes him a major character in Lawless's story. We'll see more of George Selwyn in later pages. —M.C.

8

The Hanging of the Chevalier

THE day had yet to dawn, but Father Collins was up and abroad, hurrying along the empty streets. He scurried through Dunster Court and down Mark Lane to Tower Street, then up Great Tower Hill, presenting himself to the warders who guarded the Outward Gate.

"The papist priest to pray for the Irish rebel!" announced the guard, and the gate was opened. Father Collins was led within, across the drawbridges, through the Middle Tower and the Byward Tower, along the Outer Ward to the great iron portcullis that blocked the gate of the Bloody Tower. Here the warder repeated his declaration, and the heavy barrier was raised. The priest and the jailer passed within the Inner Ward. Entering the White Tower they climbed a rough stone stairway, stopping before the door of a cell.

"Wake up, ye Irish blackguard!" shouted the jailer as he opened the door. The Chevalier stirred upon his pallet of straw, sat up, stretched, and yawned.

"Have you forgotten you're to be hanged today, man?" the jailer demanded.

"Ah, *oui*, Monsieur Eater-of-Beef, the fact had quite eloped from my mind. *Merci*, my friend. It would be unmannerly of me to fail to attend to a ceremony of which I am the guest of honor."

He rose and scratched absently.

"May I inquire as to the whereabouts of my breakfast?" he said.

"Yer breakfast!" exclaimed the jailer. "You think of breakfast on the morning of your last day on earth?"

"*Oui,* for there seems no point in contemplating supper, *n'est-ce pas?* Besides, have I not paid for it?"*

"I've brought you yer priest. I'll get you yer breakfast," grumbled the jailer. He stood back and let Father Collins into the cell, then slammed and locked the door.

"Ah, *bonjour,* Father Collins. What brings you so soon again to this melancholy place?"

"Why, I've come to hear your confession," said the priest.

"But have you forgotten that you heard my confession yesterday?"

"Of course, but do you not wish to confess again, before . . . ?"

"Before breakfast?" asked the bewildered Chevalier. "Aha, I comprehend. Before being hanged. But I fear I have no new sins to relate. You must remember very well my preferences in sinning. The hospitality of the English is not so grand as to equip their prisoners with occasions of such sin."

The priest's countenance went scarlet.

"Certainly not!" he stammered. "But I feared you might fall into a different species of sin. I speak of the sin of despair."

---

* Prisoners in the Tower were required to pay for their own meals.—M.C.

"Despair?" remarked the Chevalier. He shrugged. "I confess my prospects do not appear propitious at the moment. I did not know such reflections were sinful."

"Not despair of escaping the noose, man! Despair of gaining the kingdom of heaven! That is the sin of despair."

"Ah, I comprehend. But do not derange yourself, *bon père*." He clapped the priest's shoulders heartily. "I know you are an able priest. I do not fear you have bungled the absolution. I am certain I shall go straight to heaven!"

"But you must not be certain, my son, for that is the sin of presumption."

The Chevalier shook his head in bafflement.

"This theology is too deep for a simple soldier, especially before breakfast. You have me surrounded; if I advance, I shall be blasted by presumption, yet my retreat has been cut off by despair. What are your orders, then, *mon Général?*"

"You must hope, Desmond. Hope for salvation."

The Chevalier shrugged. "*Très bien.* Only a fool would hope for damnation." He suddenly brightened. "Tell me, Father Collins: Curiosity, is it a sin?"

"Why, I shouldn't say it was. Of what are you curious?"

"Of whether I shall go to heaven or hell, of course, since the question remains open."

The priest began to reply, but confounded, he lapsed into silence. The Chevalier continued reflectively.

"I am generally a curious fellow. It is well that curiosity is not sinful, for I believe I am steeped in it, like *le chat.* But *le chat* has nine lives. I regret that I have but one."

"To give for your country?" inquired the priest.

"Certainly not!" answered the Chevalier with some heat. "What an *idée extraordinaire*! I am a soldier, *bon père,* and it is a soldier's work to take lives, not give up his own. I regret that I have but one life because life is a great joy, and it is sad to have but one."

"This life is but a trial we all must suffer, Desmond. It is eternal life that you should contemplate with joyful expectation."

"What!" demanded the Chevalier. "And sin by presumption?"

Father Collins was again reduced to bewildered silence, which was broken by the return of the jailer with the Chevalier's breakfast—a meal of beef, biscuit, and coffee.

"You must join me, Father Collins," said the Chevalier. "No doubt these divine puzzlements will become lucid to my mind when I consider them from the vantage of a full stomach."

The priest shook his head.

"No, thank you, Desmond. There are others in the Tower who require my ministry. But I shall ride with you in the tumbrel to Tyburn."

"I think it may be better if you do not," said the Chevalier. "Priests of our faith are not beloved by the Londoners. Better that one be hanged at Tyburn than two be torn to shreds along the way."*

Father Collins protested, but seeing the wisdom of the Chevalier's words, he at last agreed, blessing the Chevalier and calling to the jailer to let him leave.

"God go with you, Desmond," he said as he departed.

"Good-bye, Father Collins," called the Chevalier. "I should say *au revoir,* but as I am certain you are bound for heaven, it would be presumption were I to do so."

---

* The Chevalier probably had in mind the Gordon riots, eight days of rioting (sparked by Lord Gordon's anti-Catholic incitements) that rocked London less than two years earlier.—M.C.

After the priest had gone, the Chevalier sat down to his breakfast, which he ate with gusto beneath the jailer's astonished gaze.

"Monsieur Eater-of-Beef," said the Chevalier, as he finished his repast, "there is one last little favor I ask of you, and for which, of course, I am quite prepared to pay."

"What might that be?" asked the jailer.

"My clothes are in a disreputable condition. To appear in them upon such an occasion should be a great disgrace. I would have that with which to brush my coat and polish my boots."

"I'll fetch what you ask," said the jailer, "but were I you (and I thank God I ain't), I shouldn't take the trouble. The mob don't care for yer clothes, so you'll be working for the hangman."

"The hangman? I do not comprehend."

"Why, man, 'tis the hangman that'll be getting yer clothes after he's cut you down."

"*Parbleu!*" exclaimed the Chevalier. "Then I am to be buried naked?"

"Why, you ain't to be buried at all. Yer carcass they'll take to Surgeons' Hall, where it'll be ottomized. You being such a sturdy specimen, I should think they'll keep yer bones there in a glass case."

"Ah!" exclaimed the Chevalier. "I am to be admired throughout the ages. It is a great temptation to my vanity."

"You ain't distressed by the idea?"

"I am distressed to think I shall not be buried in holy ground, as is customary to one of my faith. But I do not think there is any holy ground between the Channel and the Irish Sea, so it is as well to wait for Judgment Day in a glass case as in an English grave. But I am distressed for you, *mon ami.*"

"For me, ye say?"

"*Oui,* you who must stand the lonely watches of the night in this haunted place."

"Oh, there's some as say 'tis haunted, but I ain't seen any ghosts," replied the jailer uneasily.

"*Vraiment?* I have seen such here in the night, but we of the Irish race have second sight."

"What? You've seen ghosts here in the Tower, you say?" demanded the jailer.

"*Oui.* There is, for example, the lady who walks about at midnight."

"A lady? Likely one of the warders' wives. Why do you think her a ghost?"

"Because of her head, *mon ami.* She carries it not upon her shoulders, but here, tucked beneath her arm. I make no doubt you shall see her some night, and myself, as well, for my spirit shall certainly walk about if my bones do not rest. Pray, do not fear me when you see me walk, for we are friends, are we not? But you may not know me, for I shall likely resemble myself in the last moments of life, as I dangle at Tyburn. Mark this countenance, *monsieur.*"

The Chevalier bulged his eyes and lolled his tongue out horribly.

"When you see it coming round a corner in the midst of the night you shall know it is nothing but your old friend, the Chevalier de Lawless."

"God's wounds!" cried the jailer. "I . . . I'll be getting ye yer brush and polish," he said, and he ran from the cell.

In the opening chapter of this history, we witnessed the ceremony with which the condemned Colonel La Motte was escorted from the Tower of London to the place of his execution at Tyburn. It is the essence of ceremony that things be done in exactly the same way in every instance (or as much the same as chance and human frailty permit), and so there seems scant benefit to the reader to recount the full particulars of the Chevalier's journey from Tower Hill to Tyburn, since they resembled so closely that which he has already seen. Let it suffice to state that a great military procession of horse and foot, sheriffs and under-sheriffs, yeoman warders, the hangman, and sundry other functionaries escorted the tumbrel upon which the Chevalier stood during his ride through the London streets, and that a great throng of Londoners attended to the parade, some to wish the Chevalier well, others to wish him be damned, and most simply to gape.

Rather than rehearse the many similarities between these two occasions, let us, instead, consider the particulars in which they differed, for they are by far the more interesting.

First, the mass of onlookers that turned out to watch the Chevalier's procession was somewhat smaller than that which witnessed Colonel La Motte's final journey, a fact that doubtless should have piqued the Chevalier's vanity had he known it, despite the reasons for the lesser showing, to wit, the weather (La Motte rode on a charming day in July, while the Chevalier traveled the course in midwinter), and the king's mercy, which denied the mob the diversion of a disembowelment.

The second way in which the Chevalier's trip to Tyburn differed from Colonel La Motte's (and from all others) is that the prisoner refused to face backward in the tumbrel. When he was informed by the jailer that this ancient custom was designed for the comfort of the condemned, who was thus spared the prospect of the gibbet as Tyburn was neared, the Chevalier replied that he found the sight of the hearse (which brought up the rear of the procession) no more cheerful than the gibbet, and furthermore, he would be better comforted by a familiar view. The jailer inquired as to what the Chevalier might hope to see ahead of the tumbrel that would be in any way familiar, to which question the Chevalier replied that the backs of English soldiers were a mighty familiar sight to any that served in *La Brigade Irlandaise*.

But the third way in which the Chevalier's parade differed from his predecessor's is by far the most significant, for it was the instrument by which the ultimate ends of the two processions were completely different.

The parade had passed through the streets of the city, with the Chevalier answering the mob's cries with wit and gallantry, and had climbed Holborn Hill and onto the Tyburn Road, when it was brought to a halt near Orchard Street, in sight of the scaffold, by a great hay wagon standing athwart the road. The captain of the Life Guards galloped to the head of the parade to examine into the cause of the delay, and found the constable of the Tower remonstrating with an old bumpkin who had nothing more to say for himself than that his dray horse was near as ancient as he and so must needs rest from his labors from time to time. The beast had, in fact, sat down in the road, stalling the wagon and ignoring every importunity to get up.

The captain ordered the farmer to loose the beast's traces so his men might push the hay wagon aside, that the procession could resume. The bumpkin complied, but with such sluggishness it was apparent to all that the unforeseen delay was to be of some considerable duration. The driver of the hearse, who was that same Jack Bolt, the new porter of Surgeons' Hall we so recently met, got down from his seat and approached the tumbrel.

"Good morning to you, sir," he called to the Chevalier. "Would ye fancy sharing a pint or two of wine with me?"

Bolt held a pair of cups in his hands.

"*Merci, non, monsieur,*" replied the Chevalier. "I thank you for your hospitality, but the hour is too early for such entertainment. Later, perhaps."

"It'll go down yer throat easier now than later, if ye don't mind me saying so," said Bolt.

The Chevalier laughed and shrugged. "Very well," he said, and Bolt passed the cup up to him. "To your health, *monsieur,* and a longer life than mine." He took a sip of the potation.

The Chevalier was an Irishman, but his palate had a French education, so he expected little of the English wine, yet he was ill prepared for the miserable character of the strange vintage. Still, it was not in his nature to be churlish, so he drank down the rest of the pint in one swallow, pronounced it excellent, and handed the cup back to the porter.

"*Merci,* Monsieur Undertaker. When next we meet it will be my turn to stand the round."

Bolt laughed and, downing his own cup, returned to his seat on the hearse. Presently the obstructing hay wagon was removed and the procession resumed, passing the recumbent dray horse, which still sat in the road, and proceeding the last few yards to the Tyburn tree amidst the hoots and cheers of the assembled throng.

Mother Proctor's Pews were nearly filled, and a multitude crowded about the scaffold and had to be pressed back by the soldiers. Gin, wine, ale, and pork were hawked by peddlers, who did a brisk business in the crowd, and the festive redolence of dining out of doors seemed contrary to the wintry gray sky that hung above the scene.

As the Chevalier looked about from his place of vantage in the tumbrel, a wave of giddiness rushed to his head, and he faltered as he climbed down from the cart. Haughtily, he shook off the helping hands of the warders, and throwing back his shoulders, he drew a deep breath and marched toward the gibbet. Yet he had taken but three strides before his staggering legs betrayed him, and he stumbled to his knees. The crowd hooted, while a brace of warders lifted him to his feet.

"Steady, man," said the jailer. "There's many a blackguard as bold as yerself whose knees have turned to water when he saw the Tyburn tree."

"Bah!" answered the Chevalier. "It is not the sight of your English gibbet, but the fumes of your English wine that makes traitors of my knees. Let us hasten to the scaffold, *messieurs,* for I fear I have already been assassinated by the poison of your vineyards."

The Chevalier shook himself loose of the warders once more and resumed his march, but he stumbled and reeled, and arriving at the steps of the scaffold, he found himself unable to ascend them without assistance. A chorus of hoots and catcalls arose from the mob, for many had come in expectation of a bold display of gallantry by the condemned, yet there were others who took pleasure in the Chevalier's performance, finding delight in the terror it seemed to bespeak. Among these latter was the wizened little ghoul that last we met in Surgeons' Hall.

"See the dauntless rogue," cackled George Selwyn to those about him in the stands. "I think the fellow must be a baronet, for I'll warrant he wears the breeches of Sir Reverence."*

---

* Sirreverence, i.e., human excrement. The *Dictionary of National Biography* recalls that Selwyn "was a noted conversationalist in the clubs and the author of witticisms which set the tables in a roar," but adds, "Walpole relates that the demureness with which Selwyn uttered a good thing gave zest to it, but the savour of such of his jests as survive has long been lost." Or in other words, you had to be there.—M.C.

The Chevalier heard none of this, for a great roaring had arisen within his head and filled his ears, drowning the cries of the onlookers. Yet he was not unwitting of the sorry figure he cut as he stumbled across the scaffold, supported by the yeoman warders.

"It is disgraceful, *messieurs!*" he exclaimed. "I demand the soldier's privilege of standing upon his own feet when he goes to his death!"

"Yer spirit may be willing, but yer flesh don't look to be up to it, mate," answered one of the jailers, as he bound the Chevalier's wrists behind his back.

"A moment, *messieurs, s'il vous plaît,* and I shall stand without your kind assistance."

"In a moment you'll be dancin',* lad," said the other jailer.

The hangman stepped up and put the halter about the Chevalier's neck. The roar in his head grew louder, and a sudden darkness obscured his vision. He sank into insensibility, and a moment later the warders let loose of him, and he dangled from the Tyburn tree.

---

* "Dancing at the sheriff's ball," i.e., to hang.—M.C.

9

A Joyful Rising

THE Chevalier opened his eyes, beheld an angel, and fancied himself in paradise. Yet when he made to rise, the agony of the damned hammered within his skull. Heaven or hell, he pondered, but when he strove to give voice to the question, his throat could make no more than a croak. Indeed, the distress in his gullet was surpassed only slightly by the torment in his head.

"Pray, spare your exertions, sir," said the angel, gently pressing him back upon the pillow with a slender hand. "Rest yourself, and you shall recover the sooner."

He yielded to the apparition and, lying quite still, found that the beating beneath his brow subsided. Moving naught but his eyes, he surveyed a rank of sloping roof beams and saw that his ascent into heaven had gotten no farther than a garret room. He turned his gaze once more to the seraph hovering over him and saw that she, too, was a creature of this world and not the next, but what he saw gave him no cause to regret this discovery.

She was tall, with a pleasing figure and golden tresses. Her face was oval, with a high forehead and charming blue eyes. A tiny mark upon her cheek seemed less a blemish than an adornment; it strangely spiced her beauty. Her skin was silken, and she possessed a lovely mouth that

92

looked to smile often and easily. She was not a child, as he could plainly see, but he doubted she was more than one-and-twenty.

As the Chevalier contemplated this beautiful vision, the sound of a heavy tread upon a staircase reached his ears. The young woman turned, and following her gaze, he saw a new face, one quite unlovely, yet familiar.

"How is our stalwart?" asked Jack Bolt. "Back from the dead already?"

The Chevalier found his voice and croaked, "Hello, *Monsieur le Sommelier.*"

"Good evening, mate. You look to be in fine fettle for one as just was hanged. That parting glass went right to yer head, did it?"

"*Oui,* it did, I confess. It is the custom of English undertakers to embalm the body before death, then?"

Bolt laughed. "That it is, when such a one undertakes to swindle the hangman. Had ye not been fully lax, ye'd have capered and danced on the end of the string until ye'd been truly scragged."

"And the hangman and the jailers? They thought me dead?"

"They thought ye died of fright, mate. You weren't a-twitchin', so they gave me leave to cut ye down and cart ye off. The hangman never worries that he's left his job half done, for he knows the surgeons'll finish his work for him."*

---

* Eighteenth-century hanging did not involve the humane measure of arranging the noose and the drop to insure a quick, merciful death from a broken neck, a technique not common until the nineteenth century. Those who died on the Tyburn gibbet generally succumbed to asphyxia, i.e., they were strangled by the

"And what of the surgeons, *monsieur*? Do they yet sharpen their knives and await the Chevalier's arrival?"

"They've got a carcass and are none the wiser, I trust," answered Bolt. "A sorry young rake who scragged himself at Twickenham a fortnight past. I resurrected him from a crossroads, and he was riding behind ye all the way to Tyburn in the hearse. And it was he who made the trip to Surgeons' Hall."

"A suicide, and dead a fortnight!" exclaimed the Chevalier. "And you think to sham the surgeons to believe that such are the remains of the Chevalier de Lawless?"

"He was a sturdy fellow, near as big as yerself," said Bolt, "and well and truly hanged. And the gin that made him mad kept the worms away, for he was quite fresh this morning as if he'd been planted yesternight. Only one that was at Tyburn this morning will be at Surgeons' Hall tonight, and I warrant he'll not find anything amiss, for the phiz of one hanged man is much the same as another,

---

noose. But it was not uncommon for the condemned to survive the ordeal.

In 1709 one John Smith was revived after dangling for two hours; he lived ten more years and was known as "Half-hanged Smith." In 1740, seventeen-year-old William Duell hung at Tyburn for half an hour, only to revive on the dissecting table; he was not rehanged, but "transported for life" to the colonies. In 1763 a Thomas Reynolds pushed back the lid of his coffin and climbed out, after surviving a Tyburn hanging. And in 1782 John Hayes revived after his hanging and found himself on the table of a private surgeon who had purchased his body. The generous physician paid his passage to America (Hay, pp. 102–105).

Such accidental escapes inspired some condemned prisoners to arrange with confederates for their revival, but such attempts rarely succeeded, probably because they failed to include the precaution taken in the Chevalier's case of anesthetizing the victim before the hanging.—M.C.

eyes a-bulging, mouth a-wry, and tongue hangin' down to the knees."

"*Pardon, monsieur.* It is churlish of me to raise such difficulties when you have done me so splendid a service at so formidable hazard to your person. And a thousand thanks to you, *mademoiselle,*" he said, turning to the lovely young woman, "for nursing this unfortunate Lazarus back to life. I fear that both you kind English folk have put yourself in jeopardy in my behalf, and you may soon require my protection. But I can be of little service to you lying in bed."

The Chevalier made to rise, but finding himself quite naked beneath the bed clothes, he stopped.

"I must beg your pardon, *mademoiselle,* for I seem to be without my garments."

"I beg *you,* sir, rest yourself. We are all quite safe here, for none would think to look for you in a garret above New Street."

" 'Tis so, mate," Bolt agreed. "As fer yer clothes, they went to the hangman. We'll fit you out with some new duds tomorrow. Ye wouldn't want to be runnin' about the country in that lobster coat, anyway, as it would surely cause comment."

The Chevalier was filled with doubts in spite of these assurances, for he knew not the character of his benefactors, nor the motivation of their singular kindness, nor the particulars of their design for the future regarding himself. Yet it seemed to the Chevalier that to put words to such doubts would affront the hospitality of these good people. As he struggled with this dilemma, there came to the ears of those gathered in the garret the sound of a new pair of feet ascending the stairs.

"That'll be Himself," remarked Bolt.

Himself was a jolly old gentleman of near threescore

years and ten, who huffed and puffed from the exertions
of his ascent.

"Hoot-toot!" panted the old fellow when he had achieved
the garret. "My certie, there's muckle more steps to be
climbed than when last I roamed abune, or so it seems.
Good evening, Jane dear. Hello, Jack. How is the laddie?
Ah, restored to life already!"

"Good evening to you, Mr. S.," said Bolt. "Here, take
my arm, sir, if you please."

"Sit here, father," said the young woman, placing a
chair beside the Chevalier's bed. "You should not tire
yourself so, climbing all the way up here!"

"Hoot! Too auld to caper I may be, but too hale I am to
be carried, thank the Good Lord." He sat down and regarded the Chevalier.

"I welcome ye back to life, Major Lawless," he said.

"*Merci bien,*" answered the Chevalier. "I fear I am at a
disadvantage, for I do not know the names of my saviors."

"Let me present my daughter Jane," said the old man.
"This is Cousin Jack. And I'm yer Uncle Willie. Those are
all the names ye'll be needing, and all ye'll know, should
matters gae agley. Three may keep a secret if two are
dead, an auld friend once told me. D'ye ken?"

"*Oui.* And even those names should never pass my lips,
mon ami, no matter what agonies might be inflicted upon
me," proclaimed the Chevalier ardently.

"That may be, that may be," the old man allowed, "but
I dinna fear ye might give up our names to an enemy so
much as I dread ye might confide them to a friend. 'Tis
an unco business we're about, laddie, where the foe may
play the friend, and vice versa."

"Ah, *oui,* the secret war. A strange business, as you say.
Très bien, mon oncle. And may I inquire of your plan
regarding myself?"

"That ye may, and pleased I'll be to tell ye: Ye'll be smuggled out of England and ower the Channel to some place from whence ye'll be able to make yer own way hame."

"Ah, *magnifique! Merci bien!* And when is this smuggling to be done?"

"Nae mair than a few days hence, I shoudna say. Jack'll fetch ye some braw duds, and I'll see ye have some guid papers to give the glaiks to any that might suspect ye. Take yer ease, meantime. Ye've been dosed, dangled, and resurrected, all in one lang day. 'Tis eneuch to weary any man. I must gae noo."

He rose, and with the help of Bolt and the young woman prepared to descend the stairs.

"I'll see some supper is sent up to ye, if ye have any stomach for such, as yet. But I think ye want naething noo so much as slumber. Take yer ease, laddie. There's naething to trouble ye here."

But the old man himself might have been sorely troubled had he witnessed a scene taking place that very moment a few streets distant, within the horrid amphitheater in Warwick Lane.

The wizened little ghoul stood in his place in the first gallery and stared at the carcass in the pit below.

"That is not the same man!" he hissed.

10

The Fisher of Men

LORD Stormont stood at his desk in the library of his house in Portland Place. He did not sit, for he did not wish to invite his visitor to do the same. The little man filled him with disgust, and he wished nothing so much as that his unwelcome caller might betake himself elsewhere.

"I fail to see that this matter involves my department, Mr. Selwyn, nor any other department of this ministry," he said. "If you believe a corpse has been stolen, then you should take your suspicions before a magistrate and ask him to lend you a pair of constables to go and look for it."

"Ah, but it was not a corpse that was taken, I say, but a living man who has cheated the gallows."

" 'Cheated'? But you say you were at Tyburn and saw him hanged."

"Indeed, I did. I attend to the matter of hangings just as a playhouse critic attends to the theater. I rarely miss one, and have seen so many men hanged, and women, too, that I have fairly earned the name of connoisseur. So when I say there was much about this hanging that marked it as strange, you must take it as an expert opinion, and not a casual fancy."

"What is your point, Mr. Selwyn?"

"This is my point, my lord: This traitor, Lawless, may

well have been but half-hanged, and later revived by his confederates."

Lord Stormont shrugged. "An unlikely theory, at best. Yet, even were it true, of what concern might it be to this department? Our business, as you must know, is the conduct of His Majesty's affairs upon the Continent."

"Indeed," Selwyn agreed, "and I know something of the conduct of those affairs, for I have sat in Commons for many years.* I know that some very delicate matters fall within your province, involving the sending of spies, and the catching of spies. I shall put it as plainly as I can: This man, Lawless, was not a Londoner, nor even an Englishman. If he was rescued from the gibbet as I suspect, then he was rescued, not by friends or relations, but by clandestine agents of the French or the Americans. And if that be so, my lord, I think the matter is very much your business, and not that of any Bow Street magistrate."

Lord Stormont did not reply immediately, but stood silently beside a window for some minutes. At length he went to his desk and, taking pen and paper, wrote a brief note, which he sealed and handed to his caller.

"I do not credit your suspicions overmuch, Mr. Selwyn, but neither can I ignore them, it seems. Please take this letter to Mr. Vardill. You will find him in Downing Street at number seventeen."†

---

* Selwyn sat for the city of Gloucester, which was near his country estate of Matson.—M.C.

† Reverend John Vardill (1752–1811). Vardill had been assistant rector of Trinity Church in New York City and professor of natural law at King's College (later Columbia University) before he went to London in 1774. When the war broke out he was recruited by the British Secret Service at a salary of two hundred pounds per year and the promise of the Regius Professorship of

"I thank you, my lord," said Selwyn. Taking Lord Stormont's letter, he hurried from the house and into the street, where his chairmen waited. Within the hour he stepped from his sedan in Downing Street and entered a doorway but a few paces from the residence of the first lord of the treasury.*

John Vardill was a man of near thirty years. He was of a pious character, for he was a clergyman, serving his God publicly while he served his king with the utmost secrecy, and he searched out both the traitor and the common sinner with equal zeal, for while he wished to slaughter the body of the former, he ardently desired to save the soul of the latter. He was, in every sense, a fisher of men.

The reader may remark it a singular kind of confluence that brings together in common cause a divine such as Mr. Vardill and an infamous rake and blasphemer such as Mr. Selwyn. But if he has studied history, he may remember that the furnace of war has often forged strange alliances. Yet it was not a common enemy that created the powerful affinity that immediately arose upon the meeting of these two men, but a pair of common interests shared alike by both the theologist and the ghoul, to wit, death and damnation.

Divinity at King's College when the war was over (the latter promise couldn't be kept, of course; instead, he was given a small pension and lived out the rest of his life in Lincolnshire). Vardill's special secret service assignment was to hunt down American agents in London. (Van Doren, *Benjamin Franklin*, p. 562; *Secret History*, p. 431; and Augur, p. 171.) —M.C.

* The title Prime Minister did not come into use until later. The first lord of the treasury was the head of the government (Lord North, at this date), and his official residence was Number 10 Downing Street, as the prime minister's is today. The Foreign Office was housed in other buildings nearby.—M.C.

Mr. Vardill read the letter from his chief, introducing his caller, then listened carefully as Mr. Selwyn set before him that same evidence he had presented to Lord Stormont. When Selwyn had finished, Vardill spoke.

"You were quite right in bringing this matter to my attention, sir," he said, "for I believe you have struck upon some serious mischief. We have for our consideration a train of occurrences, each remarkable to only some slight degree, but when viewed together, presenting a most singular aspect."

He enumerated the arguments upon the long fingers of an elegant hand.

"First, we have a new porter at Surgeons' Hall, hired upon the very eve of the traitor's hanging. Next, we have the bumpkin and his recumbent dray, who effect an unforeseen delay in the Tyburn parade. Following that, we see our new porter again, availing himself of the delay to administer some unknown potation to the condemned. Fast upon the heels of this, the prisoner is enfeebled and goes quite insensible upon the scaffold. The man is cut down and hastily taken away, through the good offices of our newly hired porter, once again. Finally, we discover the traitor's body missing; not simply purloined, mark you, but replaced by another carcass craftily selected to counterfeit the body taken away from Tyburn. And who could have accomplished that exchange? None but our trusty porter.

"Yes, Mr. Selwyn, I think you are right. Tell me, sir, did you make much of this matter at Surgeons' Hall?"

"I remarked upon it to the beadle," Selwyn replied, "but he dismissed the matter, insisting that I must be mistaken."

"Then he likely did not broach the same question to this new porter. Mark you, sir, it is this Jack Bolt, as he calls himself, that will prove the key to this mystery."

"Yes, but I fear he may now be as scarce as Lawless himself. Bolt has accomplished his task, and I do not think he will be seen about Surgeons' Hall again."

"Ah, but I think he *will* be back, if he has not already returned, for his task is not quite complete. Bolt sought, not merely to rescue the traitor from the gibbet, but also to conceal the fact that there had been a rescue, the better to accomplish Lawless's escape from England, no doubt. Should Bolt abruptly quit his post at Surgeons' Hall, he would risk remark and perhaps inspire in others those same suspicions you have voiced to me. No, I think our Mr. Bolt will be back to play porter for a week or two, that the singular circumstances of the traitor's hanging may not be associated with his own departure.

"Pray, come with me, sir. We shall go to Surgeons' Hall to await Mr. Bolt's return from some place of concealment. You must point him out to me, as I have never seen him."

"You will arrest him when he appears?"

"Not at all," replied Vardill with a crafty smile. "I shall follow him when he departs, and I make no doubt he will lead us to Lawless. We shall have our traitor, and likely a nest of spies as bonus."

"Hee!" cackled the little ghoul. "Plenty of work for the hangman!"

11

A Marriage of Convenience

IN New Street, near Gough Square, stood the considerable house of Mr. Strahan, a Scotsman who had come
to London as a lad, prospered there, and as he approached
the extremity of a long and busy life, was counted among
the most eminent gentlemen of the City. The household
of Mr. Strahan was wonderfully various, embosoming
beyond the ordinary complement of wife, children, and
servants, a printing shop, several journeymen printers, a
member of parliament, and King George's own printer,
these last two persons being, in fact, but one, the esteemed
Mr. Strahan, himself.

As might be guessed, the hospitality of a prominent
gentleman of such divers affairs was shared by processions
of visitors of corresponding diversity, and many of the
wittiest and weightiest words of the age were uttered
within the precincts of Mr. Strahan's drawing room. The
gentleman was host to scholar and scoundrel, Whig and
Tory, debauchee and divine, in short, nearly every man
and woman of substance who lived in London or visited
the City during Mr. Strahan's long residence there. It might
not be counted remarkable, then, as we visit Mr. Strahan
upon a dark January night in the year of grace 1782 that
the same house that contained the king's printing press

in the cellar should also harbor a fugitive from the king's hangman in the garret.*

The hour is late, and much of the household long abed, but we find the master of the house in urgent conference with a late caller, that same Jack Bolt who has played a major part in the recent chapters of this history.

"You werena followed, then?" demanded Strahan.

"Ah, that I was, sir, followed by the two of 'em, and I

---

* Now that we know the name of the jolly old Scotsman identified thus far only as Mr. S. and Uncle Willie, we might note a little more than Lawless tells us about him. William Strahan (1715–1785), the son of an Edinburgh customs official, was an affluent printer and publisher, and a friend of some of the most distinguished writers of the eighteenth century. The *Dictionary of National Biography* notes that he was "publisher, and either banker and agent or confidential adviser" to Samuel Johnson, David Hume, Adam Smith, Edward Gibbon, and Benjamin Franklin. It says that, politically, Strahan was "rather an advanced Whig," but history records that he was staunchly Tory in the matter of American independence. The long and close friendship between Strahan and Franklin was supposedly broken in 1775, when Strahan, then sitting for Malmesbury in the House of Commons, voted for the measures which eventually led to the battles of Lexington and Bunker Hill. On 5 July 1775, Franklin wrote to his old friend:

Mr. Strahan :

You are a member of Parliament, and one of that majority which has doomed my country to destruction. You have begun to burn our towns and murder our people! Look upon your hands! They are stained with the blood of your relations! You and I were long friends. You are now my enemy, and I am

yours,
B Franklin

However, this letter was never sent.—M.C.

led 'em a merry chase before I gave 'em the slip in St. Giles. Then I waited for darkmans and the fog, and came here through the alleys. No, sir, there's none as saw me come here tonight, but there's many as seen me about the place at other times."

"Aye, I ken yer heed, Jack. Meseems the yonker* ye've described may be one Vardill, a crafty houd I dinna doot could snook out yer tracks to my door." He shook his head. "Selwyn and Vardill! A mirk brace of corbie craws!"†

"What is it, Father? What's the matter?"

The young woman stood in the doorway, a candle in her hand.

"Ah, Janie dear! Come hither and hark the dowie news Jack brings us."

Bolt quickly related matters to the young woman.

"But this is dreadful!" she exclaimed when he had finished.

"Aye," Strahan agreed. "I daurna hae the laddie tarrow hereabouts. He'll nae be safe till he's aboard a packet bound for Ostend.‡ But I dinna ken the gaet to put him there."

"The rum pad is the only way," said Bolt. "Two pops and a prancer for me, the same for him, and we'll be in Deal or Dover by morning."§

"Aye, and likely waiting at the inn for the wind or the

---

* Young man.—M.C.

† A dark pair of carrion crows.—M.C.

‡ The port of Ostend on what is today the Belgian coast was, at the time, an Austrian possession and, therefore, neutral territory. After Britain declared war on the United Provinces (as the Netherlands was then called) late in 1780, Ostend replaced The Hague as the major channel of British commerce with Europe. —M.C.

§ The rum pad—the highway; two pops and a prancer—two pistols and a horse.—M.C.

tide or the master to rouse himself, whilst every farmer in Kent is telling the soldiers of the pair of highwaymen that scampered past in the night. Nae, Jack. 'Tis the two of ye together they'll be looking for. Ye'll both be safer if ye gae yer separate ways, ye a-laying low in London, with Major Lawless in a seat aboard the Dover mail."*

"Oh, no, Father. You must not send the major off aboard the mail. They're certain to stop every mail and stagecoach that passes through Kent, for that is the most likely route to the Channel."

"Aye, for 'tis the swiftest. 'Tis a risky gaet to send him east, I'll grant ye, girl, but 'twould be riskier still to send him in any other direction, for they'll look for him elsewhere if they dinna find him in Kent, and they'll have muckle more time for the looking."

"They will look for two men, or one," said Jane. "But they will not look for a man and wife. And none should think it amiss if a Hamburg merchant bound for home with his English bride were found riding the stage to Harwich."

"Hooch! A bonnie trick! Lawless plays the German, but who plays the bride?"

"I shall, Father," Jane declared.

"Nae, I canna permit it, Janie. Dalt† ye may be, but I love ye as my own flesh and blood. 'Tis too risky an errand for ye. I'll send one of the maidservants to play the part."

"There's none with the wit for it, Father. The major should play his role best should he play it mute, for he

---

* A coach that carried mail and passengers between London and Dover every day.—M.C.

† Foster child. Strahan had three sons and two daughters; if he also adopted another daughter, the fact is not recorded.—M.C.

speaks English as a Frenchman. She who plays his bride plays the speaking part."

The old man rubbed his chin. "Aye, there's much in what ye say, Janie. Still . . ."

"I shall be perfectly safe, Father. If the major and I leave tomorrow we will be in Harwich by the forenoon of the following day, and in Ostend no more than a day later. Then I shall take the next packet for Dover and return to London in the mail."

"Begging yer pardon, Mr. S.," ventured Bolt, "but Miss Jane may be the safer playing the major's lady than staying here in New Street."

"How might that be, Jack?" asked Strahan.

"If ye send a housemaid and she bungles, she'll likely soon bring this Vardill and his soldiers to yer very door, and the whole household might end up in the Tower."

"Jack's right, Father."

The old man shook his head uneasily.

"Very well, Janie. I dinna like this business, but there's good sense in what ye say. Gae alang with the major, girl, but see that ye take care. I pray the Lord I dinna regret it!"

12

The Black Chamber

NIGHT descended over Paris, and with it came a drizzly winter rain, yet the gentleman who emerged from the elegant house in the Rue Traversière did not glance skyward, but peered about him into every quarter of the street. He set off at a brisk pace, which he sustained for many minutes, until, turning a corner, he slowed to a sauntering step, pausing often to examine a broadside or gaze into a shop, and always to direct a swift glance over his shoulder along the route he had lately traversed. He changed course often and seemingly without design, at times doubling back along his path before turning into a new street or boulevard. Had any observed the gentleman's peregrinations, they might have counted him as one who prized his exercise so highly he would not begrudge a thorough drenching, were that its price.

The gentleman's nocturnal wanderings were not observed until, at length, he turned off the Rue Coquillière and arrived at the great rotund construction which housed the municipal grain market. He walked about the building once, and then again, but he failed to discern the pair of onlookers who marked his passage from the nearby shadows.

"He is punctual," remarked Inspector de Bruguières. "I make it to be but a few minutes past nine."

"Yes," agreed Inspector Mouron, "a gentleman of regular habits. Always twice around the grain market. Next he will proceed to the Rue Saint-Honoré."

Indeed, this was the gentleman's course. When he had turned the corner, Mouron set out in his wake, while Bruguières waited a few moments before doing the same.

The gentleman and the two police inspectors following him were not the only persons abroad in the Rue Saint-Honoré, for even the discomforts of a wet winter evening could not quench the popularity of that busy quarter. The number of those in the street increased as the Rue de Richelieu was neared; here was the busy Hôtel d'Orléans and the Palais Royal (no longer the house of kings, but a place of shops and other diversions). Now the gentleman did not pause to glance over his shoulder. He had walked a great circuit of the empty streets and was confident he proceeded unobserved. He turned into the Rue Saint-Nicanse, passed through the Place du Carrousel and on to the Terrasse des Tuileries. His silent companions followed.

The gentleman consulted his watch; it was half past the hour. He moved on a few paces, stopping beneath a box-wood tree. He looked about, but failing to see the pair that watched him from the shadows, he dropped to his knees and dug his fingers into the earth, exhuming a small wooden peg and a length of twine. Pulling on the twine, he brought forth a bottle from a recess within the roots of the tree. He removed a paper envelope from the vessel, replaced it with another, then restored bottle, twine, and peg to their original places. He rose, looked about once more, and went upon his way.

He was gone but a few minutes when the inspectors went to the boxwood tree and removed the packet the gentleman had secreted there. Returning the empty container to its hiding place, Inspector de Bruguières pocketed the envelope.

"Stay and watch," he said, and swiftly strode away. He hurried past the Galeries du Louvre, crossed the Pont Neuf to the Île de la Cité, and entered the Palace of Justice. There, in a cellar chamber, awaited the commissioner of police, M. Le Noir.

"You have it?" demanded the police chief.

Bruguières presented the envelope to him.

"Aha! And without a seal! Excellent!"

"There is never a seal when the sender trusts his hiding place," said the inspector. "This was concealed within a bottle hidden in a hollow boxtree in the Tuileries Gardens. Monsieur Wentworth removed one packet and put this in its place."

Le Noir nodded. He opened the envelope, unfolded the sheet, and read.

"Bah! You have captured nothing but a love letter!"

Bruguières took the letter from his chief and read it.

"Perhaps," he said. "Let us see what Boucher can make of it."*

---

* A few words may now be in order regarding the *dramatis personae* who have come onstage thus far in this chapter. Bruguières and Mouron were senior French police detectives who specialized in political cases (Manceron, *Twilight,* pp. 347, 413n). Jean Charles Le Noir (as earlier noted) was chief of the Paris police and therefore responsible for internal security. Boucher was chief of the French Black Chamber, the department that intercepted and opened mail, broke codes and ciphers, etc. (Manceron, *Wind,* p. 431). The gentleman who serviced the "dead-drop" (to use modern espionage jargon for the boxwood tree arrangement) was Paul Wentworth, one of the most important officers of the British Secret Service.

While there is some mystery regarding Wentworth's origins, including his date of birth, it is generally believed he was related to John Wentworth, the last royal governor of New Hampshire. Before the Revolution, he was a planter in Surinam and also

Le Noir and the inspector departed the chamber and went yet deeper into the bowels of the Palace of Justice until they came to a curious kind of workshop that looked to be part countinghouse and part chemical laboratory. A dozen men were busy at desks and tables, performing sundry mysterious tasks with stoves, stills, bottles, lanterns, and an assortment of other engines which, had they names, must be known but to other practitioners of these same recondite arts. No sign betokened the place, for any with cause to visit knew it was called *Le Cabinet Noir.**

---

lived at various times in New Hampshire, Amsterdam, London, and Paris. He had been a Harvard classmate of John Adams, and he was friendly with such French and American notables as Beaumarchais and Franklin. In 1778 he approached the latter as Lord North's personal emissary in an effort to reconcile colonial affairs and prevent the then impending French-American alliance (Bendiner, p. 91). He was unsuccessful, of course, but this earned him the attention of French counterintelligence, and he was under close surveillance whenever he appeared in France afterward (Einstein, p. 33). Nonetheless, he was able to "run" a network of high-level agents in France, including several within the American ministry.—M.C.

* The French Black Chamber was organized late in the seventeenth century and was in continuous operation until the middle of the nineteenth. Its primary function was reading other people's mail, especially the correspondence of foreign diplomats, and it also was devoted to defeating similar efforts by other governments to read French communications. The opening and forging of seals, the breaking of codes and ciphers, and the detection of invisible inks were the principal arts practiced here. During nearly two centuries of its operation, the French Black Chamber opened and deciphered 2,020 pages of secret correspondence (Kahn, p. 172), including much of the communications of the American ministry during the American Revolution (Morris, p. 211). Nearly every other European power ran a similar operation, and the same function is performed by governments today, although electronics has replaced chemistry as the primary technology employed.—M.C.

As the two police officers entered the workshop, they were met by a thin, bespectacled gentleman.

"Good evening, gentlemen," said M. Boucher. "What have you brought me?"

"Tender words of love, from a gentleman to his mistress, it seems," Le Noir replied, "unless you can find something more hidden within them."

"We shall see, we shall see," said Boucher, taking the paper from the police chief and holding it up to the brilliant rays of a great lantern.

"No cipher, certainly," he announced. "Perhaps a code, but that will take some time to find, if it is there. Let us first see if there is white ink* on the paper."

He held the sheet close to a candle flame, rapidly passing it back and forth. Then he brought the paper near the lantern and examined it closely.

"It bears no natural stain, at least," he said. "Perhaps a sympathetic ink, then."†

Boucher took the sheet and placed it atop a table upon which stood a wooden rack holding a score of glass vials. A fine-tipped brush, of the sort that might be used in the painting of miniatures, stood in each vessel, and he took one of these and touched it to the paper. Seeing no result, he repeated the procedure with the brush from a second

---

* Invisible ink.—M.C.

† Some organic fluids, such as fruit juice, vinegar, milk, and even urine can be used as invisible ink; the writing becomes visible when heat is gently applied. Sympathetic inks are chemicals that become visible only when treated with certain other chemicals. These inks are more difficult to detect because the "developer" may be any one of a large variety of chemicals, and each must be tested in turn upon the suspected sheet. Both types of invisible inks were used by British and American agents during the American Revolution.—M.C.

bottle, then a third and a fourth. Abruptly, as if by magic, a line of writing appeared between two lines of the "love letter."

"Aha!" Boucher exclaimed. "Brown tincture discovers the stain. The hidden message is written between the lines in essence of nutgall."*

Swiftly he brushed the tincture over the sheet until the full message was discovered:

> Mr. Edwards,
>
> Lord S. wishes his warmest regards conveyed to Moses and begs to be apprised of whatever, short of independency, the American Congress might now accept to end hostilities. He also wishes to hear of the French disposition to make further loans to the Americans.
>
> I remain your faithful friend and colleague,
>
> W.

M. Le Noir read the letter and passed it to Inspector de Bruguières.

" 'Mr. Edwards!' 'Moses!' " Le Noir exclaimed. "Would that Monsieur Wentworth had more faith in his boxtree and his white ink, that he might give us the true names of those persons.

"Monsieur Boucher, my thanks and congratulations. Is it possible now to work a second miracle and make this secret writing disappear again?"

---

* Gallic acid, which is derived from gallnuts, i.e., swellings or excrescences of tissue of a plant or tree, resulting from attacks of parasites such as insects, fungi, or bacteria. Its use as a sympathetic ink dates back to ancient times. The "brown tincture" Boucher used to develop the ink was probably ferrous sulfate.—M.C.

"Ah, no, that is impossible, I fear," replied the other. "But it may be that I can create a copy that congrues so perfectly to the original, none will be the wiser."

Taking the letter, he flattened it and set it on an easel, upon which he directed the brilliant rays of a great lantern. Next, he selected a sheet of paper identical in size and texture to that of the letter, two vials—one of black ink, the other of nutgall essence—and a pair of pens. He stepped into a closet, shutting the door behind him.

The closet to which M. Boucher retreated was, in fact, a *camera obscura,* to wit, an optical machine constructed so that light may enter the darkened chamber only through a double convex glass. Objects, such as the letter, exposed to brilliant light and opposite to the glass, are represented inverted upon any white matter placed within the chamber in the focus of the glass. By this means, M. Boucher cast an image of the letter upon the blank sheet, and was thus able to copy it by tracing the hand that wrote the messages, using both black and white inks. The result of M. Boucher's ingenuity and labor was a copy of the letter indistinguishable from the original before the brown tincture was applied.

"You are truly a wizard, my friend," said M. Le Noir as he studied the copy. "And the white writing?"

"It is there, as well," Boucher replied. "It will look identical to its twin when the brown tincture is applied."

"Excellent! Here, Monsieur de Bruguières. Take it and restore it to the boxtree, and wait there to see the face of the one who claims it. When you have learned the name of the 'Mr. Edwards,' come and tell me immediately. I shall be with Monsieur de Vergennes at the Foreign Ministry."

The road from Paris to Versailles is several leagues long,

and the carriage of M. Le Noir will certainly require some little time to traverse it on this wet winter evening. Let us leave the commissioner of Police for the moment, then, and fly ahead to the Ministry of Foreign Affairs, which stood in the Rue de l'Intendance, adjoining the royal residence. There we find His Most Christian Majesty's foreign minister, the Count de Vergennes, conferring with his aide and chief spy, M. Baudouin.*

"Forgive me, *Monsieur le Compte*," said Baudouin, "but I think it may have been unwise to tell Le Noir to meddle in this affair."

"I did not tell him to meddle," replied Vergennes, "nor could I tell him not to meddle, without also telling him more than he has learned by virtue of his own efforts. For years he has watched Monsieur Wentworth, as did Sartines† before him. What has happened was inevitable, for even the ablest of spies will sooner or later commit some small error, as you well know. And, as you also know, espionage does not respect the boundaries of administrative jurisdiction."

"I see," said Baudouin. "What, then, has Le Noir found out?"

Vergennes shrugged. "Until tonight, he has found out nothing beyond the fact that Monsieur Wentworth goes with great stealth to the Tuileries Gardens each Tuesday at about nine o'clock in the evening. But today is Tuesday, and it is now past ten o'clock. What Le Noir may know at

---

* Charles Gravier, the count de Vergennes (1717–1787), the French foreign minister. Baudouin was coordinator of intelligence for the Foreign Ministry (Morris, p. 133).—M.C.

† Antoine de Sartines, Le Noir's predecessor as police chief, who at this time had been promoted to minister of the navy.—M.C.

this moment I cannot say. It is a matter of his skill, Wentworth's carelessness, and God's will."

"And if he learns the object of Monsieur Wentworth's rendezvous? What then?"

"Then, I suppose, I must tell him the rest and seal his lips," replied the Foreign Minister.

While Count de Vergennes and M. Baudouin wait for M. Le Noir at Versailles, let us return some distance along the road from Paris to mark the progress of the police chief's carriage. We find it but a mile short of its destination, its advance interrupted, and a blown and lathering mount tethered nearby. Within the carriage M. Le Noir is listening most attentively to the words of Inspector de Bruguières.

"We did not follow him, for there was no need. We saw his face quite clearly as he departed the Tuileries."

"And you are certain?"

"Beyond any doubt. This mysterious 'Mr. Edwards' is none other than Dr. Bancroft. You may make your own guess as to the identity of 'Moses.' "

"But, it is impossible! It cannot be!"

"Can it be otherwise? Who can 'Moses' be, but Bancroft's friend and master, Dr. Benjamin Franklin?"*

---

* Edward Bancroft (1744–1821), a native of Westfield, Mass. Scientist, politician, novelist, and master spy. As a young man he traveled to Surinam, where he practiced medicine and met and was befriended by the mysterious Paul Wentworth. In 1769 he moved to England, where he met Benjamin Franklin and became his protégé. In 1776 he was appointed secretary to the American ministry in Paris on Franklin's orders, but he had already been recruited by the British Secret Service. He proved to be the cleverest and most valuable agent in the British service during the American Revolution.—M.C.

13

Journey in a Stagecoach

IN the twilight of the morning, the Harwich stagecoach was made ready for the road. A pair of porters ran back and forth between coach and booking office, stowing the luggage with breathless rapidity. Presently the guard appeared at the office door.

"Now, gentlemen and ladies," he announced. "Five minutes behind time already!"

The travelers arose and filed out to the coach. The outside passengers—a rude-looking pair of rustics and an old wife—took their places, the pair upon the roof and the wife in the luggage basket behind. The old woman made herself comfortable amidst the trunks and parcels, lit her pipe, and smoked reflectively as she waited for the journey to begin.

The inside passengers numbered five, two ladies and three gentlemen. The coach steps were ascended with mannerly protocol: ladies first, and age before youth. Thus it was that the first to find her place in the coach was a ruddy and rotund matron of some threescore years. Next, a lovely young lady climbed the steps before the admiring glances of the gentlemen there assembled. The eldest of these, a corpulent fellow who had equipped himself for the expedition with a scarlet surtout and a large hat with a broad lace,* followed. Then went a stalwart gentleman, broad of shoulder and long of limb, whose dress and manner seemed vaguely foreign, and who seemed to be companion to the comely young woman. The last of the inside travelers was a young gentleman distinguished only by a certain look of awkward vivacity. The door was closed, and the guard removed the steps and climbed up to his place beside the coachman.

"All right," cried the guard, and as the coach started off, he blew a long blast upon his horn. "Let 'em go, Harry! Give 'em their heads!"

The Harwich stage was on its way.

Within the coach the inside passengers paid their compliments to each other with elaborate civility, then lapsed into silence, for excepting the stalwart gentleman and his lovely lady, all the travelers were strangers, none ever having seen any of the others before the early hour of this winter morning.

Silence propagates itself; the longer talk has been suspended, the more difficult it is to find anything to say, and none of the company seemed inclined to be first to propose a topic of discourse. The corpulent gentleman drew out his watch, looked at it in silence, and then held it dangling at his finger. None heeded this invitation to ask the time of day, so the gentleman announced at length that it was past five, and that in two hours they should be at breakfast. Yet this news failed to effect a general dismissal of the silence. To show that he was not discouraged, the man of benevolence hummed a tune and beat time upon his snuffbox, to the obvious annoyance of the portly matron with whom he shared his seat.

So passed the early hours of the journey and the morning.

* Surtout—overcoat; lace—braid.—M.C.

Even as prophesied, seven o'clock saw the coach to a little inn appointed by the coachman for the travelers' repast, an occasion that brought the little company of inside passengers together around the same table.

As the travelers broke their fast, the stout matron remarked upon the inconveniences of traveling, and the difficulty which they who never sat at home without a great number of attendants found in performing for themselves such offices as the road required. The gentleman of the scarlet surtout, who had meanwhile been perusing a newspaper with deep pensiveness, reflected that it was impossible for any man to guess how to act with regard to the stocks, adding that he had only last week sold out some twenty thousand pounds in the expectation that they would fall, and now noted that they had risen instead. The awkward young man volunteered that he had often been advised by the chancellor and the judges on the subject of the stocks, and those worthies reckoned them pernicious to trade, uncertain in their produce, and unsolid in their foundations. The foreign gentleman and his young lady said nothing.

As we have noted, all were strangers; thus, the matron deprived of her handmaidens did not mention the cookshop she kept in Threadneedle Street, nor did the gentleman of the stocks disclose aught of his vocation as harmless drudge who lived in a Bolt Court garret, where he scribbled pamphlets and dictionaries; nor did the young gentleman of the judges and chancellors discover that he was clerk-apprentice to a lawyer in the Temple. And the foreign gentleman withheld the revelation that, but two days past, he'd been hanged by the neck at Tyburn, an anecdote that should infallibly have amused his companions.

Their breakfast complete, the travelers resumed their journey. A mood of some conviviality, even outright garrulity, now prevailed, and the table talk was resumed within the confines of the coach. Jane and the Chevalier did not participate in the general interlocution, an abstinence that served but to whet the curiosity of the others. At length, the matron was no longer able to contain her inquisitiveness, and asked of Jane the circumstances that took her to Harwich.

Jane recounted the tale she had prepared, to wit, that the Chevalier was a German merchant, she his bride, and that the couple would embark from Harwich for their home in Hamburg. Upon hearing that the pair were yet in their honeymoon, the matron regaled Jane with a great fund of homely counsel regarding the management of households and husbands, offering the connubial advice with a candor encouraged by the woman's faith that the Chevalier understood not a word she spoke. All of this amused the gentlemen and emboldened them to venture sundry drolleries involving matrimony, Germans, and such. Jane blushed to hear this talk, and the Chevalier, forborn by his role from laughing, smiled and nodded witlessly, to the great enjoyment of the company.

So passed the first day of the journey, as the coach lumbered along the Harwich Road, making Chelmsford by noon, arriving at Colchester by nightfall, and stopping at an ancient hostelry known in those parts as the Maypole.

The Maypole was not unique, for many like houses of public entertainment were to be found in the English countryside, not a few of which equaled the Maypole in age (it was said to have survived since the days of King Henry the Eighth), in the number of its gable ends and huge, zigzag chimneys, and in the drowsiness of its overhanging stories, which projected over the pathway and made the old house look as though it were nodding in its sleep. Nor were the old, diamond-pane lattice windows, the sunken and uneven floors, or the heavy, time-blackened ceiling beams unmatched by those of other roadside inns. Even its name was not singular, for another hostelry standing upon the borders of Epping Forest bore the same vernal cognomination.

Once again the company of inside passengers gathered about a common table to share a meal. The garrulity that had prevailed in the coach since breakfast was carried to the supper table, where it was temporarily suspended by the entrance of the roast beef. The corpulent gentleman said grace, then declared he must pay his respect to the baronet, as he called the sirloin.* Immediately he fell to with knife and fork, his tablemates did the same, and for some time not a word was spoken, though not a mouth was shut.

When supper was over and a bottle had been served, the conversation was resumed in a mood of even greater agreeableness and good humor. This geniality was owed in part to the effects of the victuals and spirits, and in part to the spirit of bawdy raillery the presence of the putative newly wed pair and the approach of bedtime seemed to inspire. Jane blushed a deep crimson to the delight of the company, while the Chevalier silently reflected upon the question of sleeping accommodations, struggling to resolve the conflicting demands of his masquerade, the trust of his benefactor, the reputation of his benefactress, and the temptations of the flesh. But these reflections and the conversation at the table were abruptly cut short by the thunderous arrival of a company of horsemen in the courtyard without.

There was a hammering at the door, and the innkeeper, a burly, large-headed man, went to answer it. He was rudely

---

* "Sir Loin," a well-worn eighteenth-century pun.—M.C.

thrust aside, and a captain of dragoons marched into the public room, booted and spurred, with a brace of pistols stuck in his belt.

"We come for the Irish traitor, Desmond de Lawless!" he proclaimed.

14

The Battle of the
Maypole

THE innkeeper, the servants, the customers, and all others who chanced to be in the dining room of the Maypole at that instant stared at the soldier and looked at each other in astonishment. Jane gasped in apprehension. The Chevalier squeezed her hand reassuringly while he endeavored to appear as bewildered as everyone else, a task that presented him little difficulty, for he was quite as astonished as any other in the company, but his perplexity arose from a different cause, to wit, that his pursuers had found him in Essex when he expected them to be searching fruitlessly for him in Kent.

The Chevalier quickly put aside this mystery in favor of matters of more immediate and practical importance, but, lest the reader be distracted by the puzzle, let us briefly leave the anxious scene at the Maypole and recount the events that led the soldiers so directly to that remote place.

After Vardill and Selwyn lost track of Jack Bolt in the foggy byways of St. Giles, they returned to Downing Street to consider what next should be done. True it was, as Jane had feared, the pair believed the Chevalier would make for the Kentish coast without delay to take passage aboard some ship bound for a neutral port. But there are many harbors between Margate and Dengey-Ness,* many routes to them from London, and to search the length and breadth of Kent for one man seemed, to John Vardill's mind, an undertaking that might well require all the king's horses and all of his men. And while Vardill commanded a great battalion of spies and informers in London, he must needs beg the grace of some colonel of cavalry or dragoons for but a small troop of mounted soldiers to beat the countryside for a man counted by all but George Selwyn and himself as one already dead. But he amended his want of horse with a wealth of craftiness.

Vardill had never set eyes upon the Chevalier, but Selwyn had seen him at Tyburn, where the little man marked Lawless's height and length of limb, and the rapier cut upon his cheek, those same qualities that would be impossible to conceal, no matter what disguise the fugitive might assume. Thus the pair of hunters visited every ostelry and posthouse in London to inquire if such a giant had hired a mount or a seat in a mail coach, and by the small hours of the morning were persuaded that their prey yet lay concealed somewhere in the City.

Taking but a few hours slumber, the two went abroad once more early in the morning, to take their inquiry to the booking offices, and they happened upon the place from whence the Harwich stage departed while the blast of the guard's horn yet echoed in the empty streets. The booking clerk readily answered Vardill's inquiry, advising that a stalwart foreign gentleman, in the company of a young lady, was indeed aboard the receding stagecoach, having booked through to Harwich.

Selwyn proposed hiring a post chaise and setting out in immediate pursuit, but Vardill, to whom would fall the

---

* Dunge Ness.—M.C.

duty of confronting the mighty fugitive, judged such haste to be both imprudent and unnecessary, as they had the itinerary route of the coach from the clerk, while the Chevalier went leisurely on his way to Harwich, quite unwitting of his pursuers' proximity. Instead, Vardill suggested they betake themselves to the military officers, place the evidence before them, and request a force of men sufficient to undertake the arrest of the Chevalier. And so it was that, at ten o'clock that morning, Vardill and Selwyn set out in a post chaise escorted by a troop of light dragoons. Their destination was the sign of the Maypole on the Harwich Road, a league or two past Colchester, that same house of public entertainment at which we lately left the Chevalier, and to which we will now return.

"We come for the Irish traitor, Desmond de Lawless!" repeated the captain, in case any of the company hadn't heard him.

"Indeed," replied the bewildered innkeeper, "but begging yer pardon, m'lord, if any such be here, he be here without my knowledge nor consent. Which one will he be, then?"

The dragoon walked about the room, examining each of the company in turn.

"I cannot say," he declared at last, "but one that knows his face will soon arrive." The galloping troop had left the post chaise some way behind.

The Chevalier, having taken in all that was said, jumped to his feet.

"*Herr Hauptmann!*" he exclaimed, slapping his heels together. "*Der Irlander hinauf* the stairs *ist gehen!*"

"What's that, man?" demanded the soldier. "What did you say?"

"*Der* spalpeen you *bin versuchin!* He's *bin gehidin* upstairs! *Kommen Sie mit mir!*"

The Chevalier strode swiftly across the dining room and clambered up the staircase, closely followed by the bewildered dragoon, the innkeeper, the portly gentleman of the stocks, the awkward young gentleman of the judges, and the cook, who had come in from the kitchen to examine into the commotion.

The Chevalier led the motley procession along the upstairs corridor and, halting before the door to one of the rooms, placed a finger to his lips.

"*Hushen Sie!*" he whispered. He turned to the dragoon. "*Hier. Gibt mir ein Flashenpopper!*" he commanded, pointing to the brace of pistols in the officer's belt. The man drew one of the weapons and handed it unquestioningly to the Chevalier, then drew its mate, cocked it, and awaited further instructions.

The Chevalier quietly pushed open the door and thrust his head within the darkened chamber. Then turning back to the others, he whispered, "He's *bin geshnoozin. Stehen Sie hier, und Ich bin* grabbin' the beggar!"

And placing a finger to his lips again, he stepped into the room, closed the door behind him, and threw the bolt. He crossed the room, opened the window, climbed out, and dropped to the ground. All of this the Chevalier accomplished silently, and his companions waited before the closed door with great apprehension.

"He's a bold 'un, is that Dutchman," ventured the cook.

"Intrepid," agreed the gentleman of the stocks.

"Stout fellow," concurred the innkeeper.

"Daring," accorded the young gentleman of the judges.

"God's wounds!" exclaimed the captain, for a great tumult of shouting and shooting and cursing and the beating of horses' hoofs had suddenly arisen without. The dragoon pushed past the others and down the stairs and out into the yard.

"Some rascal's gone off with yer horse, sir!" cried the sergeant.

"Well, damn it, man, get after him!"

"Yes, sir!" snapped the sergeant, and the troop thundered off down the road toward Harwich.

"Wait!" cried the captain, running after the troop, for he now discerned that his hasty command had left him with naught but shanks' nag as means of locomotion, but his roaring was drowned in the thunder of the galloping mounts. Back he stormed into the public room, where he found the innkeeper, and demanded that a mount be readied for him, that he might overtake his troop. Presently a strapping dray horse was saddled and led out of the stables, with the innkeeper's apology that no other beast was available. With a great oath the captain climbed onto the animal, but neither his spurs, nor his crop, nor his fearsome blasphemies could persuade the horse to gallop, for that was one step it had never learned before the plow.

While the captain of dragoons was thus belaboring his reluctant charger, there arrived upon the scene the post chaise of Messrs. Vardill and Selwyn.

"Where is the Irishman?" demanded Vardill.

"To hell and gone, with my troop at his heels!" bawled the dragoon.

"And what of the wench?" asked Selwyn.

"I know naught of any wench!" cried the captain, as he lumbered away toward Harwich on the back of the plow horse. "Nor do I care to! Yer bloody Irishman is curse enough!"

"The woman is in the dining room," volunteered the portly gentleman of the stocks, who had come out onto the porch and witnessed the scene. "Come, gentlemen. I'll point out the sly baggage."

"There she sits, sirs," declared the informer when the

three entered the public room. Jane sat white and trembling at her place at the table.

"Madam, you must come with us," declared Vardill. "You are charged with abetting the escape of a traitor."

"I do not understand, sirs," she protested faintly. "I know only that some soldiers have kidnapped my husband, who is an honest gentleman, and no traitor, but a merchant of Hamburg."

"Save your tale, madam," sneered Vardill. "You'll get to tell it from the dock in the Old Bailey."

"And repeat it from a platform at Tyburn," cackled Selwyn.

Jane rose and went with the pair. She was led from the inn and to the post chaise waiting in the yard. Vardill opened the carriage door and stood aside.

"Get in, madam. Your stalwart champion has taken to his heels and forsaken you."

But even as these words were spoken, a horseman galloped into the yard and reined to a halt beside the post chaise.

"*Bonsoir, messieurs*. Permit me to present myself, *s'il vous plaît*. I am the Chevalier de Lawless, the same one you flatter with your lavish attentions. You have crossed half of England to meet me, and here I am. What have you to say to me? What? You have nothing to say, Monsieur Vardill? Then you, Monsieur Selwyn. I comprehend you are a famous wit. Has your wit deserted you, *monsieur*?"

The two men were stricken mute with fear. The coachman, at his seat on the carriage, moved his hand slowly down to the footboard, a motion that did not escape the Chevalier's eye.

"Ah, Monsieur Coachman," he said, drawing the captain's pistol from his belt. "You, at least, have found your nerve, but you should assassinate friend and foe alike, were you to discharge that blunderbuss. Throw it down, *monsieur,* and gently. *Merci.*

"*Très bien.* My apologies, *messieurs,* for I must deprive you not only of my own poor company, but also the presence of this beautiful lady. Come along, *mademoiselle.*"

He reached down and lifted Jane to the saddle.

"And now, *messieurs,* if you have not dined, you might sample the entertainment of this place. I recommend *le boeuf. Bonne nuit!*"

He raised his hat, bowed slightly, and galloped off down the road toward Colchester. Half a league from the Maypole he slowed the horse to a canter.

"You should not have returned, Major," said Jane. "It was gallant of you, but far too dangerous. I fear they now will catch us both."

"But, *mademoiselle,* I did not return, for I never left. I was but a few paces off, waiting in the darkness and enjoying many diversions. I saw a troop of English horse charging after a phantom, and an ass ride a plow horse. As I have told you, dear lady, I am of *La Brigade Irlandaise,* and we are called The Wild Geese, so it is fitting that my pursuers should be sent upon the wild-goose chase, *n'est-ce pas?*"

"In truth, sir," laughed Jane, "you are so doughty a gentleman that your wit turns me away from the peril of our situation."

"Your beauty, *mademoiselle,* is my inspiration, and I would dare any danger in your behalf. But it shames me that it is you who have placed yourself in peril in my behalf. Yet, our situation is perhaps not so perilous as it may appear."

He reined to a halt and, dismounting, led the horse some way off the road and into the concealment of a small grove.

"Shall we flee no further than this, then?" asked Jane.

"We flee without motion. Let us rest here while those who pursue do the galloping."

Even as he spoke, a gentle rumbling reached their ears, and swiftly swelled as the thunder of a summer storm. From their hidden vantage they watched the troop of dragoons course past along the road to Colchester. Some minutes later the post chaise of Vardill and Selwyn rattled by. And when yet some more time had elapsed, the plow horse ambled down the road, the unhappy sergeant now riding upon its back.

"*Bien*. Having found the road to Harwich vacant, they search for us in Colchester."

"And where shall we go?" she asked.

"Why, to Harwich, of course."

"But they know Harwich was our destination," she objected.

"*Oui,* but now they also know we know they know it. They will search for us in Colchester, and when they do not find us there they shall wonder if we might have fled to Chelmsford, or perhaps returned to London, or even made directly for some other place along the coast. They shall see that any of these courses would be reasonable for us to follow, and they shall suffer great consternation in striving to divine which of them we have chosen. But they shall not confound themselves further in wondering if we have gone to Harwich, for they know it would be a great foolishness to persist in the same design that has been discovered to them. *Alors,* they leave us no choice. It is to Harwich that we must go."

Jane laughed and clapped her hands in delight.

"Oh, you are a sly fellow, Major Lawless!" she exclaimed.

"*Merci, mademoiselle,* but it does not come to me naturally, and I have had to study slyness. I have read much of Monsieur Machiavelli, the Prince of Slyness, and he has written that it is a glorious thing to use fraud in the conduct of war. I cannot say if that is so, but I think it neither glorious nor honorable to employ fraud at any other time."

He took her hand and kissed it.

"I beg of you, *mademoiselle,* that you do not find slyness in my addresses to yourself. Should ever I find the courage to speak of my feelings for you, I pray that you will believe the words come from my heart."

Jane made no reply, but had the moonlight been ample to discover the hue of her lovely face, the bright vermilion there infused would have been answer enough.

And so it was that Jane and the Chevalier resumed their journey to Harwich, arriving there in the midst of the night, and presenting themselves to the landlord of a little inn at the edge of the town and far from the highway, as a German merchant and his English bride. We shall follow them no further than the threshold of their cozy room, for, as the reader will recall, the author of this history is the child of its hero, and one must surely grant that, regarding certain matters of great intimacy, children must respect the privacies of their parents.

Let us rest, then, before their door, and await the dawning of another day.

15

Ostend

THE day that dawned upon the Chevalier and Jane after
their arrival at Harwich offers little for the author
or the reader of this history to dwell upon. The relation of
the events of but an hour may require many pages when
matters have gone awry (as indeed they went upon the
foregoing day), while the account of an entire day in which
events proceed as desired may be encompassed by but a few
words. Such is the service rendered by adversity to narra-
tion, and were this an invented tale, its author should be
obliged to devise some obstacles to confront the Chevalier
in his eastward course. But as it is, instead, a true relation,
the author of this history is constrained to state that the
events of this day unfolded without incident (with the
trifling exception of a chance encounter in a public street
with the portly gentleman of the stocks, who, owing either
to abstraction or myopy, failed to recognize his former
coachmates).

Let it suffice, then, to relate that the Chevalier sold his
borrowed steed to the keeper of the inn (in order to avoid
suspicion, and not out of any greedy motive), located a
packet in the harbor that happily was on the point of setting sail for Ostend, boarded it in the company of Jane,
and accomplished the crossing without further complica-
tion. Night and the packet boat brought the pair to Ostend,

where they disembarked and stopped at a small hotel near the waterfront.

But if the day of the crossing from Harwich to Ostend passed with little to remark it, the same may not be said of its successor, which saw a train of events that proved quite fateful to the Chevalier. The first of these arose when, after an early breakfast, he declared his intention to go abroad in the town to arrange for a coach to convey them overland to Paris.

"But, Desmond," Jane protested with some consternation, "surely you know I cannot go with you to Paris. I must return to London."

"*C'est impossible!* You should be in great jeopardy in England, for this man Vardill now knows your face!"

"I fear he knows much more, else how did he know to look for you upon the Harwich stage?"

The Chevalier knotted his brow. "*Oui,* that is a puzzle. But whatever his means, the knowledge did him no good. Why does this trouble you?"

"I fear we were betrayed by someone in my father's household, though I cannot think who it might be. Yet there seems no other explanation. Oh, Desmond! I dread saying it, but at this very moment my poor father may be prisoner in the Tower!"

When he considered them, Jane's fears seemed well grounded to the Chevalier, for neither he nor Jane could guess the means Vardill had employed to track them so quickly.

"It is a *désastre*! But this is even more reason why you cannot return to England!"

He leaped up and paced about the room.

"It is I who must return to England and deliver your kind father from the Tower!"

He stopped and thrust his fist into his palm.

"I shall sail with the next packet to Dover and go directly to the Tower! I shall make the *reconnaissance* and devise some method for releasing him! Ah, but you must tell me his name, *ma chérie*, for I cannot discreetly inquire about such a one called Uncle Willie."

In spite of her anguish, Jane was moved to laughter by the Chevalier's unwitting drollery.

"Oh, Desmond, you are very brave, but very foolish. You would rush in where angels fear to tread."

"Ah, but you, my angel, propose to tread thusly."

"I have many friends in London," she explained. "They will hide me, and if it is possible to secure my father's release, they will assist me in it. I shall be safe, where you should be in jeopardy."

The Chevalier considered her words for a moment, then shook his head.

"*C'est impossible,*" he said. "*Oui,* you are right; I should do your kind father no service by delivering myself into an adjacent cell. Nor should I repay his kindnesses by permitting his beloved daughter to rush in where even a fool such as myself can see his efforts should be useless. There is but one resolution: I shall hasten to Versailles, place the matter before Monsieur de Vergennes, and obtain a fast ship, horses, pistols, and whatever else is wanted to equip a band of troopers of *La Brigade Irlandaise* to accomplish this deed."

Secure in his resolution, the Chevalier set out to procure a swift horse, that he might betake himself early to Versailles and to arrange for a carriage in which Jane might follow with more comfort and leisure. Such was his precipitancy that he departed without further discussion, confident that he proceeded with the consent and approval of his companion. But in this he was quite mistaken.

Hardly had the Chevalier gone off upon his errand before Jane set out upon one of her own, pausing only to pen a message to him. She was no stranger to Ostend, having visited the port in the company of her foster father, and so she knew the way to the shop of a certain bookseller who served as agent to Mr. Strahan in commercial matters, as well as sundry other affairs.

The gentleman was surprised and delighted by her unexpected visit, and he lent a sympathetic ear to her urgent plea that he assist her in returning to London at the earliest possible moment. That moment, it transpired, was the present, for the bookseller had only just returned from the harbor, where he had seen a consignment of books aboard a Dover packet, and he knew from the state of the wind and tide that the vessel was on the point of clearing port. Thus, without further delay, he escorted Jane to the waterfront, engaged a boatman to take them out to the packet, and going on board with her, arranged with the master for Jane's passage to Dover.

So it was that the ship carrying Jane was already standing out to sea when the Chevalier returned to the inn and found her note:

My Dearest, Brave Fool,

My heart must break, it seems, for part of it would follow you to Paris, while part would be in London with my father. Would that I, like my heart, could be with you both. But I cannot, and so I must return home. It may be that I can save my father, while I should certainly bring about your destruction should I abet your mad and gallant design to besiege the Tower.

Resume your mission, Dear Desmond, and if it hastens the end of the War, it will hasten us to that sweet moment when, if God is willing, we shall again be together. Until that day I pray you will remember one who loves you, and be content to know her only as

Your dearest,
Jane

The Chevalier cried out in anguish and dismay as he read these words, and he rushed to the landlord of the inn and begged to be advised of the direction in which Jane had departed. But the innkeeper could offer no such information, and so the Chevalier went abroad once more, racing through the streets in a great frenzy, and he came at last to the harbor, where he espied the distant sail of the packet as it stood upon the horizon. He hurried along the waterfront, stopping boatmen and porters to ask whether a passenger of Jane's description had been seen to go aboard the departed vessel, but his inquiries had no result.

The Chevalier's anxious search did not pass unnoticed by one denizen of the port, a stolid gentleman who was often to be seen loitering about the docks by day, and sitting in the taverns by night, and who seemed to have no occupation in life other than looking, listening, and smoking his pipe. This gentleman, having witnessed the Chevalier's passage from one end of the waterfront to the other, disposed himself to be in the Chevalier's path as he returned.

"*Bonjour, monsieur,*" said the Chevalier, and he proceeded to put his question to the gentleman.

"Indeed," answered the other, "I did see a young woman such as you've described go aboard the ship which stands far out there bound for Dover."

"Ah, for Dover!" exclaimed the Chevalier in despair. "Tell me, please, *monsieur,* is there another ship in the harbor making ready to sail for that same destination?"

"Another will sail in two or three days, I think. Is anything amiss? Who was the young lady, if I may inquire?"

"Amiss?" The Chevalier was at a loss to reply to the stranger. "*Merci, non.* Nothing is amiss. The lady? She is but an English woman of my acquaintance, and I promised her family I should see her safely aboard a ship to Dover. Now I know this has been accomplished and may rest easy. *Merci bien, monsieur.*"

The Chevalier departed for the inn, and so great was his consternation he failed to observe that he was followed there by that same gentleman from the docks who had conveyed the unhappy news.

He settled his account at the inn and betook himself to the stables, where his mount had been made ready. Informing the ostler the carriage he had hired was no longer needed, he climbed to the saddle and soon was proceeding at a gallop down the highway to Paris.

The Chevalier saw that it should serve no purpose to tarry at Ostend for two days waiting for another vessel to take him to Dover, for by then the object of his solicitude would have found shelter among her nameless allies in London, or else (he faltered at the thought) have been locked in a dungeon within the Tower. His design, then, was to proceed to Versailles with the utmost dispatch, present himself to the Foreign Minister, M. de Vergennes, and implore the count to equip him with that which would insure the success of a swift sortie into England to rescue Jane and her father—a half dozen of his dauntless comrades of The Wild Geese, a guide who knew the back roads of Kent and the back alleys of London, and a swift coastal cutter to take them to some lonely place on the English coast and stand ready to whisk them all away when they returned. This much he should not be denied, of that he was certain, for he believed the Scotsman and his daughter to be the faithful servants of His Most Christian Majesty, King Louis.

While the Chevalier galloped toward the French frontier, the gentleman who had followed him from the docks to the inn, and from the inn to the stables, arrived at the house of a certain widow who resided in Ostend. The name of the stolid gentleman was Herr Hake, and the lady he visited, Frouw Wolters. Both were employed in the secret service of the English king.*

"I do not know who the woman may have been," said Herr Hake, "but I am certain the man was Lawless."

"Then the Irishman made good his escape," said the woman.

"And is, at this moment, upon the highway to Paris," said her visitor.

Frouw Wolters went to her writing stand and penned two dispatches. She handed one to Hake.

"See that this is sent to Stephens† by the next Dover packet."

She gave him the second letter.

"This one is urgent. Send it to Paris by courier immediately! Wentworth must be told that Lawless is on his way. He must warn Moses!"

---

* Marguerite Wolters had been the wife of the British Secret Service chief in Amsterdam and took over his operation there after he died. In 1780, after England declared war on the Dutch, Mrs. Wolters moved the intelligence station to Ostend, where L. C. Hake had already established an operation (Morris, p. 127). —M.C.

† Philip Stephens (1725–1809), secretary of the admiralty from 1763 to 1793, and chief of British Naval Intelligence (Morris, p. 127).—M.C.

16

Versailles

To the west and somewhat to the south of Paris, the highway proceeds through the elegant village of Auteuil and over the Pont de Sèvres, which carries it across the Seine. Thence runs the road through a rustic dale beneath the châteaux of Bellevue and St.-Cloud, past the stately groves of Chaville, and on to the royal city of Versailles. There, amidst a vast and splendid tract of pastoral parks and formal gardens, stands the magnificent palace of the Sun King and his heirs. As we visit the royal apartments upon this February morn, we find one of the royal posterity in residence, His Most Christian Majesty, Louis XVI.

The king is a pursy young man of near eight-and-twenty years, and we see him struggling into his coat while one of his attendants ties his hair and another arranges his sword belt. A file of ambassadors, envoys, and ministers await him in an antechamber, through which the king's foreign minister, Count de Vergennes, has just exited. We shall not detain His Majesty, for he is impatient to have done with the formalities of state pressed upon him by his visitors and to get on to more diverting matters, to wit, his library, his locksmithy, and his dinner.* Let us, instead,

---

* Louis XVI was much more interested in reading, tinkering with locks, and eating than in the business of running his kingdom, a job he usually was content to leave to his ministers.—M.C.

follow M. de Vergennes as he crosses the Rue de l'Intendance to the Foreign Ministry, where he is met by his
secretary, M. de Rayneval.

"You have a visitor, Your Excellency," said Rayneval.
"The Chevalier de Lawless awaits you."

"Really? It must be his ghost. Bring him to my chambers."

The Chevalier strode into the office of the foreign minister and made his obeisances.

"Good day, *Monsieur le Compte.* I must beg your pardon
for presenting myself to you thus, but I have been a-saddle
for most of two days racing here from Ostend on a matter
of the greatest urgency."

The Chevalier had not stopped to dress himself properly
for court, but wore his boots and spurs and a great amount
of dust from the highway.

"You are a welcome sight, regardless of your condition,
Major Lawless," said Vergennes. "We had heard the British
hanged you. I'm pleased to see the report was in error."

"The report was entirely accurate, Your Excellency," said
the Chevalier, and he proceeded to relate the events that
had befallen him in England and the circumstances that
had brought him in such haste to Versailles.

"I see," the count remarked when he had finished, "and
not content with your astonishing exploits, you now would
undertake the singlehanded invasion of England."

"Forgive me, *Monsieur le Compte,*" ventured the Chevalier, "but I had in mind more a descent* than an invasion, and had I proposed to accomplish it alone, I should
have undertaken it already, and not come here to ask your
assistance, for it is, as I have explained, a matter of the
greatest urgency."

---

* Raid.—M.C.

"Quite so," agreed Vergennes with a sigh. "You know, Major Lawless, that His Majesty has remarked to me that the officers of his Irish Brigade cause him more trouble than all the rest of his army in combination?"

"I fear that may be so, Your Excellency," answered the Chevalier, "for His Majesty's enemies have often made the same complaint."

Vergennes nodded and smiled. "Well spoken, *monsieur,* and with truth enough to warrant my faith that, can any accomplish so daring a mission, it must be a party of The Wild Geese. But before I give you my answer, let me first confirm that the undertaking is truly necessary." He turned to his secretary. "Rayneval, find Monsieur Baudouin and ask if he has any news of this Scottish gentleman who is the occasion of the Chevalier's apprehensions."

M. de Rayneval left the chamber and returned after some time had passed.

"Your Excellency, Monsieur Baudouin is aware of the Scotsman of whom the Chevalier has spoken and begs to assure you that, but two days past, that gentleman was yet safe in his own house, and had not been put in the Tower."

"Two days," remarked Vergennes. "If I understand you correctly, Major Lawless, two days ago you were already in Ostend, and two more days had then elapsed since you were apprehended on the road to Harwich. I think your fears for the Scottish gentleman and his daughter must be groundless."

"I shall be overjoyed if they are," said the Chevalier carefully. "But is Monsieur Baudouin certain of his information?"

"It is his profession," answered Vergennes. "I require nothing of Monsieur Baudouin but that he be certain of the information he furnishes me. I shall direct him to make further inquiries, of course, to confirm that the daughter arrived safely home, but I bid you make yourself easy, *monsieur,* for it seems the English discovered your escape through some means other than a spy in the gentleman's household. I am confident that both father and daughter are quite safe, and thus you are free to turn your attentions to the matter that occasioned your return from America. When you departed Philadelphia, did not Monsieur de La Luzerne give you a letter to deliver to me?"

"He did," answered the Chevalier, "and it shames me that I did not think to throw it into the sea before we engaged the British frigate."

"The British have read it, then?"

"I cannot say. I kept it within a book—*The Discourses of Machiavelli,* which Monsieur de La Luzerne presented me—and I presume it and all else aboard the *Aurore* fell into British hands."

Vergennes smiled. "I trust the letter shall remain unread, then, for the English have no need to study Machiavelli. Did Monsieur de La Luzerne acquaint you with the contents of the letter?"

"He informed me of the affair of Moses, and of his suspicion that Monsieur Franklin is a traitor."

"Speak softly of such things when in France, *monsieur!*" Vergennes cautioned. "Sounds carry farther along the corridors of Versailles than they may in the American wilderness. Very well, he told you of Moses. Did he inform you, as well, of our plan to second you to the American ministry so you might discover who this Moses may be?"

"He did."

"Then, is there any reason why we should not proceed in this design?"

"None, if the Highland gentleman and his daughter are quite safe, as you say. But, as I told Monsieur de La Luzerne,

I am a soldier, not a courtier, and I know nothing of intrigue."

"That is to your advantage. A famous courtier should put our man on his guard, while a famous soldier shall not."

"An advantage, I agree. But I fear I know little of how to profit by it. Moses has small reason to guard himself against an adversary such as I, who am so unschooled in the ways of the secret war. Your Excellency cannot share Monsieur de La Luzerne's suspicions, for you surely cannot think my wit any match for that of Poor Richard."

"Unhappily, there is much reason to suspect Monsieur Franklin," said Vergennes. "He has met often and in secret with agents of the English. We might put that down to the normal course of diplomatic negotiation, were it not for the fact that his dear friend, Monsieur Deane, has already proved himself a traitor. And of course, there is also the matter of Monsieur Franklin's son."

"His son?"

"Yes, had you not heard? It is an American scandal. Monsieur Franklin's son is an infamous Tory.* Some say he learned his treachery at his father's knee."

"The sins of the sons are to be visited upon their fathers?" quipped the Chevalier. "Then we must blame Adam for all the wickedness in the world."

---

* William Franklin (1731–1813), illegitimate son of Benjamin, was appointed royal governor of New Jersey by King George in 1763, and his loyalties remained with the king after the Revolution began. He was arrested by the Americans and imprisoned until 1778, when he was exchanged for a British prisoner of war. He spent the duration of the war in New York (which was occupied by the British), where he became president of the Associated Loyalists, a Tory group.—M.C.

"Ah, a swift parry and a clever riposte," Vergennes remarked. "Your wit seems as ready as your famous sword, Major Lawless. I think you have been unduly modest. Whoever he may be, Moses shall find you a formidable adversary."

"But one little skilled with the Italian cloak."*

"Then I shall see you are provided with such, that you may practice," said Vergennes. "Rayneval, see that the Chevalier receives anything he requires, and obtain for him another copy of Machiavelli, for he wants instruction in things Italian."

Taking up his pen, he wrote a short note, sealed it, and gave it to the Chevalier.

"Here is a letter that will introduce you to Monsieur Franklin. You will find him at the Hôtel de Valentinois at Passy, which will be your own temporary residence."

Vergennes arose and came round his desk. Taking the Chevalier by the arm, he walked with him to the door of the chamber.

"It is clear to me, Major Lawless," he said, "that you are not well pleased by this task we have given you."

"It is not necessary that a soldier find his orders pleasing," replied the Chevalier. "It is sufficient that he execute them. You may be assured, *Monsieur le Compte,* that if it is within my ability to unmask this Moses, I shall do it."

"Of course, Major. But as a student of human nature I have observed that a man is best able to obey those orders he finds closest to his own heart. There is a side to this affair of Moses I think you have not seen. Had you com-

---

* The use of a cloak, in combination with a sword or dagger, in personal combat was an ancient Italian custom (Angelo, p. 96).—M.C.

prehended it, you should set forth upon your mission with greater zeal."

"What might it be?"

"Consider this, Major: You have come in great haste from Ostend because you believed the Scotsman and his daughter were in peril. Very well. Now you have been assured they have not been discovered to the English spy catchers. Nonetheless, they remain in jeopardy."

"What is this you say?" demanded the Chevalier in dismay.

"The names of the Scotsman and his daughter and those others in England who serve us are not known to this Monsieur Vardill, but they are well known to some here in France. One English spy at Passy is far more likely to learn those names than an army of spy catchers in London. It is Moses, not Vardill, who puts your friends in peril."

"*Parbleu!*" exclaimed the Chevalier. "I see that you are right! But then you must send another to Passy in my place, one who is seasoned in this secret war!"

Vergennes smiled and shook his head.

"Believe me, my friend," he said, "no man in France is better suited to carry out this task. I wish you good hunting, Major Lawless."

17

A Council of War

A bleak wintry sky lowered upon Windsor Castle, matching the mood of those gathered in conference in the king's drawing room. King George and Lord Stormont listened in gloomy silence as Lord North read from the papers before him.

"We shall require something in excess of twenty million pounds for the present year, which is an increase of three million over the past year, and five million over the year before. I shall propose some new taxes, of course, but once again taxes can supply only a part of what is wanted. We shall have to go to the bankers again, borrowing some thirteen million more. I must point out that a loan of thirteen million will require a repayment of some twenty-four million at liquidation."

He set down his papers.

"I am very sorry to bring these tidings to Your Majesty, but the war grows more costly each year."

"I make no doubt the opposition will be better pleased than I by your budget," said the king, "for it will lend strength to their clamorings for defeat. When must you present your proposal to Parliament, Freddie?"

"No later than the last of February, I fear."

"Let us hope we shall have news of some victories by then," said the king, "to put a better face upon your figures."

"I fear that nothing but an end to the war could improve the countenance of these balance sheets, Your Majesty. The fortunes of war are uncertain, but certain I am that, should this war survive another twelvemonth, its costs shall have grown even greater, and we shall have no choice but to resort to the bankers again for a loan of a sum greater even than what we must borrow this year. We fight this war on credit, but there is a limit even to the credit of Great Britain, and I fear we approach it."

"Are we to suffer the dismemberment of the kingdom, then, because we cannot bear the cost of its preservation?" demanded the king, to which Lord North could make no reply.

"The Americans fight with borrowed money as well," ventured Lord Stormont, "but their bankers are France, Spain, and the United Provinces. We are forced to match, shilling for shilling, the treasuries of three great states."

"But can it be," reflected Lord North, "that our enemies are so fond of making mischief for us they would suffer even a third part of its great price without persuasion? And the French support far more than their third share of its cost. Who can it be who solicits them so eloquently?"

"Who can it be but Moses?" said the king. "It suits his masquerade to play the role of beggar, for the French alms he sends his countrymen blind them to his treachery. Yet he forces us to match with an equal sum the steep price of his mask. Tell us, Stormont, what intelligence has this fellow given to support so great a cost?"

"Moses' value to us is that of potentiality, Your Majesty. 'Tis not so much a question of what he has done for us already as what he shall do for us when the critical moment arrives."

"The critical moment?" said the king. "Of what moment do you speak, Stormont? Is it that moment when we must bargain with rebels and traitors? Then I bid you do not speak of it to me, for I am resolved such an infamous moment shall never come to pass. But if it is the moment when we must command Moses to sunder the French alliance, then I put it to you that the moment is now!"

"I speak of both sundering and bargaining, Your Majesty," replied Lord Stormont, "of achieving the one by undertaking the other. Perhaps the moment *has* arrived."

"What is this you say?" demanded the king. "Speak plainly."

"Let us suppose the Americans were to treat with us, yet never consult their allies at Versailles. Let us suppose they were to bargain with us for a separate peace and leave the French to their own devices. What, then, does Your Majesty suppose might be the fate of the French and American alliance?"

"Why, there should no longer be an alliance," replied the king, "nor any need for one, for the Americans should have extorted from us their prized independency."

"Forgive me, Your Majesty, but they should not have done it. They should have no more than a piece of paper upon which that word 'independency' was writ, and for it they should have traded the friendship of their powerful ally. And they should have none to come to their aid when such a worthless treaty were abrogated."

"What treachery do you propose, sir?" demanded the king. "Sign a treaty with the Americans today and annul it tomorrow? Would you ransom the kingdom at the price of my honor?"

"What claim have rebels and traitors upon Your Majesty's honor?" replied Stormont. "A treaty with the Americans should be no solemn compact between two sovereign states; it should be no more than a promise wrested through force by cutthroats and mutineers. What sacred obligation can such a promise entail? I say none!"

The king shook his head.

"A tempting argument, Stormont. Perhaps it is as well there is none among the Americans so foolish as to be deceived by such trickery."

"There is none so foolish, Your Majesty," Stormont agreed, "but there is one treacherous enough to lead his accomplices into this trap."

"You speak of Moses," said the king.

"I do."

"But should we execute such a design, what guarantee have you that Moses will do as he is bid?" asked the king. "Does he love his pay so dearly he would venture his life for it?"

"He does, for we pay him not only in money, but with silence."

"Silence?"

"It is a very sordid business," said Lord Stormont, "and I do not think Your Majesty wishes to hear the particulars of it. Suffice to say it involves the indecencies and outrages of the Hell Fire Club of the late Lord Le Despencer,* and an infamous paper which Moses had rather die than suffer the publication."

---

* Sir Francis Dashwood (1708–1781), afterwards Lord Le Despencer, founded a secret society of prominent Englishmen who met in the ruins of Medmenham Abbey, where they staged elaborate sexual orgies and satanic rituals, including the Black Mass. The group was known by various names, including The Hell Fire Club and The Monks of Medmenham. Dashwood, who later served a brief term as chancellor of the exchequer, was earlier postmaster general, in which capacity he met and befriended his American counterpart, Benjamin Franklin.—M.C.

"I see," said the king, and his face registered surprise and repugnance. He reflected a moment.

"You have this paper?"

"It is in the possession of Lord Sandwich, who is ready to surrender it whenever required," Stormont replied.

"Very well," said the king. "I accept your assurance that Moses will do as he is bid. As to your design for treating with the Americans for a separate peace, I must reflect upon it before giving you my answer. For now, I shall demand but a smaller service of Moses."

"And what might that be, Your Majesty?" asked Stormont.

"That he cease from working against us. That he lift his siege of the French treasury. If this flow of French gold can be stemmed, there shall be no need for trickery. Then we shall treat with the Americans in earnest, but the word they write upon their paper shall not be 'independency' but 'surrender.' "

18

Poor Richard

THE luxurious suburb of Passy stood upon the lower part of the hill of Chaillot, to the west of Paris. The little town of some few hundred families nestled among vineyards, pastures, and great estates. Charming villas and chateaux stood above terraced gardens leading down to the Seine, and among these could be found the Hôtel de Valentinois.

The Hôtel was a great mansion of wings, pavilions, gardens, pools, and tree-lined lanes, all commanding a magnificent view of the river and the city of Paris, which lay beyond. It was the home of M. de Chaumont* and his guests, the ministers and envoys of the infant American republic. Many Americans lived here for a time during the years of the War of Independency, but the most eminent of these was a constant resident. The lightning rods on the roof served as his ensign, proclaiming that below dwelt Benjamin Franklin, the Sage of Philadelphia.

The Chevalier rode up the Rue de la Paroisse and dis-

---

* Jacques-Donatien Leray de Chaumont, a wealthy businessman and commissary of the French Army. In French the word *hôtel* can mean either an establishment offering accommodation to the transient public or simply a large house. In the case of the Hôtel de Valentinois, the word had the latter meaning; it was Chaumont's private mansion.—M.C.

mounted in the courtyard of the Hôtel. A stableboy took his mount and directed him to the wing that housed the American ministry. The Chevalier presented himself there and delivered over to the servant who answered his knock the letter M. de Vergennes had written to introduce him to Dr. Franklin. He waited for some minutes in an ante-chamber before being led into the office of the American minister plenipotentiary.

Benjamin Franklin came forward from behind his lit-tered desk to greet his visitor. His step was quick and his carriage straight, and he might have been esteemed younger than his threescore and sixteen years but for the marks time had left upon his face. He wore no periwig, and his head was near bereft of hair; that which remained was long and brushed back from his high, wide forehead. His eyes were bright and quick, the line of his mouth firm, and though the flesh of his face was somewhat slack, his coun-tenance proclaimed he had gotten the better of his years.

"Good morrow to you, Major Lawless," he said. He bowed, peering up at the Chevalier through his spectacles. "I welcome you to Passy."

The Chevalier returned the bow. "*Merci,* Monsieur Frank-lin. It is a great honor to be welcomed by so illustrious an American patriot."

Franklin held Vergennes's letter in his hand. He raised his chin, peered down at the paper, then nodded again toward the Chevalier.

"I have heard of your exploits, Major, and those of The Wild Geese. They are legendary."

The Chevalier bowed deeply again.

"*Merci, monsieur,* but I fear that legends are often more magnificent than life."

Franklin leaned back, read further, then, inclining his head forward, gazed at the Chevalier again.

"You are too modest, Major. To be hanged at Tyburn and live to tell the tale is surely the stuff of legends."

Once again the Chevalier bowed deeply.

"*Merci, monsieur,* but as it is a distinction I did not seek, I cannot boast of it."

Franklin put down the letter. "Please be seated and make yourself easy, Major. I assure you there is no need for so much courtly bobbing, for I am the minister of a republican state."

"Forgive me, *monsieur,*" replied the Chevalier in some confusion, "but I thought it unmannerly not to reply in kind to your own courteous gestures."

Franklin was puzzled, but then burst out in laughter.

"I am sorry, Major. Only my first curtsy was meant as a civility; the others were in deference to my double spectacles."*

He removed the glasses and exhibited them to the Chevalier.

"The bottoms of the lenses are for reading and seeing objects close at hand; the tops are for viewing things beyond arm's reach. Thus one pair of spectacles does the work of two, but at the cost of a little nodding."

"Ah, *très ingenieux!*" proclaimed the Chevalier.

Franklin replaced the spectacles upon his nose. "Tut, Major. Merely the contrivance of a lazy old man who loves his comforts and conveniences. But I'm pleased to find they confer a benefit I hadn't intended; they make my manner seem more courteous and agreeable. Happily, I set the lenses atop one another; had I placed them side by side I'd be counted a very obstinate fellow."

He made a droll face and shook his head, and the Chevalier could scarcely contain his mirth.

---

* Bifocals, which Franklin invented.—M.C.

"Well, enough of such trifles," said Franklin briskly. "Lost time is never found again." He reread Vergennes's letter, then set it down upon his desk.

"In all candor, Major Lawless, I've no idea what I shall do with an adviser on military affairs. You see, we seldom have any military affairs here at Passy. We are besieged only by mendicants and creditors."

"Perhaps Monsieur de Vergennes was mistaken," ventured the Chevalier hesitantly.

"Monsieur de Vergennes is seldom mistaken," said Franklin, "though at times he moves in mysterious ways to perform his wonders. I make no doubt he had excellent reason to second you here, while I can think of no reason at all to send you away. Do you play at chess?"

"*Oui,* I play at chess," replied the Chevalier in surprise, "but I am no master of the game."

"Excellent. You are recommended as much by the latter as the former, for while I love to play, I hate to lose. But you should perfect your skill at chess, Major, for it is more than an idle amusement. It develops foresight, caution, and circumspection. Life is a kind of chess, and by playing one game we sharpen skills useful in playing the other."

"A fascinating notion, Monsieur Franklin," said the Chevalier, "but is there not a great difference between the moving of wooden men and the deeds of those created in flesh and blood? The world is full of craftiness, even as on the chessboard, but there is also courage, honor, and fate."

"I own there is that difference," said Franklin, "but is there not a like difference between exercise with the foil and combat with the smallsword? And did you not acquire your famous skill with the latter through practice with the former? When a fencer enters the gymnasium, does he not leave fate outside? And does he require courage, or even honor, when his face is covered by a mesh and his body protected by a plastron?"

"*Touché,* Monsieur Franklin," laughed the Chevalier. "You have quite disarmed me, and put me in check as well. *Alors,* I must study the game of chess."

"I propose a bargain, Major: instruction in chess in return for lessons in the art of the foil."

"You wish to learn *l'escrime?*" asked the Chevalier in surprise.

"I should wish to, were I fifty years younger," Franklin replied. "No, it is my grandson, Temple,* whom I propose as your pupil. He has lately become very much the young gentleman of fashion, but has little skill at fencing. The French esteem skill with the foil and smallsword as essential to a young man's tuition, and I do not wish him to be regarded as one whose education is incomplete. You should greatly oblige me by instructing him."

"I shall be honored to teach your grandson, *monsieur,*" replied the Chevalier. "Instruction in the art of the blade is, after all, a species of military advice, although perhaps not what Monsieur de Vergennes had in his mind."

---

* William Temple Franklin (1760–1823), illegitimate son of Benjamin Franklin's illegitimate son, William Franklin, the Tory royal governor of New Jersey. Temple, as he was called, was born in London while his father was studying law at Middle Temple; the name of his mother is not known. Temple was raised by his grandfather so that the fact that William had sired a bastard would not be known to Franklin's family in America, or detract from the respectable image William needed to advance in the king's service. Temple accompanied his grandfather to Paris, where he completed his education and became Benjamin Franklin's private secretary.—M.C.

The colloquy between the Chevalier and Dr. Franklin was interrupted by the abrupt entry of a coarse-looking fellow wearing a dirty apron over his great belly, which garment he proceeded to unfasten from about his person and cast onto the floor.

"I abdicate, Monsieur Franklin!" the intruder cried. "I have been insulted most atrociously!"

"Insulted?" asked the startled Franklin.

"*Oui,* atrociously, by Mademoiselle de Chaumont. She contests the honesty of my accounts, and says I embezzle from you, *monsieur.*"

"Ah, but I know you are an honest man, Monsieur Finck. Have you not often told me so yourself?"

"*Oui,*" the fellow admitted grudgingly.

"Then you must not take the young lady's words to heart. They arise from an excess of vigilance for my welfare, and not out of any malice towards yourself." He took the fellow by the arm. "Pray, take up your apron and resume your dominion, Monsieur Finck. I shall draft a treaty of peace between Mademoiselle de Chaumont and yourself, affirming your independency in all affairs of the kitchen. Major Lawless, may I present my trusty majordomo, Monsieur Finck."*

The Chevalier bowed politely.

"The major will be my guest," said Franklin. "He is to advise me on military matters."

"Another mouth to feed!" exclaimed Finck. "It is not possible, Monsieur Franklin, unless . . ." He rubbed his hands together.

---

* Jacques Finck, to whom Franklin paid a monthly stipend of 1300 francs to buy and prepare the meals for himself and the staff of the American ministry. He swindled both Franklin and the local merchants who supplied the Ministry.—M.C.

"Of course, of course," Franklin replied. "Present your bill for whatever additional expense you suffer."

"Ah, *merci, monsieur.*" M. Finck, his injured honor balmed by the prospect of greater plunder, smiled and backed from the room.

"My apologies, Major, for the little household contretemps," said Franklin. "I fear Monsieur Finck's wounded dignity caused him to forget his manners."

"It is nothing, *monsieur,*" replied the Chevalier, smiling. "One must respect the wrath of an honest man who has been falsely accused."

"Monsieur Finck has assured me that he is, in fact, an honest man," said Franklin, his eyes twinkling behind his spectacles. "I allow, of course, that he may be mistaken. Come, Major, I shall show you about the house."

He indicated that the Chevalier should follow.

"*Pardon, monsieur,*" said the Chevalier, who eyed the great number of papers strewn about the American's office. "Please do not think it an impertinence, but I could not fail to observe many documents upon your desk that look to bear upon matters of state."

"Quite so," Franklin replied. "Orderliness is a virtue I fear I've never been able to acquire in myself."

"But, Monsieur Franklin, is it prudent to leave such papers about when there are those near at hand who esteem themselves to be honest, but may be, as you say, mistaken?"

Franklin stepped to his desk and picked a paper from a pile at random.

"Here is a note from Monsieur de Vergennes in the matter of a new loan my country has requested," he said, adjusting his spectacles. "But American importunity is famous, and I should be greatly surprised if the substance of this message is not already a topic of conversation in the salons and drawing rooms of Paris."

He selected another document from the pile.

"This letter discloses that a ship laden with goods for General Washington will sail from Lorient in a fortnight, a revelation that should not surprise the lowliest idler on the docks, who may observe for himself those goods as they are stowed aboard."

He took up yet another sheet.

"Here is a letter to a bookseller of my acquaintance in London; it concerns a trifling matter, no affair of state, yet I make no doubt it shall be opened, read, and copied several times before it reaches him, the words searched for a code, and the very paper tested for invisible writing. You see, Major, there are no secrets here, and were there any, they'd be no safer within my desk than atop it, for no lock can be devised that is more clever than the locksmith."

"You have no fear of spies, then?" inquired the Chevalier.

Franklin smiled. "If I were sure that my *valet de chambre* were a spy—as he probably is—I should not discharge him, for in all other respects he is quite satisfactory."

He was suddenly somber. "The best of spies, Major, is not the servant who might steal your secrets, but the false comrade to whom you freely entrust them. If you would keep your secrets from your enemy, tell them not to your friend.

"But enough of such things! Come, sir, and I shall show you the house."

Franklin escorted the Chevalier through the wing of the Hôtel occupied by the ministry. He began with the wine cellar, which harbored an impressive collection of vintages; some twelve hundred bottles, including red and white Bordeaux, five varieties of champagne, and several Spanish wines that appealed to the American's palate.

Stopping in the kitchen, they again encountered the

volatile M. Finck, and met Coinet, the cook, and Joseph Rogey, the kitchen boy. The midday dinner was in preparation: a joint of beef, half a goose, vegetables, pastries, and sundry other victuals. Two servants—Arbelot, the coachman, and Brunel, the footman—lingered in the scullery, sampling the food and venturing culinary advice to M. Coinet.

Upstairs they entered the ministry's library, a long room lined with books from floor to ceiling. A crate of books stood upon the floor, and two carpenters were constructing additional shelves to hold them.

"I am ever buying books," said Franklin. "Hardly a packet comes to Ostend without a parcel of them for me, and I pay so much to the booksellers of London I might be charged with trading with the enemy. I shall not live to read half of them, but I trust they will be useful in America, which is their eventual destination."

Next they visited a suite of rooms in which had been established a printing shop, complete with two presses, cases of type, a great assortment of brass stencils, and a type foundry.

"When first I set out to make my way in the world," Franklin explained, "I worked as a journeyman printer. Now the trade of my youth has become the amusement of my old age. It pleases me to compose trifling discourses upon sundry topics and print them here. I call them my 'Bagatelles.' 'Tis a wicked extravagance, I fear. My eyes and my back are too old for the printer's trade, so I must needs employ journeymen for the work."

"You wield a prolific pen, Monsieur Franklin," remarked the Chevalier, "to busy so many hands setting your words into type."

"A wicked extravagance, indeed," Franklin repeated, and led the Chevalier away. "Now I shall show you your rooms, which I trust you will find comfortable. Pray, take your ease, Major, and consider this house as your home."

A servant had carried the Chevalier's saddlebags to his apartment, arranging their meager contents for their owner's convenience. Left to his own devices for the moment, the Chevalier took up the books of Machiavelli that M. Rayneval had given him at Versailles and idly perused them. He read one discourse entitled "Very Rarely Do Men Know How to Be Either Wholly Good or Wholly Bad," and another, "How Easily Men May Be Corrupted."

"Deplorable," muttered the Chevalier, and putting down one volume, took up its mate. In it he encountered an essay bearing the more promising title, "In What Way Princes Must Keep Faith," but found the advice it contained less exalting than the title:

"A prince," wrote Machiavelli, "being thus obliged to know well how to act as a beast, must imitate the fox and the lion, for the lion cannot protect himself from traps, and the fox cannot defend himself from wolves. One must therefore be a fox to recognize traps, and a lion to frighten wolves. Those that wish to be only lions do not understand this."

"You are mistaken, Monsieur Machiavelli," said the Chevalier to the book. "There are many wolves with a taste for foxes, my friend, but very few trappers with a stomach for lions, especially a lion who has been annoyed by a trap. The lion reposes fearlessly in the open, and he is trapped only if he falls into a deep hole. But the fox, he must live all the time in a deep hole. And why must he live there? Because he is not a lion. Those that wish to be only foxes do not understand this."

"Those princes that have been best able to imitate the fox have succeeded best," argued Machiavelli from the pages of the book. "But it is necessary to be able to disguise this character well, and to be a great feigner and dissembler; and men are so simple and so ready to obey present necessities, that one who deceives will always find those who allow themselves to be deceived."

"Bah!" exclaimed the Chevalier, as he cast aside the book. "The fox may disguise himself, but the lion has a nose!"

The Chevalier took up his smallsword and, assuming the guarding stance, advanced across the chamber, thrusting, parrying, and lunging against an invisible adversary. He continued thus for several minutes, retiring and advancing as he engaged his imaginary opponent. In this way he kept the muscles and sinews of his limbs in good order, and ready to serve him when next he should have need to draw his sword in earnest. To lend amusement to this exercise, he imagined his phantom adversary to be the author of the work he had just set aside.

"Aha, Monsieur Machiavelli," he panted, "I think you were better with the cloak and dagger, for the smallsword does not seem to be your weapon. Guile lends it no advantage."

He paused and lowered his point.

"What is that? The feint?" He rubbed his chin reflectively. "That is so," he admitted. "One appears to thrust on one side, but executes the thrust on the other, and so leads the adversary's wrist astray, leaving an opening in his guard. I must admit that I have often employed the feint.

"What is that, Monsieur Machiavelli? Yes, you are right. I have often left an opening in my guard intentionally, to dupe my adversary into an imprudent thrust. Very well, I admit it: I frequently withdraw when I see my opponent's balance will suffer from a sudden advance. Very well, *monsieur*! Enough!"

He put down his sword.

"It is not enough to have the heart of a lion; one must

have the head of a fox. As Monsieur Franklin might say, fencing is a kind of chess. He who believes his victories have all been won without deception deceives himself above all others."

The dialogue between the Chevalier and Machiavelli was interrupted by a servant, who knocked at the door and announced that dinner was to be served. The Chevalier paused to make himself presentable (for he had disarrayed his person by his exertions) and went down to the dining room.

Word that the Chevalier de Lawless had taken up residence there had spread swiftly among the other dwellers in the Hôtel de Valentinois, and Monsieur Finck was compelled to set more places than usual for the afternoon meal. Franklin greeted his guest once again, explaining that most of those present had come to meet him.

The Chevalier was duly flattered by this attention, mistakenly attributing it to his fame as a warrior. But heroes were no novelty at Passy, where John Paul Jones and the Marquis de Lafayette were frequent visitors; the Chevalier was of interest to those gathered in the dining room because he bore the special distinction of having been hanged by the neck at Tyburn. Franklin presented his guest to each of the company in turn.

M. de Chaumont and his wife were present with their three charming daughters, and there were also three young men, each of about twenty years. The first of these was the son of M. de Chaumont; the second, an Irish lad named Carey, whom the Chevalier had seen working in the printing shop; and the third was Temple, the minister's grandson, who was to be the Chevalier's pupil.

As the Chevalier set eyes upon the young Franklin, he was strongly impressed he had met the handsome youngster sometime in the recent past, but before he could examine his memory regarding the matter, he was introduced to a distinguished gentleman of about his own age, Dr. Bancroft, the general secretary of the ministry.

A pleasant and leisurely repast ensued, replete with toasts to America, King Louis, the victory at Yorktown, and the remarkable deliverance of the Chevalier.

"It is a double pleasure for me," proclaimed Dr. Bancroft as he raised his glass. "As a patriot I celebrate our guest's valiant service to my country, and as a physician I am fascinated by his happy resurrection. When I lived in England, I was told the Tyburn gibbet had been erected for the lawless; I count it a singular thing that one of that very name should have dangled from it and lived to tell the tale."

"Defiance to tyrants is obedience to God's law," proclaimed Franklin. "The Chevalier has broken but one law, the law of gravity!"

When the meal was finished, the party repaired to the drawing room. One of the Chaumont daughters played the spinet, and Franklin called for his chessboard.

"I have promised to instruct the Chevalier in the game of chess," said Franklin. "If you are in the mood for playing, Major, the first lesson may now commence."

The Chevalier took his place across the board from Franklin, and as the company looked on, the game began.

"Tell us, Major," said Franklin, as he pondered a move, "as one who has returned to life, did you see aught of the Elysian Fields during your sojourn in the netherworld?"

"No, *monsieur*," replied the Chevalier, "though when I first beheld those saintly persons who contrived my deliverance, I thought I had come to heaven."

"And where had you, in fact, come?" inquired Franklin.

163

"I do not know, *monsieur*. I was already there when I awoke to find myself alive, and I departed the place blindfolded, and in the midst of the night."

"And the saints who delivered you?" Franklin prompted. "Were they French saints, or English saints?"

"Forgive me, Monsieur Franklin, but a very wise gentleman once counseled me to keep my secrets from my friends if I would not have my enemies learn them."

"Of course, Major," laughed Franklin, "but when Lazarus comes forth from his tomb, the living shall certainly ask him of the next world."

"Ah, Monsieur Franklin," replied the Chevalier, "Scripture does not report what Lazarus may have answered. For true wisdom we must look to the words of Moses."

The Chevalier glanced about him, examining the face of each of the company. All seemed confused except Franklin, who sat frowning at the chessboard.

"Moses?" said Bancroft. "I fear the allusion escapes me."

"I believe I comprehend it," said Franklin. "When the Chevalier speaks of Moses, he refers to me. 'Tis only fitting. I am, in fact, Moses."

Mlle. de Chaumont had stopped playing, and a long silence followed upon Franklin's words. At length the old man picked up his bishop and moved it across the board. He looked about at the company and smiled.

"Have I not led my people into the Promised Land and confounded the English Pharaoh?"

He turned to the Chevalier.

"I have you in check, Major, and I shall mate you in another move. You must learn to be more prudent, for you make your moves without sufficient deliberation."

19

Figaro

IT is morning, but not too early. At a fashionable hour, in a fashionable house, in a fashionable quarter of Paris, a beautiful woman sighs beneath the caresses of a merchant, a lawyer, a soldier, a banker, a playwright, a publisher, an inventor, a watchmaker, and a spy. But lest the reader be unduly scandalized by this scene, the author hastens to add that the throng of lovers sharing *Mademoiselle*'s bed and favors have been stuffed by God and fate into the body of a single creature, that most remarkable issue of a most remarkable age, Pierre-Augustin Caron de Beaumarchais.

"Marie-Thérèse, my dear," said Beaumarchais, "you have been embraced by a two-hundred-year-old man. How did it feel?"

The woman laughed. "I have been loved by a madman whose lips claim he is two centuries old, but whose other parts perform as a boy of twenty."

He took her hand and kissed it. "The calendar announces that today I am twoscore and ten, yet if time is measured by the events that constitute it, I have been alive for two hundred years."

"You are so weary, then?"

"Of course not! I am so busy! What time is it?"

He took his watch from the table.

"Eleven o'clock! It cannot be right! Wait! I invented it! It cannot be wrong!"

He leapt from the bed.

"I must be up and abroad! A thousand affairs await my attention!"

He hurried from the bedchamber, then ran back and took the woman's hand again.

"Until the next time, my love, twenty years hence. In other words, tonight!"

He dashed away.

Lucas, the valet, was waiting in the antechamber with his master's clothes. As Beaumarchais dressed, his secretary, M. Gudin, entered.

"Gudin, my friend, why so grave?"

"The Count de Mirabeau is here to borrow twelve thousand francs," the secretary began.

"Then show him in! Do not stand on ceremony!"

Beaumarchais was leaning on his valet as he pulled up his breeches.

"Ah, good day, *Monsieur le Compte!*" exclaimed Beaumarchais as his visitor entered. "Do you hope to borrow money from a poor fellow who cannot cover his nakedness?"

He was struggling into his shirt.

"Beaumarchais, my friend, you know you could easily lend me twelve thousand francs," said the count.

"That is probably true, but as I should have to fall out with you on the day your bill came due, I prefer to do so today and save twelve thousand francs!"

Beaumarchais left the perplexed count in the antechamber and hurried to his study, with Gudin close at his heels.

"Who else?"

"The Duke de Chalnes is here to kill you," said Gudin.

"What, again? He'll kill nothing but my fleas! Send him in!"

"Beaumarchais, you rascal!" cried the duke as he burst into the room. "Do you think I have forgotten?"

"If you have not, I have! What is it this time? A woman? An insult? Never mind! Do you think you are the only man in Paris who wishes to kill me? You shall have to wait your turn, even though you have a title! Besides, my sword is at the cutler's again; it is nearly worn out!"

"Pistols then!" cried the duke.

"Bah, pistols! Are we Englishmen? Gudin, give the duke an appointment."

Lucas, who had entered the room stealthily and placed himself behind the duke, now encircled him with his massive arms.

"Unhand me, you wretched blackamoor!" cried the duke as the valet carried him to the front door.

"Who else?" demanded Beaumarchais.

"The brothers de Montgolfier."

"Did they arrive by carriage, or in their flying machine?"

"Neither. They came on foot."

"Then they want money. Ask them how much and give them half. Who else?"

"Monsieur Le Tellier."

"Send him in! Good morning, Monsieur Le Tellier! Have you brought me proofs? No? Bound volumes? No? What, then?"

"Difficulties, *monsieur*," explained Le Tellier. "The margrave has made objections to some passages in the texts."

"The margrave? What is a margrave?" demanded Beaumarchais.

"Why, he is the ruler of Baden," replied Le Tellier. "He demands the right to delete those passages that may offend God or religion."

"By the milk of the Virgin! Do you mean that some

German insect proposes to tamper with the words of Voltaire?"

"Indeed," replied Le Tellier.

"Lucas, get my horse! I shall go to Baden immediately and horsewhip this impudent cockalorum!"

"But you are due at the Louvre in an hour," Gudin objected, "to try your lawsuit."

"You are right, Gudin, I had quite forgotten. I shall send this margrave a letter, instead! No, I have no time! You write it, Gudin! Make it very insulting! Tell him that should he persist in such outrages I will remove our establishment a few yards off to some other German pea patch where there is a fitting respect for the greatest writer of the French language!*

---

* Pierre-Augustin Caron de Beaumarchais (1732–1799) has not permitted me to slip in a footnote thus far, but I'm afraid he'll leave the reader far behind if I don't stop him for a moment and interject a few words of explanation.

Beaumarchais has taxed the abilities of a small army of biographers, so it seems futile to try to deal with him in a footnote. However, here are some of the salient details of his career for those who may not have met him already:

He was the son of André-Charles Caron, a watchmaker, and he took up his father's trade, inventing at an early age the escapement since used in virtually all mechanical clocks and watches. Through his skill and audacity he became watchmaker to Louis XV and a court favorite, purchasing the title "de Beaumarchais" to add an aristocratic appendage to his name. He became a prosperous merchant, as well as a secret agent for Louis XV and, later, Louis XVI. When Franklin and Deane came to Paris to solicit aid for the Revolution in 1776, they presented a dilemma: The French wanted to help, but they were not yet ready to take a step, such as openly supplying the rebels, that might lead them into a war with England. The Foreign Ministry turned to Beaumarchais for a solution, and the scheme he devised will seem very familiar to the student of twentieth-century clandestine

"My carriage, Lucas! I must be off to the Louvre!"

"But there is someone else," said Gudin.

"What, another? Who is it?"

"The Chevalier de Lawless."

"Desmond? Here? By the nails of St. Joseph! Why did you not announce him, Gudin, rather than entangling me in all these trifles? Send him in! No, I cannot wait!"

He rushed into the antechamber.

"Desmond, my dear friend!"

He threw his arms about the Chevalier.

"The English hanged you! Thank God it did not take!" He seized him by the arm. "Come along! We must celebrate!"

"But, *monsieur*," objected Gudin. "The Louvre! Your case!"

"Who is the plaintiff?" Beaumarchais demanded.

"Why, you are, sir."

"Splendid! Drop the suit! Send word to the court that I withdraw from the case, whatever it is!"

---

paramilitary operations. Beaumarchais set up a dummy corporation, Hortalez et Compagnie, to funnel French and Spanish money and arms to the Americans. It is likely he expected to make a personal profit on the deal; it is certain he lost a fortune in it; and it is strongly suspected he came out ahead through stock trading, guided by inside intelligence of political and military developments of the war. The whole affair was only a minor incident in the life of Beaumarchais, which was filled with more duels, deals, lawsuits, love affairs, friendships and enmities, successes and quixotic blunders than the careers of a hundred less remarkable people. Of Beaumarchais, Voltaire wrote, "That brilliant, harebrained fellow is in the right against the whole world."

In giving us a glimpse of an hour in the life of Beaumarchais, Pierre-Augustin Lawless (who, it will be recalled, was his godson) has thrown together several representative anecdotes and incidents which, while true, are a bit off chronologically. The quarrel with

Beaumarchais ordered a coach and four brought round to the house and insisted the Chevalier ride about the city with him, racing up and down the boulevards at breakneck speed, alternately pointing out public works completed since the Chevalier's departure for America, and quizzing his guest regarding his extraordinary adventures.

"That is the new grain market; magnificent, is it not? — I heard you captured Cornwallis; is that why the English hanged you? —See what they do to the Palais Royal? — What happened; did the rope break?"

He thrust his head out the window. "Lucas, drive up the Rue Saint-Honoré, and faster!" He dropped back into his seat.

"Why are you so quiet, Desmond? Ah, I see! The noose injured your throat! By the beard of St. Peter! I swear your neck is longer! And you already so tall! If you cannot speak of your exploits you must write them! We shall stop somewhere to get pen and paper!"

The Chevalier laughed and shook his head. "No, thank

---

the Duke de Chalnes, and Count Mirabeau's request for a loan, occurred well before this date, while Beaumarchais's interest in the Montgolfier brothers' plan to build a man-carrying balloon was somewhat later. But Beaumarchais's project to publish the complete works of the late Voltaire in the tiny margravate of Baden (they were banned in France) commenced about this date.

Beaumarchais occupied some of the quieter moments of his life by writing a pair of plays, *The Barber of Seville* and *The Marriage of Figaro,* upon which Rossini and Mozart, respectively, based their operas. One of Beaumarchais's many biographers, Grendel, points out that the final consonants and nasal vowels were pronounced differently in eighteenth-century French than today; *fils* (son of) would be "fi," while Caron (the name of Beaumarchais's father) would be "Caro," hence "fi Caro." Thus, the truest portrait of the magnificent madman may be the one he drew of himself, in the pages of his plays.—M.C.

you, my friend. My throat is in fine working order, I assure you."

"Ah, then it is modesty that binds your tongue! Don't be humble, Desmond! I myself sometimes boast! I must! To do any less would be to lie! Your exploits, Desmond! Out with them!"

He paused, at last, to catch his breath, and the Chevalier began a brief relation of some of the incidents that had recently befallen him. From time to time Beaumarchais underlined the Chevalier's words with oaths and exclamations, but so great was his fascination with the tale, he rarely interrupted it, and he even failed to notice that Lucas, without further advice from his master, had driven beyond the city walls and far into the country.

". . . and so I rode from Ostend to Versailles without further incident," finished the Chevalier.

"Magnificent!" exclaimed Beaumarchais. "An adventure truly worthy of von Münchausen himself.* I shall compose a great epic based upon your adventure and publish it! No! I shall make it a play for the theater! No! I shall do both! We must collaborate on it! We must begin immediately! Of course, you will be my guest while you are in Paris!"

"Alas, I cannot," said the Chevalier. "I must reside at

---

* Some readers may know that R. E. Raspe's *Baron Munchhausen's Narrative of his Marvellous Travels and Campaigns in Russia* was not published until late in 1785, but they may also know (as I did not) that there really was a Münchausen—Karl Friedrich Hieronymus, Freiherr von Münchausen (1720–1797), a famous cavalry officer and raconteur, who recounted his exploits with only slightly less imagination than his "biographer," Raspe. Beaumarchais probably had heard of Münchausen and may even have met him; the baron was a friend of Benjamin Franklin. Franklin also knew Raspe. Small world.—M.C.

the American ministry at Passy, where I have been seconded by Monsieur de Vergennes to advise on military
affairs."

"Of course! I see! You are a spy!"

"By blue!" exclaimed the Chevalier. "How did you
guess?"

Beaumarchais shrugged. "It is obvious. At the American ministry there are only two sorts of men: Americans
and spies. You are not an American. Therefore you must
be a spy."

"What?" demanded the Chevalier. "Do you say that
every Frenchman living in the Hôtel de Valentinois is a
spy?"

"Certainly! Every Frenchman, and some Americans as
well, I believe."

"Yes," agreed the Chevalier. "Some think Monsieur
Franklin himself is an intrigant and a traitor."

"An intrigant? Certainly! A traitor? Impossible!"

"There is a difference?"

"Of course! By the thumbs of St. Thomas! You would
be a spy, yet you are ignorant of the difference between
intrigue and treachery?" He rapped upon the roof of the
carriage and Lucas reined the team to a halt. "You will
surely come to grief, my friend, if you do not learn the
difference. I shall explain it to you."

"Very well," said the Chevalier.

"Let us walk," suggested Beaumarchais, opening the carriage door and stepping onto the road. "Like Aristotle and
other great teachers, I instruct best in the peripatetical
mode."

The Chevalier joined him, and the pair set off on foot
while the coach followed behind.

"Very well," began Beaumarchais, after they had walked
for a while. "Intrigue and treachery: Let us examine this

notion that Monsieur Franklin is a traitor, for example; from whence does it originate?"

"From Monsieur Arthur Lee, I am told," replied the Chevalier.

"Exactly! But when Monsieur Lee served at the American ministry at Passy, he did his best to frustrate Monsieur Franklin's patriotic works."

"Ah, that was treachery?"

"No, intrigue. Lee was envious of Franklin and wished to have his post. But Lee sent his secretary, Major Thornton, to spy upon the English."

"Intrigue?"

"Treachery. Major Thornton was, in fact, an English secret agent sent to spy on Monsieur Lee. But the major was denounced to Franklin by a pair of Englishmen, the brothers Wharton."

"Treachery?"

"Intrigue. The brothers Wharton were in the secret service of Monsieur Franklin. Franklin informed Monsieur de Vergennes that Monsieur Lee had employed a British spy as his secretary, and Monsieur de Vergennes demanded of the American Congress that they recall Monsieur Lee."

"Intrigue?"

"Treachery, if one puts a fine point upon it. Monsieur Franklin had known all along that Major Thornton was a British spy, and it was he who recommended him to Monsieur Lee as his secretary."

"By the faith!" exclaimed the Chevalier. "That *was* treachery, and treason, as well!"

"On the face of it, perhaps," Beaumarchais admitted with a shrug. "But in fact it was merely intrigue, and magnificent intrigue, at that. With splendid economy, Monsieur Franklin rid himself of a British spy and an American troublemaker in a single move. It was a necessity of war. With Lee making difficulties at Passy, Monsieur de Vergennes could hardly lend more money to the Americans."

"The count does not have His Majesty's confidence?"

"The count does not sleep with His Majesty. Vergennes pleads the Americans' cause by day, but Marie Antoinette is their prosecutor at night. She opposes the war."

"Surely not treachery!"

"Certainly not! Intrigue! The queen took a lover, Count von Fersen. His Majesty did not care for the idea, so he awarded the count a regiment and packed him off to America."

"I know the count; he is aide-de-camp to General Rochambeau."

"And will remain as such, so long as the war continues. Thus, the queen murmurs in His Majesty's ear each night the monetary arguments for peace, which she has learned from Monsieur Necker. *Voilà,* intrigue!"

"And this Monsieur Necker; does he deal in intrigue or treachery?"

"Both. He is a Swiss banker who was made director general of the treasury and finances. I never trusted him, and I was right. It seems he lined his own pockets and undermined the alliance, all the while carrying on a correspondence with the British spy chief, Lord Stormont. He was found out and forced to resign."

"His letters were read?" asked the Chevalier.

"Everyone's letters are read," replied Beaumarchais. "That is all the more proof Monsieur Franklin is no traitor."

"What! Franklin's letters opened by his allies? Treachery!"

"Certainly not. It is simple intrigue. The British spies read Franklin's letters! Should his friends know less than his enemies? Ah, Desmond, have you understood nothing of my words? Do you fancy the war is fought no nearer than Saratoga or Yorktown? Do you think there are no armies but those of Washington, Rochambeau, and Cornwallis?"

"No longer, my friend," replied the Chevalier. "I see now there is a secret war, as well, a war fought by invisible soldiers within the covert passages of hidden labyrinths."

"Indeed, Desmond, there are intrigues, dozens of intrigues! A lovely, tangled web of them! Intrigues, treacheries, and secret services!"

"I despair of it all, Pierre-Augustin," sighed the Chevalier. "It is all beyond a simple soldier such as myself."

"Nonsense! Intrigue can be learned, even as one learns fencing."

"Or chess? No, my friend, it is hopeless. I have even studied the works of Machiavelli, but to no avail."

"Machiavelli! Bah! I can teach you intrigue in a single breath: Pretend not to know what you do know, and to know all of what you are ignorant! Pretend to understand what baffles you, and to be confounded by simplicities! When you overhear something of interest, act as though you were deaf! Make a great secret of that which is obvious to all, and hide your real secrets in plain sight! Above all, put aside your Machiavelli and take up Cervantes, for the best of spies learns less of his craft from the cunning prince than from the Mad Knight of La Mancha!"

Beaumarchais halted and turned, signing to his coachman.

"Come along, Desmond. There is, in fact, a British spy within the American ministry. I shall show him to you tonight."

20

A Fateful Misstep

HAD the Chevalier known the particulars of Jane's journey home, he might have proceeded to Versailles with less haste and a more easy mind. Jane had crossed to Dover and ridden the mail to London without incident, arriving safely and unobserved at the house of her stepfather in New Street. Three full days elapsed before the dispatch from Mrs. Wolters reached Mr. Stephens at the Admiralty, and the message reported nothing more than that the Chevalier had proceeded to Paris, while some unknown woman traveling with him had departed for Dover. And so vast and intricate was the labyrinth of His Majesty's Secret Service, two more days passed before a copy of this item found its way into the hands of the Reverend Vardill. And so it was that Jane dwelt in safety beneath the roof of Mr. Strahan while Vardill rushed to Dover in the forlorn hope of picking up her trail, already four days cold. All these things might have quieted the fears of the Chevalier had he known them. But perhaps not, for as the Chevalier himself remarked, the Irish are sometimes blessed (or cursed) with second sight.

The guard and the driver of the Dover mail remembered Jane (she was not a woman any man was likely soon to forget), yet they could not say where she might have gone after she alighted from the coach in London. Vardill lingered in Dover, boarding each packet that entered the harbor, until he found the master of the vessel in which Jane had returned to Ostend. This man, too, recalled his comely passenger.

To each, Vardill presented five golden guineas, and promised a hundred more to whichever one might see her again and send word to him promptly. Indeed, the parson would have gladly paid ten times the sum for his prey, for he was confident she could be forced to give up the names of her accomplices, and so lead him to a great nest of traitors hidden in London. But there was nothing more for him to do in Dover, so he returned to London, to sit in his chambers in Downing Street and wait.

But a few streets away, the object of his search was conversing with her stepfather.

"Ye shouldna hae cam back, Janie. Ye'd be muckle safer haed ye stayed with Mr. Wiggins and his wife at Ostend."

"I could not stay there, Father, with no word of you and every reason to think you had been betrayed by someone in this house. I don't know what I should have done had it been so, but I couldn't bear to remain in Ostend and know nothing of what might have happened here."

"There's nae treachour beneath my roof, thank the Good Lord. But I dinna ken the gaet Vardill snooked out ye and the laddie upon the Harwich Road."

"And what he has once done he may again do, for all that we know," said Jane. "Oh, Father, you are right! I should never have returned, for it may be I shall lead that dreadful man to your door!"

"Hoot-toot!" uttered the old man. "Ye'r safe in this house, girl, and ye've no cause to vex yerself ower me. But 'tis in this house I fear ye must remain, day and night, for this Vardill is like to have his spies and informers abroad in the town."

"Yes," said Jane, "and any trader or vendor or grocer's

man who comes to the door could be such a one. Safe in this house I may be, yet peril is my handmaiden, and none who dwells beneath your roof shall dwell here in safety until I am gone. I must leave, Father. I shall return to Ostend."

Mr. Strahan rubbed his chin and reflected upon her words.

"Right ye may be, Jane, for all I know. I dinna ken what risks ye may suffer here, but certain I am ye'll be snug and safe with Wiggins. I shall miss ye, girl, but we'll all be easier. I'll send for Bolt; he'll see ye safely to Ostend."

"No, Father, there's no need, and Bolt himself is hunted by Vardill. I shall be far safer if I travel to Ostend even as I returned from there. I shall send a maid to book a seat for me in tonight's Dover mail."

21

Le Pot de Vin

NIGHT had fallen when Dr. Edward Bancroft departed the Hôtel de Valentinois to stroll in the terraced gardens that ran down to the Seine. At first his step was leisurely, but when he was sufficiently distant from the Hôtel to be secure from observation, he moved with more speed and deliberation. The boathouse at the foot of the hill was his destination, and when he achieved it, he glanced about to make certain he was alone, then, climbing into a skiff, he cast loose its line and pushed off into the river.

He rowed the little boat against the current, upstream toward Paris. On his right, a constellation of lights scattered along the dark mass of the hill of Chaillot marked the chateaux and villas of Passy; well off to his left he could make out the regular rows of illumination of the Royal Military Academy. He pulled upon the oars with long, powerful strokes, and the skiff soon passed abeam of the Place de Louis XV. He steered the craft to his left, crossing toward the farther bank, then resumed his journey against the flow, but a few yards off the Quai d'Orsai. A few minutes more and he shipped his oars and looked about him.

He was opposite the Tuileries and near the Pont Royal. He peered through the dimness and made out the form of a large, white wooden building standing upon a barge moored on the bank. Dipping his oars silently, he propelled the skiff toward the floating house.

Dr. Bancroft's destination was *Le Pot de Vin*, a public bathhouse moored in the Seine off the fashionable Faubourg Saint-Germain. In summer it was a pleasant and refreshing refuge from the city's heat, and in winter a gentleman might come there to hire a room and soak for an hour in a tub filled with steaming water heated in great kettles over brightly glowing coals. It was a place of comfort and seclusion, and its patrons could come and go by either land or water, and, should they wish, do so unobserved. It was a perfect rendezvous for spies.

Bancroft tied up the skiff, boarded the barge, and went directly to a certain room which he entered unannounced. Within, nearly obscured by the steam which filled the air of the chamber, a man reclined in a tub.

"Ah, good evening, Mr. Edwards,"* said Paul Wentworth. "I trust I caused you no great inconvenience in begging you join me here. Take your ease, sir. I'll ring for another tub and more hot water."

"No, do not," said Bancroft. "I've no wish to linger. Let us conclude our business quickly and I'll be away. Have you brought my money?"

Wentworth laughed. "'Pon my word, Mr. Edwards, do you ever think of money? Yes, I've money for you, but that is not the reason for this meeting. A matter has arisen that wants more discussion than can easily be done in a bottle beneath a tree."

"What is it, then?"

---

* Bancroft used the pseudonym Edward Edwards in all his dealings with the British Secret Service, and he insisted on the use of this name, not only in secret reports and dispatches, but even in face-to-face meetings with Wentworth and other British agents. —M.C.

"Instructions for Moses, new ones. His Majesty is sorely distressed by the great sums the French lend the Americans."

"And what would His Majesty have Moses do about it?"

"His Majesty would have Moses do nothing at all. That is just the point. There are many in France who argue loudly against the loans, yet still the loans are made. Quite reasonably, I think, His Majesty imagines there must be someone who argues more eloquently on the Americans' behalf, and believes such eloquence is commanded by none but Moses."

" 'Twould seem passing strange in Versailles and Philadelphia were Moses to beg no more gold from the French."

"Perhaps, but one who can beg to such great effect must needs also know the way to beg to no effect at all."

"Such treachery would be transparent," said Bancroft. "Should Moses abandon his zeal in courting French gold it should cause remark. No, sir! We are already at too great a hazard! As you well know, it was discovered to the French that there is a traitor at Passy, and they have introduced a spy into the ministry to learn his name. Were Moses to do as the king asks, he would deliver himself into the hands of this man, Lawless, and myself, as well!"

"The king does not ask," reproved Wentworth gently. "He commands. Come, my friend, this Lawless fellow is no danger to Moses or to you. Perhaps he is formidable upon the battlefield, but he is as innocent as a babe in the subtleties of our style of warfare."

"Why, then, was he sent, rather than one more cunning? I think his innocence is merely an artful domino* to hide his true craftiness."

---

* A type of mask worn in masquerades.—M.C.

Wentworth shrugged. "Be that as it may. If you have no wish to linger I shall not belabor you with appraisals of the Chevalier de Lawless. Such discourse should serve no purpose. I repeat: His Majesty does not 'wish'; he commands. You shall convey that command to Moses."

"Very well, but you may take your answer now, if you wish, for I know Moses' disposition in the matter. He will not do as he is bid, for the hazard is too great. His Majesty may command in Britain, but Passy is beyond his realm."

"What is this, now?" demanded Wentworth softly. "Moses defies his king, you say?"

"He recognizes no king. To Moses, George is not king but client, who pays for services rendered."

"Indeed! And he pays more than specie! He pays with silence!"

"Silence? What silence?"

"You know very well of what I speak," said Wentworth heatedly. "An infamous memorial* of crimes, indecencies, and outrages in the Hell Fire Club. I cannot believe Moses has forgotten the thing, or the hand that wrote it, or that it reposes in the custody of Lord Sandwich, who will cause it to be published at the pleasure of Lord Stormont."

"Can it be you do not know?" asked Bancroft incredulously. "Can it be Lord Stormont does not know? Go and ask Sandwich to produce this famous, or infamous, memorial!"

"What! Sandwich does not have it, you say?"

"He does not. It was taken from his house when it was ransacked by Lord Gordon's rioters near two years past."

"Who has it, then?" Wentworth demanded.

---

* Memorandum.—M.C.

"Have you heard of one who calls himself Montagu Fox?"

"I have, God damn me! You say he has the memorial?"

"He says he has it, and he has produced enough other secret papers stolen from Lord Sandwich to give credence to his claim. Were there any doubt, he has given Moses a verbatim copy of the thing. He certainly has it, and he means to sell it, but he has not yet named his price."*

"But if this be so," said Wentworth, "why has not Lord Sandwich related the loss to Lord Stormont?"

---

* Whatever his true name or allegiance, "Montagu Fox" remains one of the most baffling mysteries of the American Revolution. Less than a week after the Gordon riots of June 1780, an Englishman going by that name appeared at The Hague, claiming to the French and Spanish ambassadors that he had raided both Sandwich's home and Admiralty offices during the riots, and had taken away many secret naval plans and other papers. In addition to offering these documents, "Fox" also proposed that he be supplied with four thousand guns to start an uprising against the British government in Cornwall. "Fox" was referred to Versailles, where Count de Vergennes seemed inclined to take him seriously. The mysterious Englishman also visited Franklin at Passy, where he was apparently met with nothing but some skepticism regarding the feasibility of the proposed Cornwall revolt. The "Montagu Fox" affair dragged on through 1781 and into early 1782, during which period "Fox" received some money from the French and turned over an assortment of the papers he claimed to have stolen from Sandwich. Some proved genuine, some were suspect, and others were obvious frauds. "Fox" then dropped out of sight for six months; he turned up next in Hanover, calling himself "M. Montagu" and claiming to be a British naval officer ready to sell his services as a spy to the French legation. His offer was declined, and history heard no more of him, whoever he may have been. For a complete account of the "Montagu Fox" affair, see Morris, pp. 113–127.—M.C.

Bancroft laughed harshly. "Perhaps he finds nothing to boast of in the matter. I think the means whereby the paper came to his hand twenty years past is a thing he'd rather forget than have set before the king. His Majesty should hardly be amused by a full relation of Lord Sandwich's own peccadillos among the Medmenham Monks. When he found it missing, I'll warrant he resolved to say nothing and hoped it had been used to light the kindling in some hovel in Gin Alley. After all, it was enough that Moses *believed* him to have the memorial, and no harm if Stormont thought the same. But it seems Sandwich never reckoned it had fallen into the hands of this sly Fox."

Paul Wentworth sat in his steaming tub and was silent for a long while. "Well, well, well," he said at last, "this is a most distressing development. Mr. Edwards, I trust you shall look to protect His Majesty's interests in this affair."

"How do you mean?" inquired Bancroft warily.

"I simply mean that when this mysterious Fox is ready to sell this paper to Moses, you shall likely know of it. Isn't that so?"

"It is."

"Very well. I shall put it to you plainly. Whatever Moses is prepared to pay for it, His Majesty will pay more, and he will pay a generous bonus to the one who purchases it for him and keeps it out of Moses' hands. His Majesty will be most grateful to you. There is your current payment, upon the table. Take it and go, but do not forget what I have said. It will please your pocket very well, Mr. Edwards."

Bancroft smirked. "I understand," he said, and taking the bag of money, he departed. When he was gone, Wentworth rang for the attendant, dried himself, dressed, and took his leave. As he walked down the ramp to the Quai d'Orsai, the proprietor of *Le Pot de Vin* went to the room next to the one in which the two spies had met.

"Here, Monsieur Landlord," said Beaumarchais, handing the man twenty livres, "your reward, even as I promised you."

He turned to the companion with whom he had shared the past hour of silent attention to the conversation that came through a chink in the wall between the rooms.

"That, Desmond, is great intrigue and great treachery!"

22

The Chevalier d'Éon

CERTAINLY the reader must now wonder how the Chevalier and Beaumarchais came to know the time and place of the carefully concealed rendezvous between Wentworth and Bancroft, and the author here digresses temporarily to satisfy whatever curiosity this timely cognizance may have inspired.

In an earlier chapter of this history, we saw the Paris police discover (by the tried and true methods of police the world over) that Wentworth and Bancroft exchanged messages written in invisible ink between the lines of putative love letters hidden in a bottle within a hollow boxwood tree in the Tuileries Gardens. Next we saw the commissioner of police, M. Le Noir, rushing to Versailles to inform the foreign minister of his discovery. But then we learned that the Wentworth-Bancroft correspondence was already well known to the minister, M. de Vergennes, and to his chief of espionage, M. Baudouin. Further, we saw that Vergennes and Baudouin were not pleased that the police commissioner now shared this secret, and they prepared to order M. Le Noir and his men to desist from further meddling in the matter, and to seal their lips to any word of what they had learned. (The motives of M. de Vergennes in this matter were mysterious, but they shall presently be discovered to the reader.)

Now, although we may presume that M. Le Noir desisted

from further interference in the Wentworth-Bancroft affair, it would fly in the face of what everyone knows of human nature to suppose he sealed his lips. As it happened, M. Le Noir related the matter in its full particulars to his friend and mentor, M. de Sartines.

Antoine de Sartines was minister of the navy, a remarkable achievement in a gentleman absolutely lacking in nautical experience. M. de Sartines was never a sailor, but had long been a policeman, having been M. Le Noir's predecessor in the post of commissioner of police. (The appointment of a policeman as chief of the navy may seem extraordinary until we reflect upon the intimate conjunction of espionage and naval affairs in a great nation such as France or Britain, which conducts so much of its commerce and warfare upon the seas. Spies go forth in ships, return in other ships, and report on the arrivals and departures of yet other ships, and one might fairly measure the importance of a harbor to the business of the world by counting the number and variety of spies in residence along its waterfront.)

M. de Sartines, sea lord and spy master, was not promiscuous with his secrets, including this one that had been whispered into his ear by his protégé, M. Le Noir. Indeed, he spoke of it but to one gentleman, a trusted friend of Sartines and an erstwhile associate of Benjamin Franklin, and he spoke of it to an important purpose, to wit, to inquire whether M. Franklin could possibly be a traitor.

The confidant of M. de Sartines could make no answer to his friend's question regarding M. Franklin, but he resolved to examine into the matter. He took up where M. Le Noir had left off, observing the comings and goings of Edward Bancroft and Paul Wentworth, and in this way he discovered that a pebble left in the bottle beneath the boxwood tree at the Tuileries on a Tuesday night signaled a

G. J. A. O'TOOLE

meeting between the two spies in a certain room of *Le Pot de Vin* on Wednesday night. As the reader may have guessed, the name of M. de Sartines's trusted friend and confidant was none other than Pierre-Augustin Caron de Beaumarchais.* Thus, when the Chevalier went to his friend for advice on the means of examining into the true allegiance of Benjamin Franklin, it happened that Beaumarchais himself was already pursuing that very question.

Intrigues! as Beaumarchais said. *A lovely tangled web of them! Intrigues, treacheries, and secret services!*

As we rejoin the Chevalier and Beaumarchais, we find them on horseback, riding through the Burgundian countryside some twoscore leagues southeast of Paris. The road they travel runs beside the river Armançon. It is late in the afternoon of the day following their adventure aboard *Le Pot de Vin,* and as they sight the walls of the ancient town of Tonnerre, Beaumarchais reins his horse to a halt.

"No, it is impossible! I cannot proceed!" he exclaims.

"What is the matter, my friend?" asked the Chevalier.

"I cannot encounter this person! I am too terrified! Yes, I, Beaumarchais, am daunted by the prospect of this interview! Of course you do not believe me, Desmond! I do not believe myself! Nonetheless, it is true! You must encounter this person without me!"

"Make yourself easy, Pierre-Augustin," said the Chevalier. "I shall certainly proceed without you, if that is your wish. But you have not told me the name of this person we visit, much less the grounds for your belief that we may

---

* Beaumarchais was, in fact, a longtime friend of Sartines. The claim that Sartines, when naval minister, involved himself in domestic intrigue through his protégé and successor, Le Noir, is also supported by the facts (Manceron, *Wind,* p. 22).—M.C.

return from our journey enlightened somehow in the question of Moses and Monsieur Franklin."

"What? I have not told you? Of course I have not! I could not make my mouth speak the name of this person!"

"But now you must," said the Chevalier, laughing. "Is it the Sphinx of Egypt to whom we take our riddle? No, it must be some fearsome dragon to frighten so doughty a fellow as yourself."

"Ah, you have guessed the species, but missed the gender!" exclaimed Beaumarchais. "But perhaps you are right about the gender, as well, for *that* is a riddle worthy of the Sphinx! I blush for my cowardice, Desmond, for she is only a little *dragonne,* the Tiny Dragoon!"

"The Chevalier d'Éon!" exclaimed the Chevalier.

"Mademoiselle de Beaumont, as she now must call herself."*

---

* Charles Geneviève Louis Auguste André Timothée D'Éon de Beaumont (1728–1810), soldier, diplomat, secret agent, fencing master, blackmailer, and most of all, enigma. A male, according to his baptismal records and the doctors who examined his body after death; a woman, according to Beaumarchais, Louis XVI, a surgeon who once treated her, and her own private diaries. While the Chevalier d'Éon's gender remains a matter of dispute among historians (most believe d'Éon was male), the undisputed facts are also remarkable:

Dressed as a woman and calling herself Mlle. Lia de Beaumont, she was sent to Russia as an agent of Louis XV's secret service, where she was received at the court of St. Petersburg, became the close friend and confidante of the Empress Elizabeth, and was instrumental in obtaining a treaty of alliance between France and Russia. Shortly thereafter, attired as a captain of dragoons, d'Éon repeatedly distinguished himself in battle during the Seven Years' War. Next, he was a French diplomat at the court of St. James's, for which service he was rewarded by the king with six thousand

"Very well, *mademoiselle* or chevalier, what does she—
or he—have to tell us of the affair of Moses and Franklin?"

Beaumarchais shrugged. "Perhaps nothing; perhaps everything. Last night, Desmond, you heard Monsieur Wentworth say that the British power to command Moses derived from some incident involving him in the Hell Fire
Club. Have you heard of this club?"

"I have heard of many clubs of that name. They are
coteries of rakes and libertines who debauch themselves in
each other's company."

"Yes," agreed Beaumarchais, "there are many, but only
one truly deserving of the name. It is known by other
names, as well—the Monks of Medmenham and the
Knights of St. Francis of Wycomb."

"Those names sound more pious than profligate," remarked the Chevalier.

"Indeed," said Beaumarchais. "It is part of their blasphemous design. But they are neither monks nor knights,
but disciples of Satan. Their debauchery takes the form of

---

livres and the Royal and Military Order of St. Louis. However,
while in London, he had a falling-out with the French ambassador,
leading to a sordid intrigue involving French efforts to kidnap
him and take him back to France, and to d'Éon's blackmailing of
the French government with diplomatic documents potentially
embarrassing to Louis XV.

D'Éon remained in England under British protection, his/her
gender becoming a matter of great public curiosity, speculation,
and wagering, while he supported himself as a fencing master (he
was reputedly one of the greatest swordspersons of the eighteenth
century). Meanwhile, Louis XV died, Louis XVI succeeded him,
and Count de Vergennes became foreign minister; d'Éon and the
embarrassing documents remained in London. Vergennes resolved
to see the matter to a conclusion, so he called upon his ablest
secret agent, perhaps the only creature in France as remarkable as
d'Éon, Pierre-Augustin Caron de Beaumarchais. Beaumarchais went

an obscene parody of the most sacred rite of the Church. You have heard of the Black Mass, Desmond?"

"May the saints protect us, I have!" said the Chevalier. "If the Chevalier d'Éon is of this Hell Fire Club of which you tell me, I do not wonder that you shrink from her presence!"

"Bah! That is not what repels me from the woman! I should not hold a little satanism against her, if it were to her taste! *De gustibus non est disputandum,** as the ancients wisely observed. The Black Mass has even been celebrated at Versailles. Not lately, of course!"†

"At Versailles!" exclaimed the Chevalier. "And that is the place of this Hell Fire Club of which Monsieur Wentworth spoke?"

"No, no, Desmond. It is an English thing, created by English aristocrats for their amusement."

"Ah! Of course!" said the Chevalier. "It is only to be expected that Satan is honored in his own country!"

"Perhaps. At all events, I first heard of this Hell Fire Club some years ago when a certain secret service to His

---

to London and, after much negotiation with d'Éon, arranged an agreement whereby d'Éon would return to France, surrender the sensitive papers, and resume her female garments, all in return for an amnesty and a pension. In the course of these negotiations, the romantic creator of Figaro, convinced that d'Éon was a woman, fell in love with her.

But the Chevalier d'Éon affair did not end as happily as one of Beaumarchais's plays; back in France d'Éon continued to embarrass the king, slandered Beaumarchais, and retreated to her family estate at Tonnerre. It's a shame that the subject of the Chevalier d'Éon became so personally painful to Beaumarchais; his/her story would have made a wonderful opéra bouffe.—M.C.

* "There is no disputing about taste."—M.C.

† It was a royal scandal involving, among others, two of Louis XIV's mistresses, late in the seventeenth century.—M.C.

Majesty required I go to England. The matter involved Mademoiselle de Beaumont, who was then in London posing as a man and calling herself the Chevalier d'Éon. She had befriended several Englishmen of high station and was on very intimate terms with one of them, that same Lord Sandwich whose name you overheard from the lips of Monsieur Wentworth last night."

"Ah, yes. I recall the words of Wentworth. This Sandwich was of the Hell Fires, and he held and lost some paper implicating Moses as a brother in sin. And you hope Mademoiselle de Beaumont may know something of this?"

"I think it possible. The involvement of Lord Sandwich in the Hell Fires was notorious, but it was whispered in many quarters that even the Chevalier d'Éon had been initiated into that unholy order."*

"And if she was, you believe she will freely relate to me, a stranger, whatever particulars she may know of the Moses affair?"

---

* Whether or not the Chevalier d'Éon was a member of the Hell Fire Club is a matter of speculation. Originally there were only twelve members, each adopting as his *nom de débauche* the name of one of the Apostles. The original Unholy Twelve, as they called themselves, included Lord Sandwich; John Wilkes, the Whig politician; Paul Whitehead, a minor poet who served as the club's secretary; George Selwyn, whom we have already met; and Sir Francis Dashwood (later Lord Le Despencer), who founded the club. Later, the club enlarged its membership to include many others. No full roster of the membership remains, because Whitehead burned the club's records shortly before his death. What little that is known of the club has been pieced together by historians from a wide variety of sources, and many individuals are supposed to have been members largely because they were close friends of one or more of the original Unholy Twelve. The Chevalier d'Éon belongs in this category; so does Benjamin Franklin.—M.C.

"With Mademoiselle de Beaumont all things are possible," replied Beaumarchais. "She lives here in her ancestral estate at Tonnerre by the generosity of His Majesty, who pays her a pension of twelve thousand livres per year. If she knows some secret of state, I do not think she will withhold it from you."

"Yet she would withhold it from you?" inquired the Chevalier.

"There is a great enmity between Mademoiselle de Beaumont and myself, Desmond. I think it would be better that you call upon her alone, while I wait at the inn at Tonnerre."

"Very well, my friend," said the Chevalier. "We of the Irish Brigade are sworn to march through the very gates of hell, should such be required to destroy the English. It seems it has fallen to me to make good that vow."

The Chevalier took leave of Beaumarchais and rode alone into the ancient town of Tonnerre, where he inquired of the folk he met in the streets as to the residence of Mademoiselle de Beaumont. He was directed to a charming quarter, where stood several ancient and magnificent houses, and among them he found the gray stone mansion he sought, situated amidst the tranquil beauty of formal gardens and vineyards.

The house stood beside the river Armançon, four stories high, with large pedimented windows and a mansard roof. A balustraded balcony graced the front of the mansion, and the visitor could choose either flight of stone steps, to the left or the right, to ascend to it. The Chevalier entrusted his mount to a stableboy and presented himself at the front door. A servant received his calling card and bid him wait in a drawing room. The attendant returned at length, announced his mistress, and Mlle. de Beaumont entered the chamber.

She was a handsome woman of middle years, and she was dressed as such. Her abundant, powdered hair was surmounted by a headdress of gauze and ribbons. A lace jabot fell over a rounded bosom, and a black velvet ribbon encircled her throat. A single item contradicted the feminine essence of her costume: the Order of St. Louis, which she wore pinned to her breast.

"Welcome to my house, Major Lawless. It is a pleasure to meet so illustrious a soldier."

The Chevalier bowed. "And I, *mademoiselle*, am delighted to encounter a warrior whose deeds are legendary."

Mlle. de Beaumont began to inflect in the feminine way, but stopped abruptly and made a masculine bow. She bid the Chevalier be seated, but he waited for her to take her seat before doing the same.

She laughed. "This is a very awkward way for two soldiers to meet," she said.

The Chevalier smiled uneasily and began to remark upon the beauties of the gardens and the vineyards, which were visible from the window. Mlle. de Beaumont rang for a servant and ordered tea, meanwhile keeping up her side of the conversation regarding such things as the weather, the excellent wines of the district, and such. At length she made an exasperated sigh.

"Forgive me, Major, if I am rude, but I would dispense with this small talk, for I am eager to know if you have come to Tonnerre bearing good news for me."

"Good news?"

"My petition to His Majesty. Has he seen fit to grant it?"

"Alas, *mademoiselle*," replied the Chevalier, "I fear I know nothing of this matter."

"That is too bad," she said sadly. "You see, I have often begged the king for permission to put aside these women's clothes and resume my regimentals, and to go to America to fight in the war."*

"Then I am doubly wretched that I do not bring you his consent, for you should be a most welcome and valued comrade."

"Thank you for that kindness, Major," she said. "What, then, is the occasion of your visit, if not to enlist me in the dragoons?"

"I hope to enlist your advice in a certain matter of great delicacy," replied the Chevalier. "I think you are acquainted with an English nobleman, one Lord Sandwich?"

"I am," she replied, "though I've not seen or heard of him for some years. I believe he is now first lord of the British Admiralty."

"The matter of concern took place some twenty years past," said the Chevalier. "You knew Lord Sandwich then?"

"I did."

"And of his membership in a certain fraternity, the Monks of Medmenham?"

"The Hell Fire Club," she said. "Surely, Major, you do not propose so indecent a topic as suitable for conversation with a spinster, such as Mademoiselle de Beaumont?"

"Forgive me, *mademoiselle!*" said the Chevalier.

"It is a matter you must put to the Chevalier d'Éon," she said.

"I fear I do not comprehend," said the bewildered Chevalier.

"I mean that I shall not sit here in my petticoats and converse with a strange man regarding such matters as

---

* The Chevalier d'Éon did indeed make such request, not only of Louis, but also of Vergennes, the Count de Broglie, and the Count d'Orvilliers, asking to serve in the dragoons, or even in the Navy. All the requests were either denied or ignored.—M.C.

wanton orgies and lewd debauchery. But I shall be quite willing to discuss these things with you as one soldier to another, when I have donned my old regimentals as captain of dragoons."

"Ah, I see. Of course. Thank you, *mademoiselle*—that is, Captain. I shall be in your debt."

"Then I shall ask two favors in return. First, that you take supper with me."

"Certainly! And the other?"

"There is one who dwells beneath this roof who is regarded as a fencer of some accomplishment, and who would greatly prize the opportunity to meet so famous a swordsman as yourself with foil and mask."

"I shall be pleased to do so," said the Chevalier.

"Splendid." She arose. "I shall send one of my attendants to lead you to a dressing room where you will find an assortment of foils, masks, and plastrons to choose from. And I shall see that your challenger awaits your pleasure in the courtyard in a quarter of an hour. Until supper, then, Major."

She left the room and soon an elderly servant came and led the Chevalier to a little chamber containing a great assortment of foils and fencing paraphernalia. The Chevalier selected a foil, examined the blade for flaws and found none, and tried its temper by grasping its feeble with the fingers of one hand and bending it, while he held the pummel in his other hand.

Having found a satisfactory foil, he removed his coat, waistcoat, and riding boots; then, locating a leather plastron of sufficient size to cover his torso, he donned it. Next he selected a pair of soft leather shoes which fit his feet snugly, and lastly a strong mesh fencing mask, which, after fitting it over his head to assure it was of a proper size, he removed and placed beneath his arm.

"Very well," he said to the waiting servant. "You may lead me to the courtyard."

He followed the attendant onto the balcony. In the courtyard below, his adversary stood alone and waiting. The Chevalier descended one of the flights of steps and advanced to meet him.

The challenger was dressed entirely in black: black shoes, black hose, black breeches, black blouse, and black leather plastron. He was small and slight of build, and the Chevalier guessed him a boy, though his face was hidden by the fencing mask. As the Chevalier approached, the challenger raised his foil in salute. The Chevalier halted and replied in kind with his own weapon, then put on his own mask.

The two fencers went to the guarding stance and approached each other. An instant later, steel slithered upon steel.

From the moment their blades met, the Chevalier knew his opponent to be no dilettante of the local *petite nobilité* who dabbled with the foil whenever he was bored with his pen or his fiddle or his Latin verses. Here was a fencer par excellence who daily spent long hours in the *salle d'armes* in compensation for the inadequacies of nature—the shortness and slender sinew of his limbs—and had triumphed over these disadvantages.

The challenger attacked in carte; the Chevalier executed a swift glizade, disengaged, beat the opposing blade, and thrust at his opponent's breast. The challenger retired smartly, but instantly returned to the offensive, engaging the Chevalier in tierce. The Chevalier disengaged and withdrew, drawing forward the challenger, who engaged him again in carte. The Chevalier disengaged and executed a feint, making a wide opening in his guard. Instantly the challenger lunged, even as the Chevalier expected. The

Chevalier parried with no more than a deflecting touch, and stepped swiftly forward within the challenger's guard. The point of his foil touched his opponent's plastron over the heart.

The challenger said nothing, but stepped back, dropping his point and bowing to acknowledge the touch. Then he resumed his guard and advanced once again, but this time more cautiously.

He was small, but he was swift and supple, and he knew the way to use these qualities to advantage against an adversary with longer limbs and a stronger sword arm. He was wary now; the Chevalier could not lure him a second time into some imprudent move. Indeed, try as he might, the Chevalier now found his opponent's guard impenetrable, and could not touch him again.

The pair moved back and forth across the courtyard, their blades whirling in the waning light of the winter afternoon. A quarter hour passed, then another, and yet another. The challenger had not touched the Chevalier, but the Chevalier had not touched the challenger a second time. Yet the smaller man had begun to tire; the Chevalier could see that his opponent no longer moved as smartly as before. Fatigue should soon make an opening in his guard. The Chevalier stepped back and dropped his point to the ground.

"Please stop," he said. "*Monsieur,* whoever you may be, you are as good a swordsman as I; perhaps a better one. You made but one mistake when we began: you underestimated me, believing you saw an opening in my guard, which, in fact, was merely a trick; thus I was able to touch you once, but not a second time. We have fenced for the better part of an hour, and neither of us has touched the other. But though we are equal in skill, I think you know I am stronger, and you will tire first. Soon exhaustion shall accomplish what my skill has failed to do and I shall touch you a second time. I would prevail in our contest, but I will not do so if I must needs enlist trickery and weariness as my comrades, and I cannot do so through skill alone.

"I beg your leave to call an end to our match."

The challenger removed his mask, revealing the noble features of Beaumont, no longer crowned by the powdered wig and headdress. He bowed.

"Thank you, Major Lawless," said the Chevalier d'Éon. "You are indeed a gallant soldier."

He turned and left the courtyard.

23

The Hell Fire Club

"SERVING one's king upon the battlefield and serving him in a foreign court are two different things," said the Chevalier d'Éon, when he and the Chevalier de Lawless had repaired to the drawing room after supper. "I know, for I have done both."

The Chevalier de Lawless murmured agreement and waited for his host to resume.

"Some twenty years ago," began d'Éon, "I was sent upon a diplomatic mission to the court of St. James's. Every court has its factions and its intrigues—the English court was no exception—and the astute envoy will insinuate himself into as many cliques as he can without permitting himself to become the partisan of any one of them. This may be accomplished through discretion and amiableness, which is to say, one speaks seldom and superficially, listens always, and suffers the company of persons one finds revolting. Indeed, the art of statesmanship might be said to consist of nothing more than cultivating friendships among scoundrels. Lord Sandwich, the English nobleman whose name you spoke when you came here today, was such a one.

"Sandwich was a coarse, awkward fellow, with little wit and gross appetites. He occupied himself in drinking, gambling, and seducing little girls, and the only thing I can think of to say in his favor is that he was a fair swordsman and a dead shot, but even these qualities he perverted by playing the bully.

"It was curious to discover in Sandwich a great animosity toward the Christian religion; curious, I say, because such fellows as he are generally too dull-witted to reflect upon theological matters, and are usually content simply to ignore such things. Sandwich was different in this regard. I do not think he was an atheist; atheists hold religion in contempt, but there is a great difference between contempt and rabid hate, and Sandwich hated Christianity with a great passion. I could illustrate this to you with many examples, but I think it sufficient to mention but one bizarre instance in which he populated an empty chapel with a great congregation of cats."

"Cats?"

"Cats. He then ascended the pulpit and commenced to preach a sermon to them."

"In a chapel of the Catholic Church?" demanded the Chevalier de Lawless.

"No, it was of the Church of England," replied d'Éon.

"Ah, well," remarked the Chevalier with a shrug.

"In any case," d'Éon continued, "it was not surprising that a man of this disposition should become the friend of one Sir Francis Dashwood, a gentleman of much greater wit and quality than Sandwich, but who shared with him this one idiosyncrasy, this burning animosity toward the faith. But Sir Francis, as I say, possessed a much greater wit than Sandwich, and so had devised a much more ingenious and elaborate insult to the Christian Church. He founded a society in imitation of a religious order, calling it The Knights of St. Francis of Wycomb. (Wycomb, you see, was the seat of Sir Francis' ancestral home.)

"Sir Francis purchased the ruins of Medmenham Abbey,

a monastery situated at a secluded place upon the banks of the Thames near Wycomb, and which had been occupied by the Cistercian Order in the twelfth century, but had long since been disused. At great expense he refurbished the place according to his own peculiar tastes, which were far from pious.

"He took away the statues of the saints he found in the gardens, replacing them with the pagan gods of Greece and Rome, posed in every conceivable posture of lewdness. He decorated the interiors of the buildings with bawdy frescoes and obscene mottos carved in apothecary's Latin. One phallic design, for example, bore the inscription *Peni tenti non penitenti.**

"Sir Francis restored the chapel, which, like the other buildings, lay in ruins. The original walls contained a dozen windows, and he guessed they had once been graced by pictures of the twelve apostles, executed in tinted glass. He employed artisans to restore the windows, choosing the theme of the apostles, but with a difference: Each of Christ's disciples was depicted in the performance of some act of gross indecency. Not satisfied with this, he commissioned a fresco for the ceiling of the chapel, a travesty of the Last Supper, transformed into a scene of such wicked blasphemy I fear to describe it to you."

"Then I beg that you do not," said the Chevalier.

"Very well. I have said enough of Medmenham Abbey, but little of the Knights of St. Francis.

"Sir Francis brought together a coterie of twelve of his friends who shared his peculiar tastes in such matters. These called themselves The Unholy Twelve, and each adopted a name of an apostle as his *nom de débauche.*

---

* "A stiff penis is better than repentance."—M.C.

Sandwich was one of this number; I do not recall his pseudonym.

"The Unholy Twelve would gather with Sir Francis at the abbey at certain times the year round, bringing with them harlots from the brothels of London. Sir Francis and his unholy disciples would dress as monks, and the women would dress in the habits of nuns, but I need hardly explain that these costumes were soon removed after they had served their purpose of blasphemous parody, and the company would occupy themselves with fantastic debaucheries that often lasted for several days.

"The Medmenham 'nuns' were at first, as I have said, common prostitutes. Later, however, as rumors about the 'knights' were whispered in London society, some ladies of quality wished to partake of these depravities, and came to the abbey in the company of one or another of the Unholy Twelve, dressed in the habits of nuns, but wearing masks over their faces. The habits were removed during the licentious revels, but the masks were kept in place to hide the identities of these ladies, whose faces were often to be seen at court and in the finest drawing rooms of London. Thus it was that many an English baroness or countess danced naked before the assembled 'monks' and later coupled with every one of them."

"May the saints protect us!" muttered the Chevalier.

"Indeed," said d'Éon, "for you have not yet heard the worst. The number of the Medmenham Monks had grown as word of the order spread, and the original Unholy Twelve sponsored trusted friends for admission to the society. The newcomers added variety to the diversions of the monks, but Sir Francis and his followers eventually found that even lewdness and blasphemy become tiresome through endless repetition. And so, sated by the works of evil, the Medmenham Monks turned at last to the ultimate debauchery, the worship of the prince of evil, Satan himself. You have heard of the Black Mass, Major?"

The Chevalier nodded.

"Have you witnessed it?"

"Certainly not! Never!"

"Well, I have," said d'Éon, "and I cannot tell you of the Hell Fire Club—the Knights of St. Francis—without also describing to you this obscene parody of the holy sacrifice."

The Chevalier crossed himself. "Continue," he said.

"Very well. I have told you of the manner in which Sir Francis restored the chapel of Medmenham Abbey, but I have not described the use he made of it. It was here that the Medmenham Monks and their 'nuns' gathered together to celebrate the Black Mass.

"In order to worship Satan, one must turn away from God, for the power of darkness may prevail only when the power of light has been freely shut out by the will of man. Thus, the Black Mass, the supreme satanic rite, must be a perfect inversion of the Sacrament. A cross stands above the altar, but it is twisted, or stands upside down. The altar itself is inverted, or cracked. The celebrant wears a robe, not of white, but black; it is open in the front, and he is naked beneath it, so that his genitals are exposed. A black cloth drapes the altar, and black candles of human fat burn upon it."

"Human fat!"

"Yes," said d'Éon. "The candles of Medmenham were provided by one of the Unholy Twelve, a man named Selwyn, who has a great fondness for the bodies of the dead."

"I have encountered him," said the Chevalier.

"Then you have encountered the worst of the Medmenham Monks, for no demon of hell is more faithful to Satan than this man.

"The ceremony is not performed directly upon the black altar," d'Éon continued, "but upon the naked body of a 'nun,' who lies upon it, holding the two hideous candles in her hands, and with her legs spread in invitation to the celebrant, who couples with her during the ceremony. The Black Mass is read backwards, in the reverse of the sequence of the Holy Sacrament, with the Latin prayers read from a book in which they have been written in reverse, so that the sound of the ritual is, at the same time, awesome and ridiculous. Sacramental wafers stolen from a church are scattered upon the floor, and the congregation . . ."

"*Pardon, monsieur*," interrupted the Chevalier, "but I do not wish to tax you with too detailed a recitation of the thing. I think you have told me enough so that I comprehend the nature of the Black Mass. I should need further particulars only were I contemplating celebrating the unholy ritual myself, which, indeed, I am not."

"You are quite right, Major," agreed d'Éon, "but what more would you have me tell you of the Hell Fire Club, then?"

"I would have you tell me if you recall one of these Medmenham Monks whose *nom de débauche* was Moses."

"Moses? It is possible. But it was so long ago, I fear I do not remember the names that were used. I am sorry."

"As am I," said the Chevalier sadly. "But perhaps you can recall if there was some great scandal attached to this club. Oh, I know, the very essence of the thing was scandalous, but was there some particular event of exceptional infamy that might have occasioned its relation in some memorial or document?"

"Indeed there was," replied d'Éon. "I have described

Medmenham Abbey to you as I recall the place when I was shown about it by Sir Francis and Lord Sandwich, but in fact, at that time, the monks had ceased using the abbey, and had removed to a vast labyrinth of subterranean chambers on the estate of Sir Francis, which is where I witnessed the ceremony of the Black Mass and other debauchery. I was not told the reason for this remove, but I can repeat to you what was rumored in London and West Wycomb.

"It was said that one of the Medmenham Monks—I know not which—took a fancy to a young girl of common birth but unassailable virtue. He plied her with gifts and every possible attention, but he was unable to have his way with her. Finally, through a ruse, he lured her to Medmenham Abbey, where he drugged her with some recipe which he supposed to possess aphrodisiacal powers. Its only result was to render the poor girl insensible, but the monk had become so crazed with lust he vowed to have her in that fashion, if in no other. Then, at the suggestion of some other members of the order, a Black Mass was celebrated by this monk, using the girl upon the satanic altar.

"While the preparations for the ceremony were made, the girl recovered her senses and cried out for her clothes and made to leave the chapel. The monks put a gag in her mouth and bound her hand and foot to the altar, and the Black Mass was performed. It was thought by this monk who brought her there that, after she had lost her maidenhead, she would be ready to listen to his overtures and agree to become his mistress. Such was not the case, however. When the ceremony was completed and the deflowered girl released from her bonds, she cursed them all and vowed to take the matter before a magistrate.

"The monks were very frightened by this declaration, for, while an English gentleman is nearly immune from the force of the law in his own country, that immunity is not total, and there are limits to the outrages even the most corrupt magistrate dare turn a blind eye. Some of the monks were for murdering the girl, but most were afraid to take that step. In the end it was decided to hold her prisoner in the abbey in hope she would eventually forgive her ravisher, or at least acquire a kindlier disposition toward her captors. However, it soon transpired that the coupling upon the altar had left her with child.

"In the meanwhile, the girl's father, who was the landlord of a tavern and a man of some means, had raised a hue and cry over his missing child, and offered a great reward for her return. The monks became even more fearful lest some harlot who had served as 'nun' at Medmenham, or some servant or other menial who knew of the girl's captivity, might betray them for the innkeeper's gold. But nine months passed and this did not happen. Finally, her term complete, the girl gave birth, some say to twins, a boy and a girl. But the mother did not survive the delivery, which was bungled by some midwife brought too late to the abbey.

"It is said that the monk who fathered the infants saw that they were placed in good homes, and that the mother's body was concealed in an unmarked grave. But all of this was not accomplished without some remark, and eventually word of the affair reached the innkeeper, who went to Sir Francis and Lord Sandwich and threatened trouble. It is said that Sandwich paid the man a considerable sum for his silence, then went and demanded of the monk who had ravished the girl that he make a written confession of the affair in his own hand, delivering it to Sandwich as a security that he would eventually reimburse him for the amount the affair had left him out of pocket.

"And that, according to rumor, is how the monks of the Hell Fire Club came to remove from Medmenham Abbey to the caves of West Wycomb."

"Ah, my friend, could you only remember the name of this ravisher who penned the confession for Lord Sandwich!" sighed the Chevalier.

"I fear I cannot remember it, for I never knew it," said d'Éon. You must remember, Major, that this is a tale tattled in the drawing rooms of London. Different tattlers ventured different theories as to the name of the wretched fellow, but the aim of such speculation was to titillate the listener, not divine the truth. In any case, I can recall none of those named, for as I say, all this is twenty years past."

"But," persisted the Chevalier, "can you at least recall whether all the candidates proposed as having been this hapless ravisher were Englishmen?"

"Englishmen? I suppose they must have all been Englishmen," said d'Éon, "for of those who were often guests of Sir Francis at West Wycomb, only I was not an Englishman. Of course, there was one frequent guest who was an American."

"And who was that?" inquired the Chevalier.

"Why, it was Benjamin Franklin," replied d'Éon.

24

The Fencing Lesson

THE stamping of two pairs of feet and the ringing of steel upon steel marred the early morning quiet of the Hôtel de Valentinois. A large banqueting room in the pavilion housing the library had been cleared of tables and chairs, and the carpets had been rolled back to the walls, from which had been removed all *objets d'art*. It was quite a satisfactory *salle d'armes*.

The Chevalier and his pupil, dressed in plastrons and masks, moved back and forth within the confines of a long rectangle chalked upon the floor. Benjamin Franklin stood in the doorway, leaning on his walking stick and observing the practice with an approving eye.

"*Touché!*" cried the Chevalier. He stepped back and removed his mask. "*Très bien*, Monsieur Temple. That is the proper execution of carte-over-the-arm. Now let us repeat the exercise holding our foils in the left hand."

"The left hand!" said William Temple Franklin in dismay, as he removed his mask. "Why, I can scarcely manage to hold my foil properly in my right hand. Why on earth should I try to hold it in the other?"

"There are two reasons," replied the Chevalier. "First, your right arm may not be ready on some occasion; perhaps your opponent has succeeded in transfixing it. And second, the left-handed fencer holds a great advantage over his right-handed opponent, and you may some day meet such a one. Thus, you should strive for capability with both hands."

"I believe that in such circumstances I should prefer to withdraw and concede the match," said Temple.

"Ah, *oui*, that would be wise," agreed the Chevalier, "providing it were a match and not a fight to the death. We exercise with the foil, Monsieur Temple, which is but a harmless substitute for the smallsword. But it should not be mastery of the foil you seek, my young friend, but mastery of the smallsword."

"I do not wish Temple to study at being an assassin," laughed Franklin from the doorway.

"There may be times, Monsieur Franklin, when one must choose between the role of assassin and the situation of a corpse. *L'escrime* is a fine exercise for the body, of course, but it is a great waste to study it yet fail to learn the art of defense. I am told that you and your grandson are splendid swimmers, and that you swim often in the Seine when the weather is amiable. Is this not so?"

"It is," Franklin agreed. "Like fencing, swimming is fine exercise for the body."

"*Oui*, but do you instruct Monsieur Temple only in those strokes that best exercise the body, and omit others that could save him should he suffer the shipwreck? Even a wise man who wishes to avoid shipwrecks and deadly engagements may yet find himself involved in them. One should learn both to float and to kill, for it is better to have these talents and not require them, than to require them and not have them."

"I must concede the point, Major," laughed Franklin, "for you have made it with a tidy eloquence worthy of

Poor Richard himself. Temple, you must do as the major says and learn to hold your blade in the left hand."

"*Très bien*," said the Chevalier, "and I shall later instruct him in the methods of fighting with the cloak, the dagger, and the lantern."

"The lantern," said Temple. "How the devil does one fight with a lantern?"

"It is a despicable trick practiced by brigands and highwaymen, who descend upon their victims in the night, blinding them with the light of a lantern so they cannot defend themselves."

"It is, as you say, Major, a despicable trick," said Temple. "I do not think I wish to learn it."

"Certainly not!" exclaimed the Chevalier. "I propose only to teach you the means to defend yourself against it. You shall learn to fence blindfolded."

"Blindfolded! But that is impossible!"

"Indeed, it is entirely possible," said the Chevalier. "This morning, Monsieur Temple, before we began, you asked whether I advised that a fencer watch his opponent's eyes or his arm during an engagement. I did not answer you then, but I shall answer you now: It does not matter. When you have learned all else of *l'escrime*, when you think yourself a master of the blade, then you may learn *le sentiment du fer,* the feeling of the blade, a thing which enables the swordsman to defend himself even though he may be blind, or face a dozen adversaries. And when you have learned that, you will have learned all there is to learn of swordsmanship."

"I believe Major Lawless makes us the butt of his whimsy, Grandfather," said Temple good-naturedly.

"*Mais non,* Monsieur Temple," protested the Chevalier.

"I assure you I do not. You should not doubt me had you ever encountered Monsieur Langford, who, though quite bereft of his sight, is yet a *maître d'armes*."*

Temple smiled. "I should not doubt it, Major Lawless, if ever you wish to demonstrate such a feat yourself."

"Then I shall do so this instant," replied the Chevalier. "Bind my eyes with your handkerchief, Monsieur Temple, and satisfy yourself that I cannot see. Then take up your foil and try to penetrate my guard."

"And will you defend yourself with your right hand or your left?" laughed Temple.

"Whichever you say, my doubting Thomas," replied the Chevalier. "I shall hold my foil in the left hand, if you wish, for it will make no difference. I promise you you shall not touch me."

"I pray you, Major, save such wonders for another occasion," said Franklin. "I fear there can be no more fencing today, for I must take your pupil and press him upon an errand of great urgency."

"*Très bien,*" agreed the Chevalier, although Temple's disappointment was evident. "I think we have exercised sufficiently for today. Until tomorrow, then."

"The day after tomorrow, I think," said Franklin. "I must send Temple off upon a brief journey."

The Chevalier nodded, and removing his fencing cos-

---

* Langford, the blind fencing master, who, according to the *Antiquarian Repertory* of Francis Grose (London, 1775), "being blind, was yet able to teach others the Noble Science of Defence, only he desired to know the length of the weapon of his fellow combatant, with a guess at his posture, and then he practised with good success." Lawless was not alone in demanding that his fencing students practice blindfolded; John McArthur, an English fencing master of the late eighteenth century, advised the same exercise.—M.C.

tume and resuming his regimentals, he departed, leaving Franklin and his grandson in earnest conversation.

"The teacher now becomes the student," said the Chevalier to himself as he crossed through the gardens of the Hôtel, on the way to his rooms. "I shall apply myself to the study of Monsieur Machiavelli's calculations; perhaps he knows some formula I may use to discover whether Moses equals Monsieur Franklin."

Then he stopped and turned back.

"No," he said, still addressing himself, "I shall put aside Monsieur Machiavelli and take to heart the advice of Pierre-Augustin. This secret war is surely madness, is it not? Then there is one who will make a better teacher than *The Prince,* and I am certain he, too, is a guest of Monsieur Franklin."

The Chevalier returned to the pavilion of the library and the *salle d'armes,* entering now through a different door than the one through which he had recently departed. He stood amidst the shelves and crates of books and regarded the vast congregation of volumes. The voices of the old man and his grandson came to him from the gymnasium at the other end of the pavilion, and the Chevalier turned his steps in that direction. As he approached the doorway between the two chambers, the conversation became distinct.

"There is no time to send it by packet boat," said Franklin. "You had better resort to the smugglers at Calais. Hire the same fellows we've used in the past, and pay them a few extra guineas. They know the house in Dover."

"Very well, Grandfather. Is it ready?"

"Mr. Carey has been up all night setting the type. He will have it printed and bound within the hour. Tarry here no longer than that, for the dispatch must be in London in two days' time."

The Chevalier paused for a moment; no further words escaped from beyond the door. He coughed politely and knocked.

"*Pardon, messieurs,*" he said to the startled pair, "but I hope to discover one of your secrets."

"A secret?" said Franklin in unaccustomed confusion. "What secret do you mean, sir?"

"The secret," replied the Chevalier, "of where, in this great collection of books, you have hidden *Don Quixote de La Mancha.*"

25

The Hell Fire Memorial

DR. Edward Bancroft arrived in the city of Rotterdam on the Sunday following his rendezvous with Paul Wentworth at *Le Pot de Vin*. He stopped at the inn of the Sign of Parliament, taking a room after a hurried and whispered consultation with the landlord. He remained in this room throughout the afternoon and evening, taking his supper there, which was brought him by the landlord himself.

"Where is he?" demanded Bancroft, when the man entered and set the tray upon the table.

"He shall be here presently," replied the landlord. "Within the hour, I should say. I have given him your message."

Bancroft picked at a few morsels of his meal, then set the thing aside and arose, pacing the confines of the chamber, an exercise in which he had engaged unceasingly since his arrival. At nine o'clock he heard a knock at his door, and he lost no time answering it.

"Good evening, Dr. Bancroft," said his visitor, entering.

Bancroft shut the door behind him.

"Well, where is it, Fox?" he demanded brusquely.

"A little patience, if you please, Doctor, and I wish that you would call me Monsieur Montagu, for that is the name by which I am known hereabouts."

"Whatever you please," snapped Bancroft. "Have you brought the thing?"

"I have brought this thing," said the man, drawing a small pistol from beneath his cloak. "Pray, do not be alarmed, for it is but a precaution. The landlord of this place assures me you have come alone, as I insisted; but I must assure myself that it is not lead or steel, rather than gold, that you have brought to trade for my prize. Remove your coat, if you please, Dr. Bancroft, and turn away from me."

Bancroft did as he was bid, and Montagu (let us call him that; it is not his own name, of course, but neither is Fox, and we have never learned any other) satisfied himself that the doctor wore no weapon about his person. Then he examined the other articles in the room, even searching Bancroft's portmanteau.

"What is this?" he asked, his hand resting upon a small leather box lying upon a table.

"Merely a writing case," replied Bancroft. "Open it and satisfy yourself." Montagu did so. The box contained some sheets, a goose quill, and a small bottle of ink.

"Very well," he remarked. "No pistols or daggers, but no gold, either. I hope you did not forget the gold, Doctor."

"I trust you, sir, no more than you trust me. The sum you named has been deposited in a bank of this city, and I shall deliver it to you when I have the document."

"Well, that is a shame," said Montagu, "for we shall have to wait till morning for this bank of yours to open its doors."

"We shall," Bancroft agreed. "In the meantime, I would see the paper, that I may be assured the wait is worth my while. Some of your famous documents, Mr. Montagu, have transpired to be crude forgeries."

"But this one is genuine," said Montagu. He reached within his coat and withdrew a packet, which he handed to Bancroft. He kept his pistol ready in his hand and watched as the doctor unfolded the sheets. Bancroft read the memorial in its entirety, then set it down upon the table.

"Well, what say you, Dr. Bancroft? Do you doubt its authenticity? Do you not recognize the hand that wrote it?"

"I am not overly familiar with the hand that wrote it," Bancroft replied, "but I have brought a true example of that hand. With your permission, I shall compare it to this memorial."

Montagu nodded his assent and Bancroft withdrew a letter from his writing case and set it beside the other paper on the table. He carefully compared the writing and the signatures. Then, picking up the memorial, he handed it back to Montagu.

"Well?" demanded Montagu.

"It appears to be authentic," Bancroft replied.

" 'Appears,' you say. You cannot mean you suspect it! No forger, however skillful he might be, could duplicate that signature so perfectly."

"Nonsense," said Bancroft. "Even I could do it. Here, I shall show you."

He sat down at the table and took a blank sheet from his writing case. Then, uncorking the ink bottle, he dipped the goose quill and began to write. Montagu stepped closer, standing behind Bancroft. He leaned forward, resting his hand upon the table. Bancroft dipped the quill again, then swiftly stabbed its point into Montagu's wrist.

"God damn you!" exclaimed the man, seizing his wounded wrist and jumping back. "What stupid prank do you play?"

Bancroft said nothing. Montagu raised his pistol, but it dropped from his hand and fell to the floor. He staggered back and sat down upon the bed. He stared at Bancroft and opened his mouth, but he could not speak. The doctor arose and approached the bed. He placed a hand upon Montagu's shoulder and gently pressed him down, then grasped the man's feet and lifted them to the bed.

"Make yourself easy, sir," said the doctor. "You shall feel no pain, though it will cost you an effort to breathe."

He pulled up one sleeve of the man's coat and rolled the cuff of his shirt well back from the wounded wrist, exposing the full length of the forearm. He arose, went to his writing case, and returned to the bed with the ink bottle and the goose quill. Montagu lay silent and wide-eyed, his gaze following the doctor's movements.

"This ink of mine contains the essence of a juice extracted from a plant that grows in Surinam," he explained in a very casual manner. "The savages there call it 'woorari,' and some pronounce it 'curari.'"*

---

* Some writers attribute the discovery of curare to Bancroft, but Asimov (*Asimov's Biographical Encyclopedia of Science and Technology,* by Isaac Asimov; Doubleday, 1964) accords that distinction to Charles Marie de La Condamine (1701–1774). There is no doubt, however, that Bancroft was thoroughly familiar with the poison, having encountered it during his stay in Surinam, and having written of it in "An Essay on the Natural History of Guiana," which he published in 1769. Apparently he had in his possession a considerable supply of the stuff and offered it to his fellow scientists for the purpose of experimentation (Bendiner, p. 58). A plausible theory has been advanced that the death of Silas Deane in 1789 was from curare or some other rare poison administered to him by Bancroft (Boyd).

As previously noted, "Montagu Fox" was never heard from again after 1782.—M.C.

He drew a quantity of the fluid into the quill, then thrust the point into the flesh of Montagu's forearm.

"It does nothing more than make lax the muscles of the body, but that it does totally."

He withdrew the quill, drew more of the deadly ink into it, and returned the point to the tiny wound in Montagu's forearm.

"Every muscle of the body, as I say, totally lax. I fear you have befouled yourself, Monsieur Montagu. No matter. The odor cannot be offensive to you; to be offended by an odor, one must inhale it."

He took a small glass from his coat and held it beneath the man's nostrils. It remained unclouded. Montagu's eyes stared sightlessly at the ceiling.

"And I think you are done inhaling and exhaling," said Bancroft quietly. He opened the man's shirt and put his ear to his breast. Then, satisfied, he did up the shirt again, and taking a handkerchief from his pocket, blotted away the tiny drops of blood that had formed on the dead man's wrist and forearm. Next, he rolled down the sleeve and adjusted the coat. He recovered the pistol from the floor and tucked it into the waist of the corpse's breeches. Lastly, he removed the packet from Montagu's coat and, placing it in his writing case, closed the cover.

He surveyed the room, then rang for the landlord.

"Please send for a physician," he said, when the man appeared, "though I fear this fellow is beyond help. I think his heart has failed him."

The innkeeper went to the bed and examined the man lying upon it. Then he turned a suspicious glance toward Bancroft.

"He is dead," said the innkeeper.

"I thought him so," said Bancroft. "But please summon a physician, nonetheless, that the cause of his demise may be established. I think the city authorities will require it. And please, have my possessions removed to another room. I should have little sleep in this unhappy chamber, and I wish to make an early departure tomorrow."

26

Dark Tidings

IT could not be said of William Strahan that he was a printer whose fingers were never stained with ink, that the prosperous printer to King George was content to do no more in his printing shop than oversee the journeymen and apprentices who worked there for wages. It is true that the hirelings did most of the work, but there were certain jobs of a special sort for which nothing would do but that the old Scotsman himself take up his composing stick and sit for hours at his cases setting the type. Many were the friends and strangers who called at the shop in New Street to ask for Mr. Strahan, who were greeted by that distinguished gentleman still dressed in his apron and wiping the ink from his fingers. But the caller who found him thus disposed upon this March morning was not a friend, nor was he quite a stranger, for Strahan well knew the reputation of the king's spy catcher, the Reverend John Vardill.

"Good morrow to ye, Parson," said Strahan, in a voice so calm it betrayed none of the alarm he felt at the sight of this man in his shop. "Micht there be a job of printing ye want?"

"No, Mr. Strahan," replied Vardill. "I've come upon a pastoral errand concerning a certain young woman."

"A young woman, ye say? And how micht I help ye?"

"The young woman in question seems to be afflicted by a species of lunacy."

"A madwoman?"

"Her mind seems quite sane in every respect save one: She cannot remember her name, nor any other thing concerning herself."

"Hoot-toot! An unco madness, indeed! But I dinna see how I can help ye."

"Perhaps you can, however. The young woman chanced to be apprehended at Dover, where the military authorities seem to have mistaken her for some spy they are seeking. When it transpired she was not the woman they sought, but rather an unfortunate victim of the malady I have described, they entrusted her to my care in hope that I might ascertain her family, who are undoubtedly searching for her, and see to her safe delivery to them.

"After making some inquiries, I established that the woman arrived at Dover in the mail from London, and I have spoken to a porter at the booking office who recalls fetching the portmanteau of a woman of her description. He says that it was to this very house he was sent for it. And so I thought the young woman might well be a member of your household. Is that possible, Mr. Strahan?"

The Scotsman shook his head. "It canna be," he said. "Nane of my housemaids is missing."

"She is a gentlewoman, I judge, from her speech."

"Aweel, then it canna be. My wife and dochters are all the gentlewomen of this house. My certie! I've lost nane of them, thank the Lord!"

"But I understood you to have a foster child, as well," said Vardill. "Is that not so?"

"It is," Strahan replied, "but she is at Ostend, visiting with some friends. Hoot! There's the answer to your puzzle! She went off by way of the Dover mail but a few days past. Nae doubt this porter of yours has confounded one girl with the other. It may be they are of a like resemblance."

"Are you certain your foster child arrived at Ostend?"

"Oh, I am! I've e'en had a letter from her."

"A letter? After but a few days?"

"Sent back in the same packet boat in which she crossed, to make me easy. Here, I'll show you the thing! Where can it be?" He shuffled through some papers atop his desk. "Aweel, it's someplace about, nae doubt. Nae, Parson, I canna help ye. This poor woman is nae o' this house."

"Very well, then, if you are certain," said Vardill, rising to go. "I am sorry to have troubled you, Mr. Strahan."

"Hoot, 'tis no trouble, Parson. What will ye do with this madwoman, if I may inquire? Put her in Bedlam,* I suppose?"

"No," Vardill replied. "A kind Christian gentleman has offered the sanctuary of his household should I be unable to find her family. I fear I shall have to accept his offer and make her his ward."

"A kindly Christian gentleman, ye say?"

"Why, yes. You must know him, in fact, for he is one of your fellows in Commons. He is Mr. George Selwyn."

---

* St. Mary's of Bethlehem, the London insane asylum.—M.C.

27

A Brief Engagement

BENJAMIN Franklin moved a pawn.

"Major Lawless," he said, "I have considered what you told Temple this morning, and I find it very difficult to believe a blind man may fence to effect."

The Chevalier considered his situation upon the chessboard.

"Nonetheless, it is true, Monsieur Franklin, but there is a trick to it."

His hand hovered above his knight, but he drew back and did not touch the piece.

"Ah, a trick," said Franklin. "That is something else. I did not think trickery a part of fencing."

"Yet it is," said the Chevalier. His hand returned to the knight, moving it to take Franklin's pawn. "Trickery and cunning."

"Indeed," said Franklin, taking the Chevalier's knight with his bishop.

"Indeed," echoed the Chevalier, ruefully eyeing his lost piece. "A fencer studies his opponent while he engages him, quickly appraising his style and the degree of his skill. If his own skill is great, he will foresee his opponent's maneuvers even before the other has decided upon them. He will do exactly as you have just done, Monsieur Franklin, foreseeing that I should be so eager to capture your worthless pawn I should fail to see doing so should cost me a knight."

"I should not call a pawn worthless, Major," said Franklin, smiling gently, "if it is of aid in capturing a knight."

"You are right," said the Chevalier. "I think you might have been a great fencer, Monsieur Franklin, for *l'escrime* and the game of chess seem to have much in common."

"Then it must follow that you shall master the game of chess, Major."

"Ah, no. I fear I am too good a swordsman ever to be master of chess."

"I do not follow that," said Franklin.

"Fencing is a game, like chess. Deadly combat with the sword is not. It is true that the swordsman must have the skills of the fencer, but he needs another thing, a thing which is of advantage upon the field of battle, but a great hindrance at the chessboard."

"And what thing is that?"

"A certain madness," replied the Chevalier.

"Indeed?" remarked Franklin. "I find that a singular notion."

"In every deadly engagement there are three parties," explained the Chevalier, "the two who face each other, swords in hand, and fear. Fear is a strange creature, for it makes itself the ally of whoever ignores it. The man who faces death ignorant of fear must be called mad, and a madman is a formidable opponent, so the one who faces him must bear a double burden of fear, which is often too much. Thus, madness in a swordsman is a great asset."

"I cannot dispute your remarkable reasoning, Major," said Franklin, "but you must allow me to count it a very disagreeable idea that ability at chess bespeaks a want of bravery."

"*Mais non!* I said nothing of bravery! Bravery is a noble trait men use to conquer fear. But madmen have no need of bravery, for fear is their ally."

"Pray, take no offense, Major," said Franklin, "but I am unable to refrain from asking you whether you are a brave man or a madman?"

"I cannot say," laughed the Chevalier. "I do not claim to be brave, so perhaps I am mad. But have no fear, *monsieur;* if I am mad, I am mad in patches, full of lucid intervals."

"Like the hero of the book you borrowed?"

"Ah, *oui.* To read it is, for me, to look into a cracked mirror."

"Indeed. I, too, have seen a reflection of myself in *Don Quixote,* but it is not the Knight of the Sad Countenance to whom I fancy a resemblance. I see myself more in the squire, Sancho, who is a bit like Poor Richard—a practical fellow and full of proverbs."

"And faithful in his allegiance?" asked the Chevalier, smiling faintly.

"I cannot say," replied Franklin, mirroring the smile. "You do not claim to be brave, Major, so I shall meet your modesty and not claim to be loyal. Perhaps we both are madmen, but of different methods in our madness."

"Then we must leave such things for others to judge."

"I fear we must," said Franklin, "and pray they heed the scriptural admonition: 'Judge not according to the appearance.'

"But now let us finish our game, Major. I think it is your move. Put aside your madness for the moment and consider the board. Perhaps you will see how a pawn may be used to capture a king."

28

Mungo and Moses

THE twentieth of March in the year of grace 1782 was a day filled with events of consequence. In England a king lost a prime minister, and in France a little girl lost a pet squirrel. Let us begin with the squirrel, for squirrels run faster than prime ministers, and this fugitive creature may flee beyond our view if we delay.

It was the last day of winter and the weather at Passy seemed so amiable to the Chevalier that he went into the gardens of the Hôtel de Valentinois after dinner, taking along for company *Don Quixote de La Mancha*. He was seated among the early buds, engrossed in the exploits of the Mad Knight, when little Mlle. de Chaumont ran to him, sobbing and weeping.

"What is wrong, *mademoiselle?*" asked the Chevalier.

"Oh, Major Lawless, my little Mungo has run away!"

"And who might be this Monsieur Mungo?"

"He is an American gray squirrel that Monsieur Franklin gave me. He lives in the house, but he ran out today when I opened the window."

"Ah, of course, an American squirrel. Americans are very jealous of their independency. Which way did he go?"

"He has climbed up a tree at the end of the garden, and he will not come down for me. But I am afraid he will come down after I have gone to bed, and then some dog may kill him! Oh, Major, would you rescue him for me, please!"

227

"I cannot refuse," replied the Chevalier. "We knights-errant are sworn to assist in such matters." He shut his book and arose. "Lead me to the tree."

The squirrel had climbed to the topmost branch of a tall oak, a branch too slender to support any creature heavier than itself. The Chevalier surveyed the situation, then sent the child to the house to fetch a canvas bag. When she returned, he placed his book in the bag, slung it over his shoulder, and proceeded to climb the tree. He ascended through the winter-naked branches until he achieved the fork formed by the trunk and the limb chosen by Mungo. Here he stopped, making himself very comfortable.

"I must wait here, *mademoiselle*," he called down to the little girl. "Soon, I hope, Monsieur Mungo will regret his rashness and yearn for the fair hand of his indulgent mistress, or else he will look for his supper. At all events, I do not think he can descend without venturing within my reach, and when he does, I shall put him in this poke and bring him to you. Now go to your mother, *mademoiselle*, for she must wonder what has become of you."

The little girl went back to the house, and the Chevalier retrieved his book from the bag and resumed his reading of the adventures of Don Quixote, reflecting that he had equipped himself with an appropriate means of passing the time while he laid siege to a squirrel. Let us leave the Chevalier in his treetop, for the moment, then, and cross the Channel, where a different kind of siege is coming to an end.

Like Mungo, Lord North longed for a change in his situation, and for much better reason than the advent of spring. The prime minister loved his master even as the gray squirrel loved his mistress, and for this reason Lord

North had never resigned his post, even in the face of a long parade of American disasters for which he was in no way responsible, but for which he was blamed in every corner of England, especially in Parliament. Long before the defeat at Yorktown, North should have been glad to surrender his thankless post, but the king would not hear of it, for George well knew no other prime minister would do his bidding so willingly. Thus, North, like Mungo, could not leave his prison; he was bound to the king by ties of friendship (they had played together as children), and gratitude (George had paid out an enormous sum of money to rescue his prime minister from debt). But Yorktown was for Lord North what the open window had been for Mungo. That which had been impossible was now inevitable.

On February 25th, Lord North introduced his ruinous budget to Parliament; two days later Parliament passed a resolution denouncing the American war and calling for peace.

For three more weeks the king clung to his forlorn hopes of keeping both his prime minister and his colonies, but by the twentieth of March he had come to understand he must surrender both. Thus it was that Lord North, after a long conference with his king, went upon this date to the House of Commons to announce that His Majesty had decided to choose other ministers. Then, with a bow, he left the chamber, entered his waiting carriage, and departed.

The final act of the great drama that was the War of Independency had begun, though months were yet to pass before peace negotiations would commence, and more than a year was to elapse before a treaty of peace was secured. Even word of the fall of Lord North's government would be several days in reaching Passy, where Benjamin Franklin had yet encountered nothing to remark this pleasant day on the verge of spring until, while strolling in the garden after dinner, he met Dr. Edward Bancroft.

"I bid you a good afternoon, Edward," said Franklin, who had seen nothing of Bancroft for several days. "How fared you in Holland? A profitable journey, I hope?"

"Quite so," replied Bancroft. "While in Rotterdam I chanced to encounter that mysterious gentleman who calls himself Fox."

"Did you? There is a remarkable accident! And did Mr. Fox have anything of value to relate?"

"His actions were of greater worth than his words; he surrendered to me a great prize."

"What? Another paper purloined from the Admiralty? I do not think Monsieur de Vergennes will pay him anything for it. Of what he has thus far sold the French, that which was genuine proved untimely, and that which was timely proved to be forged."

"This paper is not timely," said Bancroft, "nor is it a forgery, nor is it to be offered to Monsieur de Vergennes. It was written some twenty years past. It is a thing of great value to Lord Sandwich, and I think King George himself would gladly pay a fortune to have it. But no man can possibly covet it more than yourself."

Franklin stared at the man in astonishment.

"Do not trifle with me in this matter, Edward, I beg you. Do you mean you have the Hell Fire Memorial?"

"I do."

"And you are certain it is the original and no copy or forgery?"

"I am, for I took with me a specimen of the same hand that wrote it."

"I see, I see," said Franklin. "It seems, then, that your

encounter with Mr. Fox was no accident. What price did you pay him for the thing?"

"That is of no consequence. The question is this: What price are you prepared to pay me for it?"

"Ah, so that is how it stands," said Franklin quietly. He went off a few paces, then turned and faced Bancroft.

"Suppose I should tell you I'd pay nothing for it, Edward," he said. "What would you do then, sell it to King George for a fortune? Why offer it to me at all, for you cannot doubt the king of England can pay a price far greater than any I could offer?"

"I think you know the answer," Bancroft replied. "Armed with the threat of that memorial, His Majesty and Lord Stormont will demand of you things so reckless and imprudent they should infallibly end in your discovery to the French and the Americans."

"And they cannot discover Moses without also discovering 'Mr. Edwards.' Great friends that we are, we shall hang together. Is that not it?"

"It is," Bancroft replied. "It suits me to adhere to Holy Writ and see that Moses receives his commandments from God alone, and not King George."

"Indeed. Then where shall you sell your prize should I refuse to purchase it?"

"I shall not sell it at all, then," Bancroft answered. "I shall make a present of it. To your grandson. No doubt Temple should be pleased to solve the mystery of his birth, even his conception, and to read the indecent answers to these riddles written in the hand of his Tory father, William Franklin, a faithful servant of King George and Satan."

Franklin studied the man for a moment.

"What is your price?"

"Two thousand pounds."

"What? No more?"

"Oh, I should demand more, but I am impatient, for the fortunes of war are fickle. Ten thousand pounds should be very handy a twelvemonth hence, but two thousand pounds might ransom my neck tomorrow, and who can say what hazards may intervene in the course of a year. Why, it is even possible this fellow Lawless may succeed in his undertaking."

"So you have packed your trunk and keep a saddle upon your horse, and would have two thousand pounds to add to your purse. I see. But I fear I have not even two thousand pounds at hand in France."

"But I warrant you can put your hands upon that sum, and do so by the morrow. Do not delay, Dr. Franklin. In two days' time I shall have sold you the thing at my price, or made a gift of it to Temple."

He turned and strode away. Benjamin Franklin stood in the garden for some time, then he, too, departed. And in the oak beneath which this colloquy had taken place, a hungry gray squirrel ventured down from his place of exile and crawled into the arms of the Chevalier.

"A happy ascent," remarked the Chevalier to himself. "Mungo and Moses, both in my bag."

29

The Ransom of Moses

THE day after the Chevalier rescued Mungo and returned him to his mistress, he arose early, saddled his horse, and rode into the city of Paris, taking with him that same canvas bag in which he had captured the American squirrel. He returned to the Hôtel de Valentinois some three hours later, the bag now filled and nearly bursting. Surrendering his horse to the stableboy, he lifted the bag to his shoulder, climbed the steps of the Hôtel, and went directly to the office of Benjamin Franklin, where he found the American minister in somber conference with his grandson.

"I beg you forgive this unmannerly intrusion, Monsieur Franklin," said the Chevalier, "but I must speak with you immediately of a matter of supreme urgency and confidentiality."

"Pray do so, then," replied Franklin. When the Chevalier hesitated, casting an embarrassed glance at Temple, he added, "You may speak before Temple, Major. He is my trusted secretary, and I have no secrets from him."

"Forgive me, Monsieur Temple," said the Chevalier, "but of this matter I may speak to none but Monsieur Franklin."

"Of course," said Temple. "I quite understand." He withdrew from the chamber.

"I hope that you yet reserve at least one secret from Monsieur Temple," said the Chevalier, after the young man had departed. He approached the minister's desk and set the bulging canvas bag upon it.

"And, pray, what might this be?" Franklin inquired.

The Chevalier drew his dagger and slit the bag. A mass of French banknotes flooded out upon Franklin's desk.

"Fifty thousand livres," replied the Chevalier, "which my banker assures me is the equivalent of two thousand English pounds."

"A king's ransom!" Franklin exclaimed.

"Ah, no, *monsieur*. Far too little for the ransoming of a king, but perhaps enough to ransom a prophet, like Moses. At all events, it is the price quoted to undertake the burial of an ugly truth."

Franklin bent forward and peered at the Chevalier through the tops of his spectacles.

"You quite astonish me, Major," he said quietly.

"Ah, *oui*. You did not think me the eavesdropper. I shall not ask you to believe the mad errand that took me to that treetop where I could not fail to overhear your conversation with Dr. Bancroft."

"Oh, I should certainly believe it, I assure you, Major. Yet I can scarcely believe this!" He pointed to the bursting bag of livres.

"One must believe what he can touch, *monsieur,* and I deliver these livres into your hands. You must use them to purchase this infamous memorial, so that it may be consigned to the flames of your fireplace."

"You offer your own money for that purpose?" Franklin asked incredulously.

The Chevalier shrugged. "A trifle. Besides, a soldier has little need of money." It was, in fact, nearly all the

Chevalier had saved of his pay in twenty years of soldiering.

Tears welled in the old man's eyes. He removed his spectacles and polished them with his handkerchief and did not speak. The Chevalier went to the window and pretended an interest in the garden without.

"Major Lawless," Franklin said at last, "I know no words sufficient to the task of thanking you for this. I shall not try to do so, but I give you my assurance every penny will be repaid to you."

"Whenever it may be convenient, *monsieur*. Do not concern yourself over the matter."

"No, Major, I shall repay you promptly, and with interest. There shall be no difficulty in that. Yet it seems there is another matter that may present a difficulty. I know Monsieur de Vergennes seconded you to this ministry to ferret out a traitor named Moses."

"*Oui,* but I have discovered that the one called Moses is no traitor, but a loyal gentleman who was placed in a situation of conflicting loyalties by the acts of knaves."

"And this is what you will relate to Monsieur de Vergennes?"

"A soldier such as myself who commands other soldiers must be granted some discretion in the manner in which he executes his orders. If I am ordered to capture a fortress or turn back an attack, I neither require nor welcome particular instructions in the means of accomplishing these things. It is enough that I may presently inform my colonel or my general that the fortress has been taken, or that the enemy retreats. I regard these circumstances in the same way. Monsieur de Vergennes wishes to cleanse this ministry of traitors. After I have dealt with Dr. Bancroft I shall be able to report to him that no traitors remain in the Hôtel de Valentinois."

"But if you denounce Dr. Bancroft," said Franklin, "I think he will have something to say to Monsieur de Vergennes in the matter of Moses."

"I do not mean to denounce him. His treason is already well known to Monsieur de Sartines and others. I shall merely remark upon the uncleanliness of his linen, or the untruthfulness of his tongue, and I shall do so in the presence of Monsieur de Chaumont or some other gentlemen of the neighborhood. If Dr. Bancroft takes offense at my words and wishes to dispute them upon the field of honor, then we shall hear no more from him. And if he refuses to demand satisfaction for the insult, then what he may say of Moses or Monsieur Franklin will be of no consequence, for he shall be known throughout France as a man devoid of honor."

"I see," said Franklin. He knitted his brows. "Would you esteem me differently, Major, were I to ask of you that you do not do this, that you do nothing in the matter of Dr. Bancroft?"

"Would I think you a traitor, *monsieur*? My head would tell me that you were, but I have never used my head in judging men. That I do with my heart, and it is never wrong. No, *monsieur,* I should not think you a traitor, but I do not know what I should report to Monsieur de Vergennes."

"Let us put aside that problem for the moment, Major, for a much greater one confronts us. I once asked you of the saints who saw to your deliverance from the English hangman, and you wisely declined to speak of them. Indeed, I asked so that I might rest assured you would not speak of them, for I knew, even as I put the question to you, that one of these saints is a Scotsman, another an Englishman, and yet another a young woman named Jane."

"*Parbleu!* How can you know this?"

"You have discovered far more of the secret affairs of this ministry than any might have expected, Major," Franklin replied. "Yet there remain a few matters you have not divined. One is that those same saints who rescued you are in my own secret service."

"Ah, the secret war! I fear I shall never comprehend it!"

"Some very unhappy news has come to hand this morning, sir; within the hour this dispatch has come from the gentleman in London you know as Uncle Willie."

He gave the letter to the Chevalier.

My dear old friend,

I send this by the hand of a trusty courier, and not in the usual way, for there is no time to lose.

Our dearest Janie has fallen into the vile hands of Vardill and Selwyn. Jack has learned she is captive in the unholy Hell Fire Caves of West Wycomb. Her deliverance can be purchased, but at a terrible price—the names of all who serve you in England. May the Lord forgive me, but it is a price I am ready to pay. Rescued or ransomed she must be, and if you cannot see to the one, then I must do the other.

Do not delay.

S.

"By the saints!" exclaimed the Chevalier when he had read the letter. *"C'est un désastre!"*

"Indeed," said Franklin, "it is a pair of disasters. Poor 'Uncle Willie' does not see that these men do not mean to keep such a bargain. He would betray every English friend of the American cause, but it would accomplish nothing. I know something of this man Selwyn, and I do not believe he means to set the poor child free in any circumstances.

"This is a sorry sort of gratitude for your generosity, Major, but when you entered this room a quarter hour ago, Temple and I were preparing to beg you to undertake a perilous expedition of rescue."

"But I demand to do so!" cried the Chevalier. "There is not a moment to lose!"

"There is not," Franklin agreed. "I shall send for my carriage. We must go immediately to Monsieur de Vergennes in Versailles and obtain all that is necessary for a descent."

"Bah! We have no time to waste at court! Is it not within your own power to provide a ship, a swift cutter?"

"Certainly, and a guide as well. The one you met in London and know as Jack awaits at this very moment at Le Havre, where he arranges for such a ship."

"Then it is to Le Havre I must gallop, not Versailles!"

"But you cannot mean to undertake such an expedition single-handedly!" exclaimed Franklin.

"Certainly not! I shall take along the O'Tooles."

"The O'Tooles?"

"Not the whole clan, of course," said the Chevalier. "We should want an armada to transport all the O'Tooles of *La Brigade Irlandaise.* I think a half dozen or so should be enough. Rescuing imprisoned ladies is a specialty of the family, you understand. Their ancestor, Luke O'Toole, once rescued a Polish princess from a German castle so that she might become the mother of Bonnie Prince Charles. The O'Tooles are experts in such things."

"And you have the authority to enlist them in this undertaking?" asked Franklin.

"Authority? I need no authority; it is a matter of personal obligation."

"I see. These O'Tooles are somehow obliged to you for a favor?"

"*Mais non!* It is I who have obliged myself to them, and I could not hope they should soon forgive me were I to descend upon England to rescue a lady and leave all of them behind!"

Franklin smiled and shook his head. "I once asked you if you were mad, Major. Now I think I have my answer. You are all mad, mad as Don Quixote, you of The Wild Geese, who roam the world fighting in the service of every prince who may quarrel with the English."

"I think you are right, *monsieur*," replied the Chevalier. "I think we Irish are all madmen. But if we are, it is history and the English that have made us so.

"*Au revoir!*"

He dashed from the chamber, and a moment later Franklin heard the clatter of hoofs as the Chevalier galloped from the courtyard of the Hôtel de Valentinois and down the Rue de la Paroisse.

30

The Descent

HALF a league off the Sussex coast, beneath an oppressive wintry sky, stood the cutter *Marianne,* her lookouts scanning the horizon for the sight of English sail, and her master, Captain Audubon, presiding from his quarterdeck over his cargo of horses and Irishmen. In the cabin below, a band of soldiers of *La Brigade Irlandaise,* a Roman priest, a pair of Irish Spaniards, and an Englishman were gathered round the chart table.

Colonel Laurence O'Toole, a gentleman of some threescore years, was there, and with him his sons, John, Matthew, Brian, and William. Two cousins, Don Danielo O'Toole and Don Jaccobo O'Toole, sublieutenants in the Waterford Regiment of the Irish Brigade of Spain, who had chanced to be visiting their kin in Paris, had joined the expedition.* Jack Bolt had come along as guide, and

---

* Naturally, I availed myself of the happy coincidence of the surname of my friend and collaborator, G.J.A. O'Toole, in attempting to verify Lawless's story, which is so thick with O'Tooles at this juncture, and he was kind enough to direct me to the relevant genealogical works (chiefly, *History of the Clan O'Toole and Other Leinster Septs,* by P. L. O'Toole, Dublin, 1890). Suffice it to say, one Laurence O'Toole (1722–1794) was an officer in the Irish Brigade of France, as were his five (some accounts say

Father Ignatius Hogan, a chaplain of the brigade, completed the party.

"I'll be damned," declared Colonel O'Toole, "if I'll let the British jack be hoist over any ship in which I sail."

"Well, ye'll be blown to hell if yer seen flying French colors whilst sailing up an English river, begging Yer Excellency's pardon," said Jack Bolt.

"My sons, I beg of you," pleaded Father Hogan. "Speak not of hell and damnation when on an errand such as this."

"Did you not say, *monsieur,* that this wharf was disused and deserted?" asked John O'Toole. "What does it matter, then, what colors we fly?"

"Aye," Bolt agreed, " 'tis not been used for many years, but I cannot promise there'll be none about the place to see when we tie up and march ashore with the horses."

"*Messieurs,*" said the Chevalier, "I propose we fly neither

---

eight) sons, four of whom are named here. Don Danielo and Don Jaccobo O'Toole were, as Lawless tells us, in the Spanish *Regiment de Waterford.* These same sources also give a more complete account of the incident alluded to by the Chevalier in the previous chapter, in which a Captain Luke O'Toole and his comrades rescued Maria Clementina Sobieski of Poland from a castle in Innsbruck in 1718, so that she could become wife to James III and mother to Bonnie Prince Charlie, but that episode deserves more than part of a footnote, and I hope G.J.A. O'Toole or some other of the clan will someday write the full story.

There were indeed a great number of O'Tooles among The Wild Geese, and one genealogical source complains that "Individual O'Tooles who distinguished themselves in the wars against England are too numerous to particularize." However, I found it interesting that one of the raiding party, John O'Toole, was later created a count, and is the ancestor of the present Count O'Toole of Limoges, France. When I asked my friend if he thought he might be related to this French aristocrat he allowed that it was possible, but he doubted it. "I've been to all the family wakes," he said, "and I've yet to meet a Frenchman at any of them."—M.C.

the French nor the British colors, but the colors of *La Brigade*. They possess some resemblance to the British jack, yet they are our true colors. Those that do not know them will think us a British ship, and those who have seen them before are not likely to annoy us."

"A fine idea, Desmond, my lad," said Colonel O'Toole. "That's what we'll do. Now, where is this river of yours, Jack?"

" 'Tis here," said Bolt, pointing to the chart atop the table. "The river Arun. The town of Arundel lies about a league above the mouth, but 'tis a small place and said to be full of papists, so I don't think we'll meet any trouble in the neighborhood. Be that as it may, we need not sail past it, for the landing's to the south, not far from the sea."

"And is this the village of Wycomb we'll descend upon?" inquired Colonel O'Toole, pointing to another place on the chart. "It looks to be some twoscore leagues to the north."

"That and a bit more," Bolt agreed. " 'Tis not the village, but the manor of the late Lord Le Despencer that we want. It lies nearby, and the Hell Fire Caves are beneath the grounds."

He unrolled another chart and set it upon the table.

"Here's a plan of the caverns," he said. "I made it from a relation of the place told me by a London strumpet who'd been there lately to play the nun."

"God forgive the poor woman!" muttered Father Hogan.

" 'Tis not a natural cave, but a maze of tunnels left when chalk was mined from a hill to make a road from the village to High Wycomb," Bolt continued. "Le Despencer had many decorations made to suit his unholy tastes. 'Tis a great labyrinth of chambers and grottos and catacombs, a-winding back a quarter mile under the hill. Here, near halfway in," he said, pointing to a place on the plan, "His Lordship made a banqueting hall of a great room some forty feet in breadth and height. And here, some way beyond, runs an underground river or stream. And at the very end of the cavern lies the Inner Temple, as the woman said it's called, and it's there the darkest things are done."

"The Black Mass!" whispered Father Hogan.

"And what manner of force defends this position?" Colonel O'Toole inquired.

"I've heard of no soldiers quartered thereabouts," Bolt replied. "Selwyn's own liverymen and some of them what calls themselves the Medmenham Monks are down in the caves, playing jailer to our poor Jane, or so says the harlot."

"So says your harlot, ey?" said Colonel O'Toole. "Well, let's hope her truthfulness surpasses her chastity by a damned sight. Still, it's a shame to come to England and not send a few of George's own lads to hell."

Father Hogan shook his head. " 'Hell and damnation,' " he said. "If you must speak so much of the devil, Laurence, you should not be surprised if you see him."

"Why, I'll be surprised if we don't," replied O'Toole. "To hear Desmond tell it, we're calling upon him at his country villa."

"I beg you do not jest of such matters, *mon ami*," said the Chevalier.

"Ah, get along with ye, Desmond!" O'Toole replied. "D'ye truly believe there's any more to this Hell Fire stuff than a gang of English dandies drinking and whoring in fancy dress?"

"That may be all they intended when first they undertook their unholy amusements," said Father Hogan, "but it is a perilous thing to call upon Satan, for he may come even when he is called in jest. I caution you, my sons, should you find, upon entering this wicked place, that the

Black Mass is being celebrated, you must abandon your quest and depart without delay!"

"Father Hogan," said Colonel O'Toole, "I've been soldiering these twoscore years and more, and I've yet to see anything that could make me take to my heels!"

"You have not seen the *visio malefica,* thanks be to God!" said the priest.

"Faith, and I have not, nor even heard of it. What might it be?"

"You have heard of the *visio beatifica,* the beatific vision, the blinding beauty of the pure goodness of God, of which all the beauties of this world are but a dim reflection. It is what every Christian hopes to see after the final judgment. You have heard of it, have you not, Laurence?"

"I have."

"Very well. The *vision malefica* is its opposite, the vision of absolute evil. It was seen by Esau when he did not repent, and by Cain, when he murdered his brother, and the sight of it drove Judas to slay himself. There are some that say to look upon it is to surrender all hope of salvation. I do not know if that is so, but I know it is a terrible thing to set mortal eyes upon the *visio malefica,* yet should a man wish to do it, there is no more powerful means of summoning it up from the depths of hell than the Black Mass."

"*Mon Dieu!*" uttered the Chevalier reverently, and the entire company, including Colonel O'Toole, crossed themselves. They were standing thus, silently reflecting upon the priest's words, when the transom above their heads opened and Captain Audubon thrust his head down into the cabin.

"*Allons, messieurs.* The river Arun is in view."

"Then put her in at your pleasure, Captain," said Colonel O'Toole. "We're more than ready, for we seem to have nothing better to occupy us down here than telling each other ghost stories!"

Audubon cast them a puzzled look and withdrew, shutting the transom.

"Very well, lads," said Colonel O'Toole, "here's what must be done. Father Hogan will stay aboard, so that makes us a company of nine for the trip, and we've brought along sixteen horses. Brian and Danielo, you will come with us this far." He pointed to a place on the map halfway between Wycomb and the coast. "There you'll wait, resting your own mounts and the extra ones, while the rest of us ride on to Wycomb. That'll make a party of seven for the descent, which is a lucky number. There'll be eight of us coming back, God willing, the girl riding pillion with Desmond. Should we be in any way of a hurry, we'll leave the blown mounts behind and make for the coast on the fresh ones. Captain Audubon will lay by the wharf, but if he meets with any difficulty there, he'll stand out to sea and come at the coast here"—he pointed to a place some leagues east of the mouth of the Arun—"and send in a boat to fetch us."

He took out his watch.

"I make it an hour short of dusk. Unless we dally, we should be there and back by dawn. Have any of you a question?"

"I would have Father Hogan bless our undertaking," said the Chevalier.

All but Bolt then knelt while the priest prayed for their success, holding his crucifix aloft and repeating that same invocation that was the motto of *La Brigade Irlandaise,* "*In hoc signo vinces.*"* His orison complete, Father Hogan

---

* "By this sign thou shalt conquer," originally the motto of the emperor Constantine.—M.C.

removed from about his neck a chain, from which depended a small golden case.

"This reliquary holds a fragment of a bone from the body of your namesake, St. Laurence O'Toole," he said to the colonel. "Carry the relic with you, Laurence."

Colonel O'Toole took the case and examined it curiously.

"What, yet another of the clan to share in the fun?" he said. "Well, I can't deny an ancestor."

He placed the chain about his neck and tucked the case beneath his waistcoat, then turned to the others.

"We'll bring the saint along with us, lads, but let none forget to carry his blade, and look to keep the sea from your powder as we land. And let none of you suppose a saint might rank above a colonel upon the battlefield. These rakes of Wycomb may be accustomed to their dreadful visions, but I warrant their hair has never stood so straight above their heads as it will when they see The Wild Geese flying through their doorway!"

31

The Battle of the Hell Fire Caves

BY midnight the moon had risen among the silver clouds that hung over the hills of Buckinghamshire, lighting the landscape with a soft and wavering radiance. The seven men walked up the Wycomb Road, leading their lathering mounts in the nocturnal silence. Bolt raised his hand and the column halted. Beyond a turning in the road they could see the dim outline of a vast Palladian mansion standing well off the road at the foot of a wooded hill.

"That'll be His Lordship's manor house," whispered Bolt, pointing. "The entrance to the cavern lies partway up the hill behind it."

The party left the road, crossing fields and meadows and giving a wide berth to the darkened mansion. As they reached the foot of the hill, Colonel O'Toole signaled a halt. He pointed to a shadowy edifice standing upon the summit.

"And what might that be, Jack?" he whispered.

"'Tis a church," Bolt replied. "'Twas built by His Lordship."

"A church, is it?" said the colonel. "'Tis a shame His Lordship is no longer with us, for I've a great fancy to have met the man. What a lovely English lord, going up the mountain to pray in his own church on Sundays, then down to his caves for whoring the rest of the week! And what did he call his church, Jack?"

" 'Tis the church of St. Laurence," Bolt replied. "We have one of our own," he added.*

"Well, 'tis glad I am to hear of something the English didn't steal from us. I doubt my sainted ancestor should have been very pleased to be venerated by Lord Le Despencer."

The party resumed their way and soon came to a Gothic archway, beyond which lay a small courtyard enclosed within a grotto in the side of the hill. A dense wood of yew trees sheltered the place, obscuring the view of the mansion below.

"Here lies the entrance to the Hell Fire Caves," Bolt announced. "The tunnel opens from the far end of this court."

"Very well," said Colonel O'Toole. "Matthew, William, you both will remain here, guarding the mounts and keeping watch. We don't want to walk home, nor to be surprised down below by an attack from without. Should any trouble arise, come to the mouth of the cavern and fire a pistol to signal us."

He turned to Bolt.

"Jack, you're a fine lad, but I've more need of your eyes and ears than your arm tonight. Take yourself up to the church, above, and keep a sharp lookout from there. If you see or hear anything queer, come back down here and tell Matthew or William.

"Desmond, John, Jaccobo, the four of us will call upon the monks."

"*Mon Colonel, mon ami,*" said the Chevalier, "you are a splendid soldier, and my superior officer as well, and I have been content that you should lead and I follow from

---

* The correct spelling of the English saint is Lawrence.—M.C.

Paris to this place. Indeed, *monsieur*, I should be content to follow you anywhere, even through the gates of hell, as the saying goes. But this errand of ours, which brings us in truth to the mouth of hell, is a matter of supreme personal significance to myself. Thus, I beg of you the privilege of leading within the Hell Fire Caves."

"I cannot refuse you that," replied Colonel O'Toole. "Very well, Desmond, lead on!"

The four drew their swords and, the Chevalier leading the way, passed through the arch and crossed the courtyard. No gate or portal barred their way, nor was any sentinel to be seen. They entered the mouth of the cavern unhindered and unchallenged.

A low, vaulted passageway led gently downward, dimly lit by flickering sconces hanging upon the walls. The air was cool and dank and bore some faint hint of strange incense. There was no sound but the dripping of water, which oozed from the stone overhead and flowed in tiny rivulets down the cavern floor. Silently the four intruders stole forward.

Presently they came to a turning in the passageway, from which the tunnel extended to the left and continued downward. This second part of the passage differed from the first in only one respect—the walls had been decorated with stone carvings, hideous and grotesque faces of demons. The four continued onward and soon reached another bend. High up on the wall to the left, the numeral *XXII* and the letter *F* had been carved into the stone. Beyond, the tunnel divided into a maze of divergent passages. The Chevalier unrolled Bolt's plan of the caverns and examined it.

"It is a kind of labyrinth," he said, "but all the passages converge again into a single one."

The party advanced down one of the passages and soon

came to the place where the divergent passageways inter-
sected and a single tunnel extended beyond. Again the
Chevalier consulted the plan.

"The Banqueting Hall lies ahead," he said.

As they proceeded, the dim light of the lanterns hanging from the tunnel walls was augmented by a glow from
ahead. A moment more, and the four men found themselves
upon the threshold of a vast chamber, lighted by scores of
candles that burned in a great chandelier depending from
the stone celing high above. Beneath it, a strange and shock-
ing sight met their gaze.

A long dining table spanned the room, with thirteen
places set along one side. In the middle sat a human figure
dressed in robe and sandals. Its blackened face was split by
a grotesque grin, and its lifeless eyes stared straight ahead.
Upon the table before it lay the carcass of a pig, an apple
in its jaws and a crown of thorns upon its head. The wall
behind it bore a vast fresco, an obscene and blasphemous
caricature of the Last Supper, a perfection of the same travesty intended in the arrangement of the figure at the table.

"*Bon Dieu!*" exclaimed the Chevalier. The others gaped
in silence.

The Chevalier approached the table and read from a card
that had been placed before the figure.

" 'St. Francis of Wycomb.' *Messieurs,* I think these are
the mortal remains of Lord Le Despencer."*

---

* Lord Le Despencer died in December 1781, some four months
before the date of this scene. He was interred in a mausoleum
beside the church he had built on the summit of the hill above
the Hell Fire Caves. It may be worth noting in this regard the
speculation of McCormick (p. 169) that a secret passage extends
from the vicinity of the Banqueting Hall and may terminate in
the vicinity of the church or mausoleum above. Before leaving
these grisly implications, we might also note the curious bequest

"*Madre de Dios!*" exclaimed Don Jaccobo. "Let us be gone from this unholy place!"

The Chevalier and the three O'Tooles passed through the gruesome Banqueting Hall and into the tunnel beyond, venturing yet deeper into the caverns. The strange redolence they had faintly perceived at the cave's entrance now hung heavily in the atmosphere, and the silence of the place yielded to a distant murmur, which seemed to grow louder as they advanced. The Chevalier stopped and cupped a hand to his ear.

"What is that?" he asked.

" 'Tis the sound of running water," said Colonel O'Toole. "Jack's strumpet said something of a brook."

"*Oui, mon père,*" said John, "it is the sound of a brook, but it is something more."

The four stood in silence, listening intently. Above the faint mutter of coursing water another sound came to their ears, a monotonous and rhythmic chanting.

"Aye, 'tis the monks singing their unholy vespers," said Colonel O'Toole.

"*Mes amis,*" said the Chevalier, "you must accompany me no farther, for you have heard the warnings of Father Hogan. You are the bravest of the brave, but it is not bravery but wicked folly to hazard your immortal souls!"

"And what's your own disposition, Desmond?" inquired the colonel. "Would you turn back?"

---

of Paul Whitehead, the minor poet who served Le Despencer as secretary and majordomo of the Hell Fire Club. When Whitehead died in 1774 he left instructions that his heart be delivered to Le Despencer, who duly received it, deposited it in a marble urn, and placed it in this same mausoleum, after a bizarre and elaborate ceremony arranged by His Lordship and described in detail by Chancellor (pp. 157–158).—M.C.

The Chevalier shook his head. *"C'est impossible.* May *le Bon Dieu* not hold me to account for that of which I am not free to choose. I must go on."

"Then I'll be coming with you, and I'll hear no arguments from you, m'lad. I've let you walk ahead of me, but I hope you have not forgot who is the colonel and who the major."

He turned to the other O'Tooles.

"John? Jaccobo? What say you? Consider it well, lads, for I own there is something to what Desmond says."

"Non, mon père," replied John. "I shall not turn back."

"Nor I!" said Don Jaccobo.

"Very well, m'lads." He turned to the Chevalier. "We O'Tooles will be going on, Desmond. Now you better get on with leading us, if you don't want to find yourself following."

"I salute the valor of your clan!" said the Chevalier, and he turned and resumed his advance down into the cavern, his three comrades at his heels.

Guided by the plan, they found their way past several turnings in the tunnel, and passages leading off to the right and to the left. At length they came upon another chamber, this one much smaller than the Banqueting Hall, and lit only by the guttering flame of a single sconce. There was no furniture in the room, and it seemed quite empty but for a shadowy pile lying athwart their path in the middle of the place. As they approached, the thing began to move.

The dim light discovered to their eyes a great serpent coiled upon the floor. The snake rose up before the Chevalier until its hideous head was level with his own. It opened its massive jaws, unsheathing a pair of long, dripping fangs, and it vented a hissing challenge at the four intruders.

The Chevalier made to pass by the reptile, going first to the left and then to the right, but so great was the length of the beast, and so swift its motion, that he could not pass beyond the reach of its awful jaws. His sword extended, he advanced upon it.

The serpent reared back its head before the Chevalier's approaching point, and its hissing grew louder and more shrill. The Chevalier could proceed no farther without treading upon the coiled body of the reptile. He halted, turned his blade somewhat to the side, and remained thus, standing motionless. But an instant passed before the serpent lunged at him.

The snake struck and the Chevalier's blade whirled, the two motions simultaneous and too swift for human eyes to follow. But at this instant the guttering flame that enlightened the scene died, plunging the chamber into darkness.

One of the Chevalier's legs was seized in a powerful grip, first near the ankle, then at the knee. His waist and chest were bound in a crushing embrace, which made to wring the life from his body. Falling to the floor, he drew his dagger and slashed at the loathsome coils encircling him.

Colonel O'Toole heard the sounds of the struggle, yet could do nothing but stand by helplessly in the darkness.

"John! Jaccobo!" he called. "Go back beyond the last turning and fetch a light from the wall!"

The Chevalier let go of his sword and dagger and seized the crushing coils with his bare hands. With a mighty effort he freed himself from the creature's deadly embrace, even as Jaccobo returned, carrying a candle to illuminate the scene.

The head of the serpent lay upon the floor, cleanly severed from the body by the Chevalier's sword. The body of the great reptile thrashed wildly about the chamber, coiling and uncoiling in the convulsions of death. Jaccobo held the light aloft and gazed at the creature in horror.

"*El diablo!*" he whispered. "Possessed of the body of a serpent, even as in Scriptures!"

"*Non, mon ami,*" said the Chevalier, arising and recovering his sword and dagger. "This serpent made to captivate my body, not my soul. It is a creature of this world and no other. I take it as a good sign, for I cannot think these Monks of Medmenham would set an earthly creature to stand sentinel could they summon one from hell."

"Aye, Desmond," said Colonel O'Toole. "That makes sense."

The Chevalier stepped over the writhing carcass and led his comrades forward. They entered the passage at the far end of the chamber and proceeded deeper into the cavern; as they advanced, the sounds of the waters and the chanting grew louder and the redolence of strange incense increased. Soon they came to a place where the tunnel excavated by the hands of Lord Le Despencer's laborers opened into a great natural cavern that had been carved from the rock by the black waters running through it.

"*Le Styx!*" exclaimed John O'Toole.

It was not, truly, a river, but a swift stream, spanned by a narrow footbridge. The four crossed to the far wall of the cavern, where their way was blocked by a pair of wooden doors. The monotonous threnody issued from beyond.

"They are barred!" cried the Chevalier in dismay, when the portals did not yield to his hand. The four struck their shoulders against the stout wooden panels, but without result. While they were thus engaged, they heard a woman's screams from beyond the obstacle.

The Chevalier turned, ran off a few paces, and then charged, leaping into the air and colliding feet foremost against the barrier. The doors were torn from their hinges by the force of his assault, and fell with a great crash into the chamber beyond. Sword in hand, the Chevalier charged through the doorway, the O'Tooles close behind. The four were brought up short by what lay before them.

The chamber was not large, but about the size and shape of a small chapel, which it resembled in its furniture and decorations. Some two dozen robed figures—the monks and nuns of Medmenham—knelt upon wooden benches before a shattered altar hewn of blackest obsidian. On the wall above the altar hung a great mirror, and above it a twisted cross. Before the altar stood a little man draped in black vestments adorned with pentagrams and other magical devices; as he turned, the Chevalier recognized the wizened features of George Selwyn. Beyond him, two monks struggled with a naked woman, pressing her upon the black altar and making to bind her to it. Two massive black candles stood beyond the altar, the light of their tall flames cast back by the great mirror, illuminating the strange scene.

Silence followed upon the crash of the shattered doors. The worshipers had stopped their chanting and turned to look to the intruders. All within the chamber seemed frozen, and even the victim had ceased her struggle for an instant, directing her imploring eyes toward the Chevalier and the O'Tooles.

"Desmond!" she cried.

"Kill him!" screamed the little man, but before any of the satanic congregation could move, an ancient and terrible Gaelic war cry burst from the Chevalier's throat and he leaped forward.

Monks and nuns scattered before the onslaught, seeking refuge in the distant reaches of the chamber as the Chevalier and the O'Tooles charged.

"They are but four!" cried Selwyn. "Kill them, I say!"

A dozen of the monks found their nerve, and drawing swords from beneath their robes, made to stand their ground and engage the invaders. The pair that had held Jane at the altar joined the battle, too, their victim now lying insensible upon the floor.

Steel crashed upon steel as the Chevalier and his comrades, standing squadrons* in the middle of the chamber, met the monks' desperate counterattack. Shrieks, oaths, and Irish war cries filled the scented atmosphere of the satanic chapel. Three of the monks engaged the Chevalier, and a moment later two lay dead and their fellow had taken to his heels. The Chevalier turned and saw John dispatch another of the enemy. Four more dead monks lay upon the floor; the others had withdrawn and fled with the nuns through the shattered portals. John and Don Jaccobo stood unscathed, but Colonel O'Toole had fallen.

"*Mon père!*" exclaimed John, rushing to his father's side.

"Is he dead?" demanded the Chevalier.

"No, thank God!" answered John. "But he has been struck upon the head and is insensible."

"Then you and Jaccobo carry him away to safety. I shall see to matters here."

As the two O'Tooles bore the colonel away, the Chevalier turned to Selwyn, who had remained at his place before the altar during the fight.

"Keep your distance, Major Lawless!" hissed the little man. "This device protects me."

He stood within a pentagram drawn upon the floor.

"Should you pass within it, you will be blasted by the forces of hell!"

---

* I.e., they drew up in a square formation, back to back.—M.C.

Without hesitation the Chevalier stepped inside the figure and grasped the little man by the neck. He squealed and struggled and broke free, leaving the Chevalier holding his black vestment, while he cowered naked in a distant part of the chapel. The Chevalier took the robe and, wrapping the yet insensible Jane in it, made to depart.

"Will you not kill him, *monsieur*? He is a detestable little creature."

"Who is that who speaks?" demanded the Chevalier, his sword at the ready. The voice had come from beyond the black altar, which was wreathed in the smoke of the perfumed incense. Through the haze, the Chevalier dimly discerned the figure of a man.

"What, do you not know me?" the figure demanded. "Can it be you have never heard of the Chevalier de Lawless?"

The smoke cleared a little, and the Chevalier saw that the figure was but his own reflection in the great mirror beyond the altar.

"What trick is this?" exclaimed the Chevalier. "Where are you, the one who speaks and claims to be me?"

"I am here, at the very place you look," said the voice, "and you can see my claim is true, if you know the handsome countenance of *le beau Irlandais*, as the ladies of Paris and Versailles are pleased to call the Chevalier de Lawless."

The Chevalier ventured behind the altar, but found no one there. The chamber was empty of any other living creature but for the insensible Jane, and Selwyn, who yet cowered in a distant corner of the chapel.

"What is this, Monsieur Selwyn?" demanded the Chevalier. "Do you practice *la ventriloquie*?" The frightened little man made no reply.

"It is I who speaks, *monsieur*," said the voice from the altar, "and not that loathsome little insect. Why do you not squash him? I should do it myself, but the Chevalier de Lawless is too proud to slaughter an unarmed man, is he not?"

"You answer your own question, Monsieur Whoever-you-are," said the Chevalier.

"I have told you my name, *monsieur,* but you seem to forget it," said the voice. "I am the Chevalier de Lawless, and it is my pleasure to slaughter Englishmen. My sword has drunk their blood in half the nations of Europe, and in America at Gloucester and Yorktown, and upon the high seas. I cannot tell you the number of Englishmen I have slain, for I am too proud to count their bodies, but it is a great number. I am the mightiest swordsman alive, for I have bested even the Chevalier d'Éon, and I am invincible, for even the English hangman could not kill me."

The Chevalier leapt upon the black altar and faced the figure in the glass. The smoke had cleared, and the light of the two great black candles revealed his own image in the mirror.

"I do not fear you, *monsieur*!" cried the Chevalier.

"No," replied the vision, "for there is none so brave as the Chevalier de Lawless."

"Then you do not know him," said the Chevalier, "for he is not brave at all. He is a madman, and you are as like to find him catching squirrels in treetops as upon the field of battle!"

"You are right, *monsieur,*" said the vision. "You have found me out. I am not the Chevalier de Lawless, but Prince Balberith, the mightiest champion of His Satanic Majesty.* Look on, mortal, and I shall show myself to you."

---

* According to the lore of demonology, Balberith is prince of the fallen cherubim, a demonic angel who tempts men to murder. —M.C.

The vision in the glass began to change, transforming itself into a thing of supreme hideousness. The Chevalier remembered the words of the priest and understood that it was the *visio malefica* that formed itself before his eyes. With a swift blow of his sword, he cut the two great candles and plunged the chamber into blackness.

"Ah, *oui,*" said the voice, "the Chevalier de Lawless needs no light to defend himself, for he knows the trick of fighting in the darkness. *En garde,* Monsieur de Lawless!"

"I shall tell you the trick, that you may know it as well, for, as we have said, I am a madman," said the Chevalier. "The trick is this: Never disengage, so that you may at all times know the situation of your opponent's blade!"

So saying, he whirled his point in the darkness, but his blade struck glass, not steel. The sound of the shattering mirror filled the chamber, then all was silent. A light appeared in the doorway, where Don Jaccobo now stood, a torch in his hand. The vision had fled, or else lay in shards upon the black altar.

"What is wrong, Señor de Lawless?" asked Don Jaccobo. "Why have you not yet departed this unholy place?"

The Chevalier made no answer, but picked up Jane's recumbent form and followed Don Jaccobo from the Hell Fire Chapel.

Dawn found the *Marianne* well out in the Channel, running before a fresh westerly. In the cabin, the Chevalier ministered to Jane, who slept fitfully in a narrow bunk, while John O'Toole replaced the bandage on his father's head. Jack Bolt, the other O'Tooles, and Father Hogan pressed John, Jaccobo, and the Chevalier for particulars of their descent into the caverns.

"Don Jaccobo and I bore my father, yet insensible as

he then was, back through the tunnel," said John, "and we came again to the chamber of the serpent."

"It was *el diablo,* even as I said," proclaimed Jaccobo, "for it had mended itself together and threatened us again."

"By all the saints!" exclaimed Father Hogan. "What did you do?"

"We drew the relic of the saint from the waistcoat of my father," said John, "and the serpent retreated."

" 'Tis nonsense!" said Colonel O'Toole. "It was no devil, but another snake, and you frightened it off."

"Then what became of the carcass of the first serpent, *señor?*" demanded Don Jaccobo.

"The second one ate it!" answered the colonel.

John and Don Jaccobo looked at each other and shook their heads.

"And what of the devilish church itself?" asked the priest. "You broke in upon the unholy ritual against my warnings, but I trust you saw nothing of the *visio malefica.*"

"I saw something quite hideous there," ventured the Chevalier, "after the O'Tooles had departed."

"Did you indeed? What did you see?"

"A strange and ugly thing in a mirror. But I did not look upon it."

"And 'tis well you did not," said the priest. "In a mirror, was it? Well, we should not be surprised at that."

"*Vraiment?* Why do you say so, Father Hogan?"

" 'Twas vanity that moved Lucifer to rebel against God, Desmond," explained Father Hogan, "for he preferred to reign in hell than serve in heaven. The devil created the sin of pride, and if he's to be seen in this world at all, he's more likely to be found peering out at you from your looking glass than peeping in your window."

The Chevalier considered these words and said nothing.

"And how many did you kill?" inquired Brian O'Toole.

"No more than was required," replied the Chevalier. "The taking of lives is a terrible thing, *mon ami,* and we should not glory in it."

"What? Even the lives of Englishmen?" demanded Brian.

The Chevalier nodded. "*Oui,*" he replied. "I have come to believe this."*

---

* But can we believe this part of Lawless's story? The Hell Fire Caves were sealed for more than a century and a half, until 1952, when they were opened to be explored by curious tourists. Lawless's description of their shape and dimensions corresponds generally to what may be seen today. There are some differences, of course—nothing remains in the Banqueting Hall but the hook in the ceiling from which the chandelier was hung, and the "river Styx" is today just a small subterranean stream. Some of these differences can be attributed to the changes wrought by time, while others may be the sort of minor errors inevitable when a story is passed along by word of mouth. It is the more magical elements of the story that jeopardize its credibility.

The snakes (let's assume, along with Colonel O'Toole, that there were two) are plausible; pythons and boa constrictors, while not native to England, could have been imported. As to the Chevalier's vision in the mirror, it may be worth noting Lawless's frequent references to the strange incense that filled the air in the caves. The burning of strange substances in imitation of church incense was a part of the Black Mass, and we cannot discount the fact that opium was well known and widely used in eighteenth-century England. Nor should we overlook the fact that Lord Sandwich, one of the original Unholy Twelve, had traveled extensively in the Middle East, and could not have been ignorant of marijuana and hashish.

Of course, some may say we are too ready to offer a pharmacological explanation for the Chevalier's reported vision, and too quick to reject the metaphysical one he apparently accepted. In any case, there's no point in speculating about it. All we can say for sure is that this is what Pierre-Augustin says his father told him of the incident.—M.C.

32

The Courtship of the Chevalier

THOSE who have read the lives of the saints and other pious biography will know that many a man whose lot it has been to come face to face with the devil has thenceforth put aside all worldly matters, going forth to preach against the Fiend, or else has retired to a monastery or hermitage, devoting himself entirely to prayer and meditation. It should not have been surprising had the Chevalier done such a thing, not only from the motives of traditional hagiography,* but out of several other considerations not commonly of influence among those destined for canonization.

The Chevalier had crossed swords with the devil (if not Satan himself, then one of his chief lieutenants), and if he had not conquered, neither had he been vanquished. Indeed, a swordsman may fairly claim victory when his opponent withdraws, as did Prince Balberith. Thus, like Alexander, the Chevalier had no more worlds to conquer. When an Irish warrior has made Old Nick himself take to his heels, he can hope for little future diversion in the pursuit of mortal foes, nor any glory whatsoever in the prospect of slaying Englishmen, when he has been moved,

---

* Biography of saints.—M.C.

as was the Chevalier, to regard such glorying as sinful. The Chevalier did not mean to leave off warring with the English, but he sadly reflected that what had once been his great joy was now no more than drudgery.

But it was not alone the moral lesson learned by the Chevalier in his encounter with the Tempter in the Hell Fire Caves that made him waver in his ancient and cherished heritage of enmity toward all Englishmen. Heretofore he had met his Englishmen only upon the battlefield, and those who had approached close enough for introduction had not lived long enough for acquaintance. Yet it had lately been his lot to encounter several Englishmen in other circumstances, and to discover, much to his astonishment, that some of them were quite agreeable fellows. Indeed, M. Franklin, of whom the Chevalier had become very fond, had for threescore and ten years been an Englishman (albeit of the American variety), and it seemed unlikely that all of the old gentleman's splendid qualities had been acquired so late in life, and as a result of a quarrel with the English king. But more than any of this, the softening of the Chevalier's heart toward the English derived from his reflection that, whatever else an Englishman may be called a son of, he is undoubtedly the son of an Englishwoman, and it was for one of this species that, as we have seen, the Chevalier had acquired the tenderest of feelings.

Thus, the Chevalier gave no thought to the prospect of turning hermit or preacher, for he had already set himself upon another course, to wit, to become a husband.

The house of Colonel O'Toole was situated in the Faubourg Saint-Germain, and it was there that Jane was taken by her rescuers upon their return to Paris, that she might be cared for by Mme. O'Toole and the colonel's daughters. Such is the resiliency of youth, and such was the courage of this young woman, that but a few days had passed before Jane had fully recovered both in body and spirit from her terrible ordeal, and was up and about, and ready to greet visitors, the first (and it need hardly be added, the most welcome) of whom was the Chevalier.

"Dearest Desmond!" she exclaimed, when he entered the drawing room. "I would tell you of my thankfulness and my admiration of your valor, should it not want days, no months, to speak it all. But I fear you will think me not grateful at all, for I must first ask if my father has been told I am safe."

"*Mon chérie,*" replied the Chevalier, "scarce an hour after we entered the port of Le Havre another ship set sail for Dover to bear the good news to your father. The secret dispatch had been prepared in advance by Monsieur Franklin and carried from Passy by his grandson, who awaited us at the port so he might send along these tidings upon the instant he knew them to be true. And but a day later, Monsieur Franklin and his grandson followed the first dispatch with a second, conveying a personal request that I have made of your father. It is my great joy that I have his reply already."

"A request, Desmond?"

"*Oui.* I asked of him that he rescue my veracity, for I would not be called a liar."

"I own I am baffled by your words," she said.

"But the matter is very clear," protested the Chevalier. "Upon a recent occasion I alleged you were my bride, which, of course, was an untruth. I have begged the permission of your kind father to alter matters so that the statement is no longer false."

"If I take your meaning, Major Lawless," she said indignantly, "you have offered the most singular of reasons to ask for a lady's hand. Would you marry me to make good your word to the stagecoach passengers?"

"Ah, *non*," replied the Chevalier. "It was not I who lied to the stagecoach passengers. I did not converse with them, for I was a merchant of Hamburg who spoke no English. It was to the innkeeper of Harwich I made this allegation, and it was that gentleman I had in mind."

Jane blushed a deep vermilion, yet her anger remained hot.

"I never doubted your honor, sir, yet I never dreamt you so punctilious a fellow to worry of some promise you made a landlord!"

"Ah, but now that you know that, you shall never doubt my word, *n'est-ce pas?* And I have so many words to whisper to you, *mon chérie*. You ask me for months to praise my valor. *Très bien,* you may have them, though I did no valorous thing, for a man who ventures all to recover that which in all the world he holds most dear can lay no claim to valor. I grant you these months, for I beg of you years, all that you have, that I may speak to you, not of valor, but of love."

Jane's anger melted away as the Chevalier swept her into his arms.

"You shall have my hand, Desmond," she said. "It seems I have no choice, for you already have captured my heart."

33

The Tale Unfolds

"**P**OOR Richard claims that three may keep a secret if two of them are dead," said Benjamin Franklin. "I pray he may be mistaken."

"What is the good in knowing secrets if you must also keep them?" demanded Beaumarchais. "It is like keeping a great magazine of wines in the cellar, but serving only water at your table."

"No, my friend," said the Chevalier. "Meanness and frugality are different things, and it is frugality that Poor Richard preaches."

"Quite so, Major," said Franklin. "Poor Richard preaches it, yet I have never learned to practice it. Still, I am quite frugal with my secrets, never drawing the cork from one until the occasion demands. I judge this such an occasion, but I would share this fine vintage with no others but yourselves."

The three were walking upon the bank of the Seine at a lonely place beneath the heights of Passy. There was none about to see them or hear what they said.

"As you have discovered, Dr. Bancroft is an English spy," Franklin continued. "I have known the man for a dozen years. Indeed, he was something of a protégé of mine when first I knew him in London."

"Ah, *c'est dommage,*" said the Chevalier, shaking his head sadly, "that the man should be so ungrateful."

"Perhaps," Franklin remarked. "At all events, Dr. Bancroft was engaged as secretary to this ministry when it was established here in France some five years ago. This was done on my instructions, for I had a special reason to wish him here."

"Of course," said Beaumarchais, "you were fond of the young fellow!"

"It was not that," said Franklin.

"Then you esteemed his intellect and learning!"

"Nor that."

"You admired his persuasiveness!"

"No," said Franklin, "it was none of those things. I engaged Dr. Bancroft for quite a different reason: I knew him to be a British spy."

"*C'est incroyable!*" exclaimed the Chevalier.

"*C'est incomparable!*" exclaimed Beaumarchais. "I stand in awe of your genius, Monsieur Franklin! Do you not comprehend, Desmond?"

"I fear I do not."

"Ah, but it is so clear! Monsieur Franklin addresses himself thusly: 'I know the English and their spies very well. I wonder who the English king will set to spy upon me here in France. *Parbleu!* Perhaps he will send some disagreeable fellow who will prove quarrelsome. Or it may be some stupid fellow who will be tiresome. Or even a clever fellow that will keep me busy finding him out. What shall I do! Aha, I have it! My own spies in England tell me Bancroft has turned to spying. *Voilà,* I shall engage him! If I must have a traitor in my house, it is better he be one I can trust!'"

"Is this so, Monsieur Franklin?" inquired the bewildered Chevalier.

"I should not have put it quite that way," said Franklin hesitantly, "but, yes, I own that Monsieur de Beaumarchais has stated the essence of the thing.

"I knew the English should infallibly send a spy. I had been told by highly stationed friends in London that Dr. Bancroft was engaged in secret services to King George. The English might very well have sent him here without my prompting, but I knew they should hardly neglect the opportunity of my invitation to come and serve as secretary."

"But why did you wish this?" asked the Chevalier.

"I wished it because a spy that's been found out is of no worth to his master, but he may be contrived to serve unwittingly the one he makes to spy upon. Dr. Bancroft never guesses how well he has served the American cause.

"You must understand, Major, that of the many things King George and his ministers would know of our affairs here at Passy, there are some I should be pleased to reveal to them. Early in the war they were eager to know if the French were disposed to aid us and if Louis might even send his armies to join the battle. I was as eager that they should have the answers to these questions, for I hoped the prospect of an alliance between the French and the Americans might bring King George to his senses, that he might grant us our independency and forgo a long and costly conflict. It proved a vain hope, but it was never an unreasonable one, and it was Dr. Bancroft who faithfully reported to his king that the French were disposed to ally themselves with us."

"But why did you not simply announce this to the English yourself?" asked the Chevalier.

"Ah, Desmond," exclaimed Beaumarchais, "you have no head for commerce, and what is spying but the buying and selling of secrets? Give a man something for nothing and he will count it worthless; sell it to him, and he will wonder if he's been cheated. Ah, but lock it up so that he must steal it from you, and he will prize it as a great treasure! Have you not seen how Monsieur Franklin leaves his secret papers lying about? It is the only way to keep them safe!"

"In other words, Major," said Franklin, "King George would not have believed the American minister, but he could hardly doubt his own spy."*

"Ah, I comprehend," said the Chevalier. "But is there not also some hazard that a spy may learn some secret you do not wish revealed?"

"There is," Franklin admitted, "but such things are usually revealed whether you wish them to be or not. I should not have wished the English to know of Mr. Lee's quarrels with Mr. Deane and myself, nor of Mr. Adams's insults to Monsieur de Vergennes. Such things comfort the English, but they are common tattle in Paris and Versailles, so they are soon known in London. Indeed, of the few secrets I would keep from the English, the chiefest among them had been made a present to them long ago, and not by any spy, but by my own son. And that is a matter you gentlemen already know something of, the Hell Fire Memorial. Yet I think I must recount all the melancholy particulars, nonetheless.

---

* But, in fact, he did. George distrusted both Bancroft and Wentworth, suspecting that they distorted their reports to him in order to manipulate the London stock market, in which both were heavily interested. The king was also subject to wishful thinking, credulous of optimistic reports, and skeptical of pessimistic ones. —M.C.

"When I returned to London in 1758 to serve as agent for the colony of Pennsylvania, I brought with me my son, William, hoping to guide and abet him as he set out to make his way in the world. I saw to it that he was enrolled in the Middle Temple to study the law, and I introduced him to the most influential men in England. Among these gentlemen were Lord Le Despencer and Lord Bute.

"Le Despencer—Sir Francis Dashwood, as he was called when first I met him—was a very strange man, made of the stuff of great saints and great sinners, and ever wavering between those two opposite courses. I own I was fond of the man, or of that face he showed me. That my friend possessed another, darker countenance I did not soon suspect, not even when he led me through the Hell Fire Caves and told me something of his Monks of Medmenham. He neither told nor showed me all, and so I counted him and his fellows as no worse than a curious company of revelers who chose to dress their pleasures in outlandish trappings. You have doubtless heard of me that I am not given overmuch to prudery in such matters myself. I hold, instead, with a simple piety: Serve God by doing good to man."

"But it was Satan, not God, whom Le Despencer and his monks served," said the Chevalier. "They observed the devil's commandments to do every sort of wickedness."

"They did, indeed," Franklin agreed, "but I had no inkling of that when my son announced he was to be initiated into the Medmenham Monks. I own I welcomed the news, for I thought it a great advantage to a young man that he associate himself in so convivial a way with gentlemen of means and influence. And in this, at least, I was not disappointed, for William's friendship with Lord Bute was the step upon which he climbed to the station of royal governor of New Jersey.* That his revelry amidst monks earned him a bastard, as well, was not a matter of which I was moved to reproach him, to put things quite plainly, lest he hurl his own illegitimacy back in my teeth. I need hardly say I knew nothing of the mother's ravishment and captivity at the time.

"I shouldered the burden of William's bastard and kept the secret of the boy's paternity, so that William might advance to his new station without scandal. I own it soon became a trifling burden, and then no burden at all, as Temple swiftly advanced in my affections. Nothing ever hurt me so much as William's desertion to side with the English and take up arms against me, yet I am moved to forgive him even this, when I think of the joy he chanced to bestow me when he brought that tiny bundle to our lodgings in Craven Street."

"And do you forgive him, as well, for the Hell Fire Memorial?" asked the Chevalier.

"I do," said Franklin, "for he meant me no treachery when he wrote the thing. He must look to God for forgiveness in the matter of the poor woman who was Temple's mother.

"As you may know, William wrote the memorial, confessing his crimes, in obedience to Lord Sandwich, who demanded it as surety of repayment of a loan. William needed the money to buy the silence of the woman's father, and he could hardly turn to me for help without also con-

---

* William Franklin was appointed to the post by Lord Halifax, president of the Board of Trade, at Bute's request (Van Doren, *Benjamin Franklin,* p. 302). Lord Bute (1713–1792) was a close friend of King George, serving as secretary of state and prime minister. He is believed by some historians to have been a member of the Hell Fire Club.—M.C.

fessing to me the reason he needed it. I would that he had, but he did not, and I knew nothing of the memorial or its contents until the matter was discovered to me by Lord Stormont, but three years past. Stormont sent Mr. Wentworth to me here at Passy to inform me of the unhappy particulars, and to threaten their publication should I decline to provide secret services to King George."

"*Morbleu!*" exclaimed the Chevalier. "A disaster!"

"Not at all," said Franklin. "I reviled the memorial and the affair it related, of course, but I welcomed Stormont's proposal. Indeed, I accepted it."

"By the shoes of St. Peter!" exclaimed Beaumarchais. "Do you boast to us of treason?"

"Not treason, Monsieur de Beaumarchais," Franklin replied, "but the sweet use of adversity, for should King George think me a servant, he could hardly esteem me to be master as well."

"I am baffled," lamented the Chevalier.

"I am overcome!" cried Beaumarchais. "*C'est éclatant!* Do you not see it, Desmond?"

"I fear I do not."

"Ah, but it is so clear! The great English spider, Stormont, sits in London, spinning his web across the water in France. He catches American flies, like Monsieur Deane and Monsieur Bancroft, and he thinks he has caught Monsieur Franklin. Ah, but Monsieur Franklin says to himself, 'This Stormont spider thinks me a fly. *Très bien*, I shall be his fly at Passy so that he does not see that I, too, am a spider, one who spins his web across the water in England and catches English flies! *Alors,* I shall make certain the English spider does not dine upon the English flies in my own web.' Ah, what splendid intrigue!"

" 'Tis so," Franklin agreed. "I did not wish William's memorial be published, for I have kept from Temple any knowledge of the scandalous circumstances of his birth. Still, Temple is no longer a child, and I suppose I must tell him of the matter someday, although I would not have the tale discovered to the world. At all events, it suited my design to yield to Stormont's threat, for in saving Temple from scandal, I also secured the welfare of those who serve me secretly in England."

"*Oui,* I comprehend," said the Chevalier. "Jack, and 'Uncle Willie,' and most of all my dearest Jane!"

"And a few others, as well," said Franklin. "I shall not astonish you with their names, but I may tell you that, while Stormont was well informed of events at Passy and Versailles, I was quite as well informed of events in Westminster and even Windsor."

"But did not Monsieur Bancroft relate to his masters that you were thus so splendidly informed?" asked the Chevalier.

"He did not, for he does not know it. None in the ministry knows of it, but for Temple and another young gentleman who works in my printing shop."

"You confide in a printer?" exclaimed Beaumarchais. "I do not think that wise, Monsieur Franklin. Printers are a treacherous brotherhood! You are the exception, of course!"

Franklin smiled. "Many of the trade are very trusty, Monsieur de Beaumarchais. As I think Major Lawless may lately have learned, the gentleman in London he calls Uncle Willie is of the printing trade. Indeed, were he not, I should be quite a lean spider, for I am nourished by the books he prints in his shop. And he, in turn, is guided by the products of my humble press."

"Aha!" exclaimed Beaumarchais with a crafty smile. "Invisible ink! You and your London confederate write your dispatches to each other in invisible ink between the lines of the books you print for each other. Is that not it?"

"It is not," Franklin replied. "The messages are in the books, but they are not written in invisible ink. Should Mr. Todd of the English Post Office* lay hands upon one of the volumes that I often send off or receive, he should douse it in every recipe at his disposal, and were there a line of invisible writing anywhere in the book, he should infallibly read it. The messages are not in invisible ink, but in cipher."

"In cipher? But is that not unwise?" asked Beaumarchais. "The English may not penetrate your cipher, but when they find strange letters or numerals upon the pages of a book they will know that the one to whom you send it is in your secret service."

"Indeed, but there are no strange letters or numerals, nor any other thing to seem amiss, for the cipher is concealed within the words that are proper to the book. A great scholar devised the scheme long ago, and it is a handy means for one who has a printing press at his command. But I digress. Let me return to the matter of Moses, the name by which I am known in the Secret Service of King George.

"I have said that but two in this ministry are witting of my triple role of spider, fly, and minister, and one of them is my grandson. Beyond the walls of the Hôtel de Valentinois few others share the secret.

"Though there was great advantage in King George's

---

* A. W. Todd, Secretary of the British Post Office. Todd's responsibilities included the British "black chamber," i.e., the department that intercepted mail of political importance (Augur, p. 135; Watson, p. 488, n. 69). Franklin's own prerevolutionary contact with the Post Office may have made him aware of the Secret Office and the Private Office, both subdivisions of the British Post Office; the former intercepted foreign letters, while the latter opened domestic mail (Kahn, p. 171).—M.C.

faith that I was his secret servant, there was also great hazard in it. Half the truth is often a great lie, and I feared for our valued alliance with the French should Monsieur de Vergennes's own trusty spies learn but a part of the matter. Thus, I called upon the count and told him all of it, a wise precaution as events later proved, but not a sufficient one.

"Mr. Arthur Lee is a gentleman of many excellent virtues, but neither good humor nor trustfulness are among them. To put it plainly, he is quarrelsome and suspicious, and when he was here in France he quarreled with Bancroft, Deane, and myself, and he suspected us of every crime from larceny to treason."

"But he was not wrong in suspecting Monsieur Bancroft and Monsieur Deane," said the Chevalier.

"He was not," Franklin agreed. "When a man makes it a habit to suspect everyone, he will sooner or later meet someone that deserves his distrust, but he is no wiser than the fool who trusts everyone, and I think he is more often mistaken.

"When Mr. Lee departed for America, I fancied myself delivered from further injury by his ill humor, but it was a vain hope. Indeed, his complaints against me found more sympathetic ears at Philadelphia than ever they did at Paris or Versailles. Soon the Congress had drawn up sides, dividing itself into those who believed Mr. Lee's accusations and those who did not, and soon the government of the United States of America had left off all other business to debate the question of whether Mr. Deane and I were a pair of scoundrels. Thus, Monsieur de Vergennes and I had no choice but to let two others in on the secret of Moses. He confided the matter to his emissary at Philadelphia, Monsieur de La Luzerne, while I informed my good friend and colleague, Mr. Jefferson. Both gentlemen wield great influence with the Congress, and they succeeded in extinguishing the fuse Mr. Lee had lit. This was not accomplished without some cost, however. Mr. Deane was summoned home, and while I cannot pardon his later treachery, I believe it was born of the ill use he received at the hands of Mr. Lee and his friends in Congress.*

"No sooner was the affair of Mr. Lee resolved than new adversity struck, however. One of Monsieur de Vergennes's spies in London stole papers from the British Foreign Ministry disclosing that an English spy called Moses had been placed within the American Ministry here at Passy."

"But you had made the wise precaution of informing Monsieur de Vergennes of Moses," said the Chevalier, "so this could have been no adversity."

"The difficulty did not arise from Monsieur de Vergennes, who, as you say, was not ignorant of Moses," said Franklin. "The difficulty arose from Lord Stormont, who became witting that Monsieur de Vergennes knew of Moses."

"*Parbleu!*" exclaimed the Chevalier. "Again I am confounded by the intricacies of the secret war."

"Do you not see it, Desmond?" demanded Beaumarchais. "Ah, but it is so clear! Monsieur de Vergennes thinks Monsieur Franklin his friend and ally; he is right! Monsieur Stormont thinks him his servant; he is wrong! But then the papers are stolen, and Monsieur Stormont thinks Monsieur de Vergennes now believes Monsieur Franklin serves the English; he is wrong, but he is also right! *Voilà!* You comprehend now, do you not?"

---

* Deane actually returned to America in 1778, two years before Lee went home, but most historians seem to agree that he was recalled at the instance of Lee, who had already written of his suspicions to his friends in Congress.—M.C.

"I fear I do not," said the Chevalier.

"With the theft of the papers," Franklin explained, "Lord Stormont had every reason to expect the French to expel me and the Americans to hang me. He had known I was accused by Mr. Lee, for he has his spies in Philadelphia, and he knew there were some who believed the accusations and others who did not. That much of it suited me, for I think it kept Stormont and the king from commanding that I sow disunity and mischief between the Americans and the French, lest my actions confirm what some suspected. But the papers stolen from the British Foreign Ministry should have proven those suspicions beyond question. Thus, I feared Lord Stormont should soon wonder why no action was made against me and presently conclude that his fly was, in fact, a spider in disguise."

"I comprehend . . . I think," said the Chevalier hesitantly. "How did you confront so intricate a difficulty?"

"I confronted it by sending for you, Major," Franklin replied.

"For me? You jest, of course, *monsieur.*"

"Not at all. I wrote to Mr. Jefferson and he conveyed my plea to General Washington and Major Tallmadge, letting them into the secret of Moses by way of explanation. I asked they send an officer to Passy under orders to ferret out a traitor who was called Moses. And I asked that the man they send be incapable of succeeding in his task. I have learned how badly Major Tallmadge misjudged you, Major Lawless."

"*C'est magnifique!*" exclaimed Beaumarchais. "You comprehend, do you not, Desmond?"

"I do not, I fear," replied the Chevalier.

"Ah, but it is so clear! Monsieur Franklin addresses himself thusly: 'Monsieur Lee suspects me of treachery, and he is wrong! Monsieur Stormont suspects me of intrigue, and he is right! If only Monsieur Lee would work harder at proving himself right, even though he is wrong, he should convince Monsieur Stormont he is wrong, even though he is right! Aha, I have it! I shall see that Monsieur Lee has a helper! But this helper must be one incapable of assisting him! Otherwise he might succeed in proving Monsieur Lee right, despite the fact that he is quite wrong!'

"Next, this Major Tallmadge addresses himself thusly: 'Who shall I send upon this errand for Monsieur Franklin? Aha, I know! I have heard of this Major Lawless, that he is a great soldier who distinguishes himself upon the battlefield! *Alors,* he must know nothing of intrigue, so he will succeed, for he shall certainly fail!' But Major Tallmadge knows nothing of the Chevalier de Lawless, who arrives at Passy and soon discovers Monsieur Franklin to be Moses, becoming, like Monsieur Stormont, both right and wrong at the same time, and failing because he has succeeded! It is all perfectly simple!"

"Perhaps, *mon ami,* but I fear some essential part of the thing continues to elude me."

"In asking you be seconded to this ministry, Major," explained Franklin, "it was my hope that your efforts to discover Moses should soon be apparent to Dr. Bancroft, who should, in turn, report them to Lord Stormont. In this way I hoped to demonstrate to Stormont that I was distrusted by both the French and the Americans, and so dispel any doubt he might make that I was a spider, rather than a fly, to use Monsieur de Beaumarchais's delightful figure once more.

"In the event, this was accomplished much sooner than I dared hope, when you were captured at sea, for Monsieur de La Luzerne's letter stating the particulars of your mission fell into English hands along with the *Aurore.* I had not foreseen it, but that letter in the hands of Lord Stormont immediately rescued my disguise. But I meant to see to your own rescue, as well, for I should have been very grieved had the English hanged you—to any permanent result, I mean.

"When my friends in London succeeded in procuring your escape and deliverance here, I had no choice but to see that you resumed your mission, lest Lord Stormont's suspicions be revived. Thus it was that you came to Passy, and it was then that events began to elude my control.

"The Paris police discovered Dr. Bancroft's dealings with the English. They also learned of Moses, and they suspected that he was I. Monsieur Le Noir, the commissioner of police, reported the matter to Monsieur de Vergennes, who warned him away from any further examining into it. Nonetheless, word reached the naval minister, Monsieur de Sartines, who asked his friend and ours, Monsieur de Beaumarchais, to resume where the police had mysteriously left off. This he did, joining forces with you.

"To confound matters yet further, an English adventurer who called himself Montagu Fox turned up in the Netherlands in possession of William's memorial, which he had stolen from Lord Sandwich. This left me to wonder if Lord Stormont knew the thing to be missing, and if he did, why he imagined I continued to play fly to his spider. Before I had time to reflect upon that puzzle, I received the disastrous news from 'Uncle Willie' that Jane had been captured by the British and turned over to the custody of Mr. Selwyn. Hard upon the heels of that disaster, Dr. Bancroft reappeared at Passy after a mysterious trip to Rotterdam, the infamous memorial in his pocket and a threat upon his lips that he should give the thing to Temple if I did not meet his price.

"I confess, Major, that I do not know what I should have

done at that moment had you not chosen it to climb into the top of an oak in my garden!"

"It was to rescue the gray squirrel for Mademoiselle de Chaumont," said the Chevalier.

"Indeed! Well, I must declare you are wonderful at rescuing, sir! You rescued me with your generous loan, and you rescued Jane with your gallant band of Wild Geese. I am quite astonished when I reflect upon the degree that you have improved matters in the space of but a few days, rescuing us all from the jaws of disaster."

"*Oui,*" agreed Beaumarchais, "Desmond has worked miracles! Yet, is there not a small disaster that cannot be avoided? I think these wonderful events must persuade Monsieur Stormont that his tasty fly, Moses, is, in fact, a spider."

"Perhaps," Franklin admitted, "but the matter is no longer of consequence. I have had word from London that Lord North has resigned his office, taking with him all his ministers, including Lord Stormont. King George must select a new government, and I warrant it shall be one bent, not on waging war, but on suing for peace. Oh, there yet remains some haggling to be done, and some papers to be drafted and signed, but, gentlemen, the war is finished. America has won her independency!"

"*C'est magnifique!*" cried the Chevalier. "I congratulate you, Monsieur Franklin!"

"*Oui,* as do I!" Beaumarchais said. "And when shall we have the pleasure of seeing Monsieur Bancroft hanged?"

"Hang Bancroft?" said Franklin. "Oh, I do not think that necessary. It has never been my wont to seek revenge."

"Perhaps not revenge," said Beaumarchais, "but is it not a matter of justice?"

"It is, but I am content to leave such matters to be settled between Dr. Bancroft and his Maker. He has served his country well, albeit unwittingly and despite himself, and he is yet a young man with many years before him. Perhaps he will repent and resolve henceforth to do good. If not, if he persists in spying upon America for the English, he will do good nonetheless, for as I have said, a spy that's been found out is too valuable a prize to hang. Wars may come and then pass away, but intrigue between nations ever endures. I think it better we seal our lips and return Moses to the Scriptures from whence he was borrowed."

"You are very wise, Monsieur Franklin," said the Chevalier, "but do you not hazard your own good name in keeping the secret of Moses and Monsieur Bancroft?"

"I am an old man, Major Lawless, who has spent fifty years of his life in public offices and trusts. I think posterity will judge me on the whole, and not some part that may seem scandalous.

"As a wise man once said, truth is the daughter of time."

Afterword

by
Michael Croft

THAT'S all there is. Except there's some more.
I'm sorry if that sounds like one of Beaumarchais's paradoxes. I mean that you have just read the last page of Pierre-Augustin Lawless's *History,* but not the end of his story. He wrote a little more of it—a brief postscript— and then he hid it. Why did he hide it, how did I find it, and what does it say?

All in good time. First things first.

When I was finished investigating the authenticity of the *History* (or thought I was), I typed up all the foot- notes, compiled a bibliography (you'll find it at the end of this book), and began to think about what I was going to tell my client and his client in my final report. I thought I was ready to summarize my conclusions, and I decided to organize the report under a few general headings, the major questions Marsh needed answered:

1. Did Pierre-Augustin Lawless make the whole thing up?

Not a chance. That would have been impossible, and I can prove it.

Granted that an eccentric, with plenty of time on his hands, could have researched historical literature and concocted an elaborate literary hoax bolstered by thousands of facts he found in the records of the American Revolution. Still, he could never have written Lawless's *History,* at least, not in 1836, the year it was published. The *History* contains one element that would not appear in the historical literature for another fifty years. I'm talking about Edward Bancroft's role as British secret agent.

Bancroft wasn't hanged. He wasn't even accused of anything, except, of course, by Arthur Lee, and Lee never persuaded enough people he was right about Bancroft to bring him to justice. Bancroft continued working for the British after the war. In 1783 he returned to America to assess the prospects for a counterrevolution, and recommended to his chiefs in Downing Street that they undertake covert action to overthrow the United States government and restore English colonial power. Apparently the British didn't take his advice.

He returned to England, pursued his scientific interests, raised a son, and died at Margate in 1821. During the rest of his life he was never accused of having worked for the British Secret Service.

The truth about Edward Bancroft was not made public until the 1880s, when the British government opened part of its archives to an American researcher, B. F. Stevens (B.F. stands for Benjamin Franklin, but that's just one of those strange coincidences; so far as anyone knows, Stevens was not descended from Franklin). Stevens published twenty-five volumes of facsimiles of British government documents relating to the American Revolution, including much correspondence among Bancroft, Paul Wentworth, Lord North, Lord Stormont, King George III, and William Eden (Stormont's predecessor as Secret Service chief). The documents agree in detail with what Lawless tells us of Bancroft's operation. To cite only one example, a memorandum of 11 December 1776 entitled "Engagement of Mr. Edwards [Bancroft's nom de guerre] to correspond with Paul Wentworth and Lord Stormont and the Means of conducting that correspondence" (Stevens, Item #235), specifies the hollow tree near the Tuileries, the bottle, the invisible ink, and all the other details Lawless gives us of Bancroft's "dead-drop."

Where could Lawless have gotten this information if not from his father, Beaumarchais, or some of the others he says he interviewed? Obviously not from the British government, which wasn't ready to release it for another half century. It couldn't have been Arthur Lee; he suspected Bancroft, but he never knew all the details Lawless gives us. And it certainly wasn't Bancroft himself, whom Lawless doesn't even claim to have interviewed.

Lawless didn't invent the story. It had to have been based on what he was told by his father and the others he interviewed. Whether or not he was told the whole truth and nothing but the truth remains to be seen, but the accuracy of the Bancroft material certainly bolsters the credibility of his story.

2. Was Benjamin Franklin an agent of the British Secret Service?

Lawless says he was, but that he was playing double agent (really, triple agent, I suppose), and his true allegiance was to the American side. But at least two twentieth-century historians—Richard Deacon and Cecil B. Currey—argue that Franklin was both a traitor and a member of the Hell Fire Club.

Deacon, in his *History of the British Secret Service*, claims that Franklin belonged to the Medmenham Monks, that the monks were not a satanic cult but an instrument

of the British Secret Service, and that Sir Francis Dashwood
was an intelligence officer. He offers only one source to
support all these claims, McCormick's book on the Hell
Fire Club. However, McCormick characterizes Franklin's
membership in the club as "doubtful" (p. 196) and has
nothing at all to say about links between the monks and
the British Secret Service. I think we can forget Deacon
and turn to Currey.

In his *Road to Revolution*, Currey suspects Franklin was
a member of the monks, basing his suspicion on nothing
more than Franklin's friendship with Dashwood and occa-
sional visits to his West Wycomb estate. Dashwood (later
Lord Le Despencer, in case you're confused) was British
postmaster general and later first lord of the treasury, i.e.,
he was an important and powerful man, and he had many
guests at West Wycomb besides Franklin. Even Lord North
was there (Franklin mentions meeting him there in his
letter to his son of 14 July 1773), and I doubt that the
staid prime minister was also a satanist (although Currey
suspects him, too).

There's just no evidence to support the theory that Franklin was a member of the Hell Fire Club, Currey's suspicions notwithstanding. Let's put aside that question and
return to the main one, i.e., was Franklin a British agent?

Currey presents his largely circumstantial argument that
Franklin was in the British Secret Service in his second
book, *Code Number 72, Benjamin Franklin, Patriot or Spy?*
The book falls far short of proving Franklin a spy, but it
proves Marsh's belief that, when it comes to espionage,
most historians are laymen.

Franklin met with British agents, was careless with (at
least some of) his secret papers, was mysterious in account-
ing for the disbursement of government money, and associated with Deane and Bancroft, who were later proved

to be British spies. Does all this prove Franklin was a British spy? I don't think so; British spies weren't so careless (consider Bancroft!). But it does suggest that Lawless was right, that Franklin was running his own intelligence operation against the British.

Much of counterintelligence consists of planting information (some true, some false) where it can be picked up by the opposition. A present-day intelligence officer who finds a bug in his office will probably leave it undisturbed for a long time; the opportunity it presents outweighs the inconvenience. "Secret" documents are judiciously leaked, "defectors-in-place," or "moles" (two terms in current use that describe Deane and Bancroft), are closely watched, but usually left unmolested. As Lawless says Franklin said, they're too valuable to hang. What about the great sums of money mysteriously unaccounted for? Intelligence operations demand secret budgets; otherwise the fellow you bribed yesterday may be shot tomorrow.

But what about those British secret documents? What about the gentleman who went by the code name Moses? Currey says only two documents referring to Franklin by this name have been found "so far," i.e., after two hundred years. One of the documents is not a British government paper at all, and it concerns stock speculations, not espionage, and it was written by an English banker, not a government official. Currey argues plausibly that the Moses of this letter was Franklin.

The second document is from British government archives. It bears no signature nor address, but Currey assures us it was from Lord North to William Eden (Stormont's predecessor in the Secret Service) because of the handwriting and the contents. That both Lord North and the banker refer to someone named Moses "can only" mean both referred to Franklin, claims Currey.

Well . . . maybe.

It doesn't really matter. Even if the letter was written by North to Eden, and the Moses mentioned was, in fact, Franklin, it says nothing more incriminating than this single cryptic phrase: "Moses has told his intimate friends that something good is in store for them." Who the friends might have been, what Moses might have promised them, how Lord North happened to know about it, and what significance it may have had, remain a mystery.

Still, in view of Lawless's story, the Moses reference in a document presumably written by Lord North is interesting.

If Currey could only find two instances in which Franklin was referred to as Moses, he found plenty of places where Franklin was called "72," and thus the title of his book. Benjamin Franklin was known to the British Secret Service by the code number 72, Currey says.

And he's absolutely right.

The number 72 was Franklin's "alias," Currey claims; it was his agent number in the British Secret Service, Currey seems to imply.

And that is absolutely wrong.

I don't know exactly what significance Currey really attaches to the "72" business, except that he seems to think it important enough to use it in the title of his book, and to head one of his chapters with a phrase quoted from one of Paul Wentworth's letters to his Secret Service boss, Eden, "72 received me very kindly." I found the letter in Stevens's facsimiles (Stevens, Item #489), and it was very interesting.

There is no doubt Wentworth meant Franklin when he wrote "72," because Eden or his secretary wrote in "Dr. Franklin" right above the number every time it appeared; you can see it for yourself, because Stevens published photocopies of the original handwritten pages. Eden also wrote in "Mr. Deane" above every mention of the number 51, as in "51 joined us."

The conspiracy thickens!

"I met 40 at the garden door," Wentworth continues; "Chaumont" has been written in above "40." Jacques-Donatien Leray de Chaumont, owner of the Hôtel de Valentinois and Franklin's landlord—secret agent number 40, yet another of this nest of British spies!

But wait!

"Nothing but 107 would be listened to," says Wentworth. Who might the mysterious "107" be? "Independency," notes Eden.

We read further and find even more astonishing equations: 64 = England; 45 = Congress; 144 = Paris; 110 = London; 207 = war; 3 = ambassador; etc., etc.

How right Marsh was about historians! Here is one who doesn't seem to know the difference between an agent number and a simple communication code.

So much for secret agent "72." There's just no evidence to support the theory that Franklin was a British secret agent. But there's plenty of evidence to settle the question of whether his loyalties lay with England or America.

Benjamin Franklin was both architect and caretaker of the French-American alliance. The vital flow of arms, supplies, troops, and money from France to America never stopped during his term as American minister at Passy. When the terrible-tempered Arthur Lee or the francophobic John Adams insulted or offended the French at Versailles, it was Franklin who soothed the ruffled feathers at court. When the British tried every possible diplomatic maneuver to drive a wedge between the allies, it was Franklin who countered each move and kept the alliance whole. And when the French queen and finance ministers warned (quite accurately) that the war would bankrupt the nation's treasury, it was Franklin who saw to it that Louis and Vergennes turned a deaf ear to those warnings and continued to lend even more money to the Americans.

Franklin should be judged by his actions. It was always within his power to sabotage the alliance and end the vital flow of French aid simply by sitting back and doing nothing. He never did that. He always did the opposite.

Patriot or spy? What do you think?

3. Was Benjamin Franklin running his own intelligence operation against England?

Again, a circumstantial case can be made. Franklin was in an excellent position to organize his own spy ring in London; he lived there for more than fifteen years, and knew almost everyone who might possibly be willing and able to send him information. And the American war had much less than the unanimous approval of the English people and Parliament. Franklin knew many powerful Whigs; it's quite possible some of them supplied Franklin with confidential information.

But is there any proof?

Maybe.

At least one very experienced intelligence officer believed Franklin had a highly placed agent in England. The person of whom I speak is the late Allen Dulles, OSS veteran and director of the Central Intelligence Agency from 1953 to 1962. In 1962 Dulles published a book-length essay on the subject of his lifelong trade, *The Craft of Intelligence*. In an early chapter (p. 36) on the history of American intelligence, he reviews the Franklin-Bancroft relationship and then adds:

Franklin's own agents in London were apparently highly placed. Early in 1778 Franklin knew the contents of a report General Cornwallis submitted in London on the American situation less than a month after Cornwallis had delivered it. The gist of the report was that the conquest of America was impossible. If Franklin's agents had penetrated the British Government at this level, it is possible that they had caught wind of the intelligence Bancroft was feeding the British.

Unfortunately, Dulles was not writing a historical work. If he had been, he would have cited sources to support this intriguing passage. But he does leave us some clue to the basis of his statement. In his bibliography Dulles lists a number of historical works, among them *Turncoats, Traitors and Heroes,* an account of spying during the American Revolution written by John Bakeless. Bakeless tells us the same thing we find in Dulles, plus a bit more:

> The Whitemarsh fiasco [i.e., the British defeat there] discouraged the enemy both in Philadelphia and London. Cornwallis, who left Philadelphia for a brief leave in England, reported on Whitemarsh in London the next month, adding that the conquest of America was impossible—a bit of news which an American secret agent in London was reporting to Benjamin Franklin at Passy by January 20, 1778.*

Apparently Bakeless was Dulles's source. But who or what was Bakeless's source? Bakeless was a meticulous his-

---

* Bakeless, p. 220.

torian, and his book is richly documented, but he offers no basis whatsoever for this intriguing nugget.

With the help of my friend and associate, G.J.A. O'Toole, I traced Bakeless to a little town in Connecticut, and we wrote to him there, asking him about the matter. After a few days we received a reply from the historian's widow, informing us that John Bakeless had passed away a few years earlier.

There was one clue to Bakeless's source, and that was the date, January 20, 1778. How could he be so specific about the date Franklin received the Cornwallis report? The obvious explanation is that Bakeless saw a letter Franklin wrote on that date which mentioned it. But where was the letter?

O'Toole and I searched through all of Franklin's published papers and came up with nothing that resembled such a letter. But not all of Franklin's papers have been published, although they have been compiled and will be published eventually. Where are they? At the Yale University Library, which happens to be where Bakeless did much of the research for his book (according to his acknowledgment in a preface).

O'Toole and I wrote to the present editor of Franklin's papers at Yale and explained our problem. We soon received a reply.

Bakeless's source, said the Yale historian, was not Yale, but probably a manuscript in the Harvard Library—a letter written by an anonymous correspondent in London, dated 20 January 1778, reporting Cornwallis's arrival and his pessimistic estimate of British efforts in America. The letter also contains some news from Brest of the 27th and 28th of January, proving it could not have been sent before the latter date. And it is addressed to Arthur Lee, not Franklin.

If the Harvard document was Bakeless's source, he really committed a whopper. That doesn't sound like Bakeless, but nobody's perfect. Still, there is just barely another explanation.

Maybe Bakeless wasn't Dulles's source. Maybe Dulles was Bakeless's source.

John Bakeless was once an intelligence officer, according to the biography on his dust jacket. Did he know Dulles? And in spite of the fact that Bakeless published the item in 1959, and Dulles in 1963, could this nugget have come to Bakeless from Dulles in private conversation or in a letter? If so, it certainly explains why Bakeless omitted any source for the statement when he published it in his book.

But if Dulles was Bakeless's source, where did Dulles get the thing? Where did Allen Dulles get any of his information? It's pointless to speculate, I suppose, but it's very tempting. It's tempting to imagine Allen Dulles sitting in some richly appointed room in Downing Street sometime in the early 1940s, the air filled with the aroma of old brandy and fine cigars, and across from him a familiar bulldog face.

"Dulles, old fellow, I ran across something in the archives the other day, and I think it might interest you. I have it here."

Well, I'll leave the matter there. Franklin may have been running his own high-level agents in England, but "thus far" (to use Currey's wonderful phrase) we have no solid evidence, just tantalizing hints. We'll have to wait and see. After all, Franklin himself said, "Truth is the daughter of time."

And that, curiously, brings me to Pierre-Augustin's hidden postscript, because it's the accident that led me to discover it.

If the phrase, "the daughter of time," sounds as familiar

to you as it did to me, it may be for the same reason; you, too, may have read Josephine Tey's splendid revisionist defense of Richard III, which masquerades as a mystery novel under that title. I wondered if Tey might have been quoting Franklin, so I got down my copy of her book and looked to see if she had given the full epigram. She had.

> Truth is the daughter of time.
> —OLD PROVERB

How old? Older than Franklin? It didn't seem to matter, but I get curious about little things like that. I checked Bartlett's and several other collections of quotations, but didn't turn it up. So I called a friend at Georgetown.

"Who said 'Truth is the daughter of time'?" I asked.

"I think it was Bacon."

"Roger?"

"Uh uh. Francis."

He was wrong, but it doesn't matter. In fact, it was a lucky mistake, because it brought up the name of Sir Francis Bacon, and that turned out to be the key to Pierre-Augustin's hidden postscript.

All the information I had about Sir Francis Bacon was negative: He did not write Shakespeare's plays, even though some say he did. Why was I so sure of that? That's when it hit me. I remembered the book I once read on the Shakespeare-Bacon controversy; it wasn't a book on literature, it was a book on cryptology. It took me a few minutes to locate it, and about a half hour to refresh my memory.*

I guess most people have heard of the argument that Sir Francis Bacon was the real author of Shakespeare's

---

* The book was *The Shakespearean Ciphers Examined* by William F. Friedman and Elizabeth S. Friedman (Cambridge, 1957).

plays, but few probably know much about the history of the controversy. The idea is a couple of hundred years old, but it gained popularity in the nineteenth century when an American eccentric named Ignatius Donnelly misunderstood a cipher that Bacon had invented back in the sixteenth century. Bacon had devised a way to conceal messages in printed texts, and Donnelly thought he found some of Bacon's ciphers in the Bard's plays. It turns out he was wrong.

But what has any of this to do with Lawless's *History*, or Benjamin Franklin? Just this: The cipher Franklin says he used in communicating with his friend and fellow printer in London had to be the Bacon cipher. As Franklin tells Beaumarchais in the final chapter, "the cipher is concealed within the words that are proper to the book. A great scholar devised the scheme long ago, and it is a handy means for one who has a printing press at his command." He can only be talking about Bacon's cipher.

The biliteral cipher, as Bacon called it, is a simple substitution cipher that is concealed within some innocuous text through the device of switching back and forth between two different type fonts; Bacon recommended roman and italic. This, then, was what Franklin did at Passy and Strahan did in London at their respective printing shop/ communication centers.

When Strahan had a message for Franklin, he would reset the type in a few pages of some standard work he had in stock, enciphering his message and concealing it in the text according to Bacon's formula, then rebind the book with the new pages, ship it off to Franklin by way of some third party (probably Wiggins, the bookseller of Ostend), and not worry about the British Secret Service or Post Office taking a look at the thing. When Franklin wanted to communicate with Strahan, he'd do essentially the same thing in his Passy printing shop, although the vehicle he used was probably one of his humorous essays—he called them his "Bagatelles"—that he printed in the ministry. Franklin characterized his Passy printing shop as "a wicked extravagance," but it was, in fact, an essential part of his espionage operation.

Unless you're particularly interested in codes and ciphers, I've probably told you all (or more than) you care to know about the cipher Franklin and Strahan used. (But if you are a cryptology buff, you'll find more details in the Appendix.) You may even wonder why I didn't relegate the whole business to a footnote instead of saving it to clutter up this little essay. I said something of Pierre-Augustin's hidden postscript several paragraphs back, and you probably wish I'd get on with that subject, instead of dwelling on this one. On the other hand, you may have guessed that the reason I've gone into the technique Franklin used to conceal his dispatches is that Pierre-Augustin used that same technique to conceal his secret postscript, right in the pages of his *History*.

If you did, you're right. You guessed it, but I wouldn't have, despite the italic characters I saw scattered throughout the original edition of the *History* (but which are omitted from this edition), which had no apparent reason for being there. It would have gone right past me if I didn't have an eye for coincidences, and wasn't, like the Chevalier himself, addicted to curiosity.

The coincidence I mean is the name Carey, which I noted three times in the *History*. In Chapter Eighteen Lawless mentions "an Irish lad named Carey, whom the Chevalier had seen working in the printing shop" at Passy. In Chapter Twenty-four, when Franklin is preparing to send off a dispatch to London, he tells Temple, "Mr. Carey has been up all night setting the type," i.e., we must now conclude, putting it into the biliteral cipher. The third occurrence of the name is on the title page of the *History*, which identifies Lawless's 1836 publisher as Carey and Hart of Philadelphia. I wondered if, by some remote chance, this Carey was the same as the other. He was.

Mathew Carey (1760–1839) was born in Dublin, Ireland, where he grew up and became a printer's apprentice. In 1779 he published an anonymous pamphlet criticizing the government, and the resulting furor caused him to flee to Paris. There he met Franklin, who hired him to work in his printing shop. During the war, Carey also carried out secret missions in Ireland for the Marquis de Lafayette. After the war, Carey moved to America, settling in Philadelphia, where Lafayette gave him the money to set up his own printing business. He went on to become a prominent figure in American book publishing during the early nineteenth century, and Carey and Hart was one of his imprints.

Naturally, when Pierre-Augustin decided in 1836 that the time had come to publish the exploits of his illustrious father, he turned to the Chevalier's old associate from Passy, not only for sentimental reasons, but because Carey was able to resolve a dilemma confronting him. Lawless had mixed feelings about one part of the story, and he couldn't make up his mind whether to publish it or consign it forever to oblivion. Carey enabled him to compromise; he hid the secret within the typefaces of the *History* using the biliteral cipher, and left it up to fate to decide if his hidden postscript should ever be deciphered and see the light of day. And after another hundred and forty-five years, fate decided that it should.

Bacon's biliteral cipher is simple once you know the trick, and it didn't take me long to decipher Pierre-Augustin's postscript. After I had, I knew my job was complete; any further investigation of the authenticity of Lawless's *History* would have to be done on my own time, for I had learned everything Marsh and his client needed to know regarding her proposed lawsuit. I called him and arranged to meet with them both.

Kitty Applegate turned out to be a boisterous and beautiful redhead, a southern lady of exceptional intelligence and charm. It's a shame she makes such a brief appearance in this report, and it's an even greater shame I couldn't offer her more profitable information.

"I've got some bad news and some good news," I said, after the introductions were complete. "First the bad news: Franklin repaid the debt to the Chevalier."

"How do you know?" Marsh demanded.

I told them about the biliteral cipher, and the hidden postscript. I had typed up the deciphered postscript and made several copies. I gave them to Marsh and Kitty Applegate and let them read it for themselves, and I guess you'd like to do the same thing.

So here it is.

Postscript

by
Pierre-Augustin de Lawless

THE author of this history should be remiss were he to omit from it the full particulars of a certain matter that has not, thus far, been related. It is a thing that fills his heart with pride, but he dare not reveal it, lest it fill other hearts dear to him with shame and anguish. Thus, he conceals it within the words that may be plainly read, and entrusts God to decide what eyes may ever read it.

Three years past the date of the events thus far recounted Benjamin Franklin made ready to take his final leave of France and return to the land of his birth. It was then that he sent for the Chevalier, asking him to come alone to the Hôtel de Valentinois. When the Chevalier arrived, Franklin greeted him with great affection and presented him with a draft upon a bank in the city of Paris.

"Here is but a part of what I owe you, Major Lawless," he said. " 'Tis the sum you lent me, with interest, yet I remain forever in your debt, and the ransoming of the secret of Temple's birth is the least of it."

"It is the least of a very small thing, *monsieur*," said the Chevalier. "Do not trouble yourself with such matters."

"Yet there is one thing that troubles me, Major, and I beg your advice in it."

"What might it be?" asked the Chevalier.

"Thanks to your generosity, Temple has not learned the secret of his birth. I have it here, the infamous memorial."

He took up a paper from his desk.

"I have ever believed in truth," Franklin continued, "but I own that this is a truth I should prefer to consign to my fireplace. Were the choice yours, instead of mine, what should you do?"

The Chevalier reflected for only a moment before replying.

"I think I should burn the thing, *monsieur,* and say nothing of it to Temple."

"You think it so shameful a secret, then?"

"Mais non! I do not think it at all shameful. It is a thing of which only your unhappy son, William, must feel ashamed. But who can say how Temple might receive such a discovery? And there are surely others in the world who would make a scandal of it, were it known. No, Monsieur Franklin, no good can come of that wicked paper. I should cast it into the flames and not burden your grandson with it."

Franklin handed the memorial to the Chevalier.

"Take it, Major, and do with it what you will. I must tell you that it contains one matter of which you are ignorant. I pray you will not reproach me for discovering it to you, but I fear I must.

"Two children, not one, were born in Medmenham Abbey; a pair of twins, a boy and a girl. Temple has a sister, and she is your wife."

"But of course, Monsieur Franklin," said the Chevalier. "You did not believe I knew this?"

299

"I own I did not, sir!" exclaimed Franklin.

"I may be mad, *monsieur,* but I am not blind. I guessed this secret long ago, for, as you say, Jane and Temple are twins."

"Have you told her?"

"I have not. What I have said of Temple, I should say of Jane. There was a time I wished to tell her, so that she should know the illustrious name of her grandfather, but this cannot be done without her learning the infamous name of her father. Perhaps I shall tell my son when he is a man, so he may know that the blood of Benjamin Franklin flows in his veins, but that day is many years off. As for today . . ."

He dropped the paper into the fire. It blazed for a moment, then twisted into ash, as Benjamin Franklin and the Chevalier de Lawless looked on.

"Pierre-Augustin was faced with a dilemma," I said, when they finished reading. "You see, in 1836 his mother, Jane de Lawless, was still alive. The old lady had never learned the secret of her birth, and Pierre-Augustin wouldn't take it upon himself to tell her. But he wanted to publish the *History* because he was fifty years old himself and he didn't want to risk losing the chance to tell the world about the Chevalier's exploits. This was his solution."

Kitty Applegate took out a handkerchief and wiped her eyes.

"That's very beautiful," she said.

"Well, I suppose I should thank you, Croft," said Marsh. "It would have been pretty unfortunate to have the defense turn that up after we took the thing to trial. But I really doubt there's anyone else in the world who could have unearthed it."

"Even if you're right—and I doubt it—you wouldn't

want to have been the unwitting cause of an injustice," I said.

"No, certainly not," he said unhappily.

"I'm sorry, Ms. Applegate," I said.

"Well, don't be. My goodness, I'm descended not only from the Chevalier but from Benjamin Franklin. Can you imagine how that makes me feel, when a year ago I didn't even know who my natural parents were?"

"Is the good news worth five million dollars?"

She smiled. "Five million, less fees and expenses, and that's assuming we had obtained a judgment in our favor," she said professionally. "No, I'll settle for this."

" 'A lean award is better than a fat judgment,' " I remarked.

"Who said that?" she asked.

"Your ancestor, Poor Richard."

That proverb was a bit pessimistic, I thought, as I walked back along Pennsylvania Avenue to my office. Poor Richard was practical, but he was also usually an optimist. After all, what could be more optimistic than "Truth is the daughter of time?" It's like "Murder will out." It sounds great, but it usually doesn't work.

Benjamin Franklin loved to take old proverbs, improve on them, then publish them as the sayings of Poor Richard. I wonder what he might have done with the daughter-of-time proverb if he'd tried.

"Truth is the daughter of curiosity"? No. How about "Truth is the daughter of diligent inquiry"? That didn't seem quite it, either.

Then I had it. I could almost see him, Ben Franklin, peering at me through his clever spectacles.

" 'Tis well said that truth is the daughter of time, sir, but you must own every child has two parents. If time be the mother of truth, what name shall we give the father? I say he is chance."

If you ever said that, Poor Richard, I couldn't agree with you more.

Appendix

Bacon's Biliteral Cipher

S IR Francis Bacon described his cipher in Book Six, Chapter One, of his *Advancement of Learning*. He defines a cipher as a type of alphabet, "a secret and private one, agreed upon betwixt particular persons," and specifies three requirements for such secret alphabets:

> 1. that they be easy to write and read; 2. that they be trusty and undecipherable; and 3. if possible, clear of suspicion. For if a letter should come into the hands of such as have power over the writer or receiver, though the cipher itself be trusty and impossible to decipher, it is still subject to examination and question, unless there be no room to suspect or examine it.

This is exactly the point Beaumarchais made: Even if Lord Stormont or the British Post Office had been unable to break Franklin's cipher, Strahan's cover would have been blown if they realized he was receiving messages in cipher.

Bacon goes on to describe his cipher, which he says he devised in Paris (appropriately) when he was a young man. He sets forth what he calls a "biliteral alphabet," which is simply a means of representing each letter of the

alphabet by a string of five letters, all of which are either
a or *b*.

Thus:

A	= aaaaa	I	= abaaa	R	= baaaa
B	= aaaab	K	= abaab	S	= baaab
C	= aaaba	L	= ababa	T	= baaba
D	= aaabb	M	= ababb	V	= baabb
E	= aabaa	N	= abbaa	W	= babaa
F	= aabab	O	= abbab	X	= babab
G	= aabba	P	= abbba	Y	= babba
H	= aabbb	Q	= abbbb	Z	= babbb

The keen-eyed reader will have noted that this alphabet
contains only twenty-four letters, J and U having been
omitted. The reason for the omission is simple: the letters
didn't exist in Bacon's time. As late as the late eighteenth
century *J* was considered merely to be a variation of *I*, and
U a variation of *V*. This presented no cryptological prob-
lems to Franklin, Strahan, and Carey. In deciphering, they
could distinguish between the vowel and the consonant
from the context of the adjacent letters in the word.

The biliteral alphabet multiplies the length of the
"clear" message by five. For example, the word "fly" would
be written.

F L *Y*

aabab ababa babba

Now, obviously, a strange-looking string of letters such
as this is bound to attract attention, so Bacon explains how
it can be concealed within "external writing," a dummy or
cover text which camouflages it. This is where the roman
and italic typefaces come into play.

Let's make up the following sentence as the cover text:

> Stay till I come to you.

Which would be printed,

> St*ay till I come t*o you.

For convenience in enciphering and deciphering, we treat the sentence as a string of letters, and break it up into five-letter groups. Thus,

> St*ay* i*ll*Ic *omet*o you—

Next, we write either an *a* or a *b* above each letter, depending on whether it's roman or italic. Thus,

F   L   Y
aabab   ababa   babba
St*ay*   i*ll*Ic   *omet*o you—

(Of course, the "you" at the tail of the message would result in aaa, which would be ignored by the recipient, since it's a three-letter string and therefore not part of the cipher alphabet.)

And that's all there is to it.

Bibliography

THE following sources proved useful in verifying parts of Lawless's *History*. I cited some in my footnotes, while others provided general background. I have grouped them under several headings.—M.C.

I. The diplomatic background of the American Revolution:

BENDINER, ELMER, *The Virgin Diplomats,* Knopf, 1976.

BOATNER, MARK M., *Encyclopedia of The American Revolution,* David McKay Co., 1974.

JONES, JOHN PAUL, *John Paul Jones' Memoir of the American Revolution,* U.S. Government Printing Office, 1979.

MORRIS, RICHARD B., *The Peacemakers: The Great Powers and American Independence,* Harper & Row, 1965.

SCHOENBRUN, DAVID, *Triumph in Paris: The Exploits of Benjamin Franklin,* Harper & Row, 1976.

TREVELYAN, GEORGE OTTO (Richard B. Morris, ed.), *The American Revolution,* David McKay Co., 1964.

II. Espionage and intelligence operations of the American Revolution:

AUGUR, HELEN, *The Secret War of Independence,* Little, Brown, 1955.

BAKELESS, JOHN, *Turncoats, Traitors and Heroes,* Lippincott, 1959.

BEMIS, SAMUEL F., "British Secret Service and the French American Alliance," *American Historical Review*, Vol. XXIX, 1924.

BOYD, JULIAN P., "Silas Deane: Death by a Kindly Teacher of Treason," *William and Mary Quarterly*, 1959.

DEACON, RICHARD, *A History of The British Secret Service*, Taplinger, 1969.

DULLES, ALLEN, *The Craft of Intelligence*, Harper & Row, 1963.

EINSTEIN, LEWIS, *Divided Loyalties: Americans in England During the War of Independence*, Houghton Mifflin, 1933.

KAHN, DAVID, *The Codebreakers: The Story of Secret Writing*, Macmillan, 1967.

STEVENS, BENJAMIN FRANKLIN, *B. F. Stevens's Facsimiles of Manuscripts in European Archives Relating to America 1773–1783*, 25 vols., 1889–98.

VAN DOREN, CARL, *Secret History of the American Revolution*, Viking, 1941.

III. Benjamin Franklin:

ALDRIDGE, ALFRED OWEN, *Franklin and His French Contemporaries*, New York University Press, 1957.

BOWEN, CATHERINE DRINKER, *The Most Dangerous Man in America: Scenes From the Life of Benjamin Franklin*, Little, Brown, 1974.

CURREY, CECIL B., *Code Number 72, Benjamin Franklin: Patriot or Spy?*, Prentice-Hall, 1972.

    Road to Revolution: Benjamin Franklin in England, 1765–1775, Anchor Books, 1968.

LOPEZ, CLAUDE-ANNE, AND HERBERT, EUGENIA W., *The Private Franklin: The Man and His Family*, Norton, 1975.

VAN DOREN, CARL, *Benjamin Franklin*, Viking, 1938.

IV. Beaumarchais, the Chevalier d'Éon, and eighteenth-century France:

COX, CYNTHIA, *The Real Figaro: The Extraordinary Career of Caron de Beaumarchais,* Coward-McCann, 1962.

GRENDEL, FREDERIC, *Beaumarchais: The Man Who Was Figaro,* Macdonald and Jane's (London), 1977.

MANCERON, CLAUDE, *Twilight of the Old Order,* Knopf, 1977.

    The Wind from America, Knopf, 1978.

NIXON, EDNA, *Royal Spy: The Strange Case of the Chevalier d'Éon,* Reynal, 1965.

V. The Hell Fire Club, Satanism, etc.:

CHANCELLOR, E. BERESFORD, *The Hell Fire Club* (Volume IV of *The Lives of the Rakes*), Brentano's, 1926.

MC CORMICK, DONALD, *The Hell-Fire Club,* Jarrold's (London), 1958.

ROBBINS, ROSSELL HOPE, *The Encyclopedia of Witchcraft and Demonology,* Crown, 1959.

WHEATLEY, DENNIS, *The Devil and All His Works,* American Heritage, 1971.

VI. The Wild Geese:

CULLIGAN-HOGAN, MATTHEW J., *The Quest for the Galloping Hogan,* Crown, 1979.

HAYES, RICHARD, *Biographical Dictionary of Irishmen in France,* Dublin, 1949.

    Irish Swordsmen of France, Dublin, 1934.

MURPHY, W. S., "The Irish Brigade of France at the siege of Savannah," *Georgia Historical Quarterly,* vol. 38, n. 4.

    "The Irish Brigade of Spain at the capture of Pensacola," *Florida Historical Quarterly,* vol. 38, n. 3.

O'CALLAGHAN, JOHN CORNELIUS, *History of the Irish Brigades in the Service of France from the Revolution in Great Britain and Ireland under James II to the Revolution in France under Louis XVI*, several editions, 1870–86.

VII. Eighteenth-century life:

BAYNE-POWELL, ROSAMOND, *Eighteenth Century London Life*, Dutton, 1938.

CHANCELLOR, E. BERESFORD, *The XVIIIth Century in London: An Account of Its Social Life and Arts*, Batsford (London), 1920.

HAY, DOUGLAS, ET AL., *Albion's Fatal Tree: Crime and Society in Eighteenth Century England*, Pantheon, 1975.

RICE, HOWARD C., JR., *Thomas Jefferson's Paris*, Princeton, 1976.

WATSON, J. STEVEN, *The Reign of George III*, Oxford, 1960.